"This book was a labour of love.
The drawings alone took me several years to complete.
I hope you enjoy reading it."
D.L.Lewis

Dedicated to John and Pam Lewis,
adventurers of the high seas…
and to Helen Stimpson,
the patient play tester…
Thanks to Jackson, Livingstone, Morris, Dever
and all the other great writers
for inspiring my generation…
and to all the great fans who support
the new wave of indie authors.

Battle Land Publishing
Based in England, U.K.

Book one in the Demon's Bane Series
The Demon Sorcerer

Second Edition
First Published 2018

Set in Times New Roman

ISBN: 978-1-9161250-0-1

The
Demon Sorcerer

The Demon's Bane Series
Book One

Written and illustrated by D. L. Lewis

The
Demon Sorcerer

Introduction

Your homeland is filled with peril. It is a place of haunted forests and shadowy marshes. Its people live in fear of the foul Demons and dreaded beasts that stalk its untamed regions. In order to survive, you have learnt to use a sword to great effect and you have made a name for yourself as a mighty adventurer.

You are soon to learn that a terrible evil is growing in the south, an ancient power that threatens to destroy the few bastions of good that reside in this dangerous world. From beyond the snow clad peaks of the Druideen Mountains, a plea for aid has reached your ears.

Will YOU answer the call to arms?

If you wish to embark on this perilous adventure, you should first read the **Rules of Play** which will explain how to use this book.

Rules of Play

Life Force and Striking Speed

You will be asked to enter the following scores onto your Character Sheet. The sheet is located after the rules section.

Life Force - *Roll one six sided dice. Add 15 to the number rolled and enter the total into the **Life Force** box on your Character Sheet.*
Your **Life Force** reveals how healthy you are. You have been keeping yourself fit, so you will start your adventure in good shape. However, if you are hit or injured during the course of your adventure, your health may suffer. If your **Life Force** reaches 0 you are dead.

Important note: your **Life Force** may never exceed 30, as this is the maximum **Life Force** that a mortal may aspire to. Only Gods and certain other rare or magical beings may have higher scores than this.

Striking Speed - *Enter the number 10 in the **Striking Speed** box on your Character Sheet.*
You are swift with a blade - well versed in the art of battle - hence you start with a high score in this area. When engaged in close combat, whoever strikes fastest gains the advantage.

For reasons you will discover, many of your scores will change during the course of your adventure. It is important that you keep an accurate record of your scores.

Special Abilities

Pick two skills from the list below and enter them in the special abilities box on your Character Sheet.

Picklock - With this skill you will be able to pick almost any lock.

Scale - With this ability you will be able to scale anything, be it a wall or a cliff, no incline is too steep.

Haste - With Haste you will be able to run at incredible speed, if only for a limited time.

Stealth - With Stealth you will be able to walk with the softest of footfalls, allowing you to tiptoe in virtual silence.

Sixth Sense - Only a few ancient Wizards have found the time to fully master this skill. As you are a human warrior, your **Sixth Sense** will never be perfect. You will occasionally have premonitions of danger, forewarning you of imminent perils that your other senses cannot detect (for example, a concealed trap.) But remember, because you have not fully mastered the ability, it will not alert you to every hidden danger, so you will still have to be on your guard for much of the time.

Greater Wisdom - With Greater Wisdom you will have the ability to understand all languages. Whether it is the primitive speech of the Orcs, the obscure dialect of the Fairies or indeed any other language, you are a master of them all.

Close Combat

During the course of your adventure, you will come into contact with many enemies.

When fighting opponents, you will need to look at your **Striking Speed**, **Life Force** and the chart with the headings **Focus**, **Move** and **Damage**. These can all be found on your Character Sheet.

In your homeland, invisible energy flows through the land and sky. It is in all places, moving slowly through the rocks, the trees and the rivers. No one knows what this power is, but many people call it the World's Spirit. Wizards trap small amounts of this energy in their staves and occasionally unleash it in the form of wondrous or violent spells. Other creatures - those who do not deal in magic - cannot sense the World's Spirit except at certain times. Only when in close combat can they feel the arcane power moving in the environment around them. Warriors and beasts then draw upon this energy to briefly increase their **Striking Speed**.

The rules for close combat are as follows:

1. Throw one dice to determine how much arcane energy you can draw from the world around you. Add your **Striking Speed** to the dice roll and make a note of the total. This is how fast you can attack this turn.

2. Now it is your enemy's turn to draw energy from the earth and air around it. Throw one dice and add your opponent's **Striking Speed** to the number rolled. This is how fast they can attack this turn.

If your total is higher than your enemy's, continue to number 3 of these instructions. If your enemy's total is higher, go to number 4. If both totals are the same, you and your opponent clash but neither inflicts harm on the other, so you must return to instruction number 1.

3. You strike before your opponent has time to act. Look on your Character Sheet and find the chart with the headings **Focus**, **Move** and **Damage**. Roll one dice to determine your level of **Focus**, then look at what **Move** you have performed. Reduce your adversary's **Life Force** by an amount that is equal to the **Damage** your **Move** has inflicted. Now return to number 1 of these instructions and continue fighting until either you or your opponent's **Life Force** reaches zero (death).

4. Your enemy strikes before you can act. Look at the chart underneath your opponent's **Life Force**, with the headings **Focus**, **Move** and **Damage**. Roll one dice to determine its level of **Focus**, then look at the **Move** it has performed. Reduce your **Life Force** by an amount that is equal to the **Damage** your enemy's **Move** has inflicted. Now return to number 1 of these instructions and continue fighting until either you or your opponent's **Life Force** reaches zero (death).

If your opponent dies, you may continue your adventure. If you die, your adventure has ended and you must return to the beginning of the book and start again by creating a new character.

Fighting More Than One Opponent

Unless the text specifically states otherwise, you should treat multiple opponents as though they were a single enemy.

Magical Swords and Damage Bonuses

During the course of your adventure, you might acquire some rare swords. Some of them can increase the damage that you inflict. If you come across such a weapon and lose it at a later date, you must remember to remove the damage bonuses from your Character Sheet.

Ranged Weapons

If you find a ranged weapon such as a bow, the book will tell you when and how you can use it.

Equipment

You will start your adventure with a bare minimum of equipment. Your list of possessions consists of a **Sword**, a **Blanket**, a **Backpack** and some money. To determine how much money you start your adventure with, roll one dice and add 7 to the total. Enter this amount in the **Crimson Coins** box on your Character Sheet.

Final Words of Advice

Your quest will be perilous and it may take several attempts to reach your goal. Some of your enemies will try to destroy you with brute force, others may use deception, so you must always have your wits about you. If you are unsuccessful on your first attempt, do not despair. Failure is the opportunity to begin again more wisely, so make notes of any pitfalls that you want to avoid on future attempts.

Lastly, it is recommended that you make copies of the Character Sheets so that you can have them next to you whilst playing. If you do not want to do this, use pencil (not pen) on the Character Sheets in the book.

You are now ready to start your adventure. You should begin by reading *The Story so Far…*

Character Sheet

Character's Name

Focus	Move	Damage
1	Sword Hilt Smash	1
2-3	Stabbing Thrust	2
4-5	Sweeping Blade	2
6	Heavy Sword Strike	3

Life Force
30 MAX

Striking
Speed

Special Abilities

- [ ] Pick Lock
- [ ] Scale
- [ ] Stealth
- [ ] Haste
- [ ] Greater Wisdom
- [ ] Sixth Sense

Character Sheet

Equipment

Crimson Coins

Notes

The story so far…

Night has descended over the wooded hills, covering the wilderness like a blanket of death. The sun has long since fled from sight, but all is not as it should be. You pause on the doorstep of your secluded cottage. The surrounding forest is strangely quiet and there is neither a hoot nor a rustle as you look up through the dark branches. As a cold wind passes overhead, you suddenly hear a terrible roar rumbling out of the distance. Grabbing your sword, you clamber to the top of a tree and gaze out over the moonlit scene. Far away on the edge of the forest, several towns are burning. You can see the glow from the raging infernos and the black smoke that is billowing upwards. As you watch, you notice a huge, dark shadow gliding towards you across the starry sky. It is a monstrous, winged beast, with gleaming eyes and fiery jaws. A grey Demon sits upon the Dragon's back, and an aura of flickering magic surrounds them. Before you have time to think, the winged terror soars overhead and a torrent of fire explodes from its gaping mouth. The world is lit in a searing blaze of red. The trees turn to ash, and your body is engulfed by flames…

Your eyes flicker open. You realise that you have been dreaming, but the vision felt strangely real, as if you were witnessing a terrible glimpse of the future. You sit up and view your surroundings. Grey morning light filters into the isolated cabin, and you can hear something tapping just outside the entrance to your hut. Still half asleep, you put on your clothes and open the door. A small bird is standing on the doorstep, and there are several marks in the wood where it has been pecking with its beak. You watch as it drops a rolled up parchment at your feet, then it flaps away and swoops out of the lonely forest.

You had not been expecting a message, so you unravel it with a curious expression. Your name is written at the top, and the words are sparkling with an aura of magic.

The letter reads as follows:

It is herby requested that you attend a
meeting with the Wizards of Lore.
This is a matter of urgency, and your presence
is required as soon as possible. Please do not
delay, for time is of the essence!
Yours gratefully,
Pelanthius Lesken,
Head of the Wizard's Council.

You turn the parchment over and see that a map has been drawn on the back, giving you directions to a castle in the south, but there is no further information.

For many years you have lived the life of a fearsome Demon Slayer, but in all that time of adventuring, you have never before received a message from the mysterious Wizards of Lore. Your curiosity has been sparked, and given that it has been two months since your last adventure, you prepare your backpack and set off in response to the summons.

By late evening you are already high up in the Druideen Mountains, following the route laid out on the map, but as night draws in you notice a pack of slavering Wolves approaching from the east. As the creatures come close, you draw your sword in self-defence, and a fierce battle erupts on the rugged slopes. Your blade stains the ground with their blood, and your skilled swordsmanship forces them into a hasty retreat. You stumble on through the darkness, watching the shadows with wary eyes, and at the crack of dawn you depart from the southern edge of the mountains. You follow the map into the depths of a murky forest, where huge Spiders, with legs as long as your arms, scuttle around in the gloom. Their countless eyes gleam with murderous rage, and it takes you three days to hack your way through their ranks. Finally, on a misty morning, you stagger out into a vast region of sunlit fields. The air here is filled with glittering butterflies, and when you look at your map, you are relieved to see that you are very near to your goal. As you pause to shade your eyes from the rising sun, you see the distant spires of a white castle, gleaming on the horizon, and a shiver of excitement runs through your veins. You walk up to the castle gates and pull out your letter, showing it to the lone watchmen who is keeping guard. The doors are immediately flung wide, and he ushers you through into a windowless, dark hall, where the air is shimmering with magic. The young man asks you to sit at a long table, then he hurries off to fetch his masters.

At the centre of the table, a glowing candle flickers weakly against the sea of shadows. Were it not for that light, you would be plunged into utter blackness.

You stare vacantly into the dancing flame whilst tapping your fingers impatiently on the table. The dreariness of waiting starts to make you feel tired, and the exertions of the last few days finally catch up with you. You sink back into the chair and close your eyes.

As you slumber, the magic in the hall drifts around you, healing your wounds and revitalizing your muscles, until your body feels completely refreshed.

A short while later, a loud boom wakes you up. A gust of air causes the candle to flicker, then the light goes out. You peer into the shadows and see the glow of a lantern, wading through the darkness to meet you, and the sound of approaching footfalls echoes around the vast chamber.

"At last," you murmur under your breath.

Four men, elegantly dressed in colourful robes, emerge from the gloom and place the lantern onto the table.

"I am Pelanthius. Please accept my apology for the delay," says one, as he and the others seat themselves opposite you.

The light plays on his face, and you can see that he is very old. His eyes are narrow and his long hair hangs down his back in rugged grey curls. You sense an aura of great power and wisdom surrounding him.

"I am the head of the Council of the Wizards," he says, "and these are my brothers, Carn, Kassmire and Jasil. I must thank you for coming here so swiftly. You are wondering why we have summoned you?"

"I am," you reply.

Kassmire leans back in his chair. "There is some history to the matter," he explains. "I feel it is only right that you should be made aware of the whole story."

You nod in agreement and he begins without further ado. "I must take you back to a time when our world was younger. The land was at peace back then. Humans, Wizards, the Fairies of the vast woods, even the Dwarves in their deep caverns, all had learnt the wisdom of tolerance, and a prosperous age of trade and unity had come upon us. But to the south, in the shadow haunted crags of Cair Nurath, the Demons writhed in darkness and discontent. They had no wish to be a part of this age of peace, for they were an evil race, filled always with hatred and anger. The Demon Sorcerer, Zanack, dreamt of bringing chaos and bloodshed back to the land. With that plan in mind, he united the Demon clans of the region and forged a great army that marched under his banner. He and his host of followers stormed the peaceful realms, plunging the world into an age of bloody mayhem. After a decade of violent warfare, our great ancestors, the ancient Wizards of Light, led the Humans and the Dwarves in a united front against Zanack. The Demons were strong, but their throng was pushed back, and the enemy began to weaken. Sensing his downfall, Zanack escaped before his army was destroyed. He fled into the murky and mysterious land known as the Elemental Plane of Darkness. It is a place that exists far from the realms we know, it is a land filled with poisonous ethereal skies, where the shadows are

haunted with the whispers of brooding evil. He knew that we would not follow him into that place, for it was a land of pure nightmares, and no good heart could pass across its borders… He had escaped, but with his army crushed, his reign of terror was over."

"You must understand," says Pelanthius, "that the Elemental Plane of Darkness is the most terrible place that exists in the known world. It lies far-flung to the south, beyond the sea and past the land of ice and stars; a place where the sky is filled with toxic clouds, and where upon the land, the dreaded Elementals stalk the barren terrain, feasting upon mortals who have accidentally tumbled into their dark realm. It is a place from which all believed there was no return. Yes, Zanack had escaped, but none believed he could survive long in that place. Our ancestors thought they had seen the last of him. But still, just in case he did return, the Wizards created a powerful shield to protect themselves in any future battles. Many years they toiled over it, shaping and imbuing it with mystical enchantments. When they were finished, they named this mightiest of all creations, the Doom Shield."

The flame from the lantern flickers and begins to glow in a strange assortment of changing colours, causing the shadows to stir in the haunted corners of the deep hall.

"But alas, it does not take a Wizard to guess what happened next," says Jasil. "Two centuries have passed since Zanack vanished, but just recently the old Demon has returned! He has come back, stronger even than before, and he is already plotting his revenge. The Demons of the land are flocking to him and it is said that he has also made an alliance with the Orcs. Worse still, it has been rumoured that he has convinced some of the powerful Elementals to aid him in his quest to dominate these lands."

You make a suggestion. "Can the Wizard's Council not forge an army and rise up against him?"

"It has been spoken of," says Pelanthius, "but alas, it is more complicated than you make it sound. We have spread the word but it will take time to mass an army big enough to confront Zanack. He has already moved back into one of his dark fortresses in the marshy lands to the south, and all the foul creatures near that region have been scurrying to serve under his command, drawn by the promise of war and glory. More worryingly, if he truly does have the formidable Elementals on his side, a full frontal attack on his fortress would prove suicidal. No. There is only one option available, though it is not a task for the faint-hearted. Someone will have to sneak unnoticed into his dark fortress, slip past the mighty guards that defend him, and face him one to one. Zanack must be slain before he can amass a huge army. If he is given enough time, he will ignite the fires of a new war, and I fear that his reign of terror may this time prevail."

"A hero is needed for this quest," insists Carn, "one who can leave now, one who is cunning and strong. You were an obvious choice. You have made a name for yourself as a brave warrior and you are highly spoken of across the land, even if you are too modest to admit it yourself. But this mission is by no means easy, and it will prove far more dangerous than anything you have come up against 'til now. Thus we come to the point of it, and we must ask whether you will take on this burden? We will not pressure you if the task is too great."

"First, where can I find this Doom Shield?" you ask.

"It was locked in the tower above us," says Pelanthius. "But some weeks ago, in the dead of night, a terrible creature descended from the sky. It was a servant of Zanack; a deathly shadow with wings of mist, carrying a whip of flames. It broke into the tower and stole the shield. We fought it, but it escaped and flew into the south. The shield cannot be destroyed, so I would wager that it was taken back to Zanack. The Demon Lord has probably locked it away in his dark fortress."

"You must find the shield before you can destroy him," says Kassmire. "For without the aid of the Doom Shield, Zanack will be too mighty for you to defeat." He looks at you hopefully "…will you aid us?"

You lean back in your chair. "How can I refuse?" You nod your head and readily accept the challenge.

You are glad to be out of the dark hall and back in the sunlight again, as Pelanthius escorts you through the green gardens that surround his magical castle.

"I would have offered you my winged horse, Snowfire," says the Wizard. "He is a trusty mount and a good friend, but an accident some months ago left his wing injured, and I am afraid such a journey would be beyond him at the moment. You like my gardens?"

"Of course," you answer.

"Birds twitter in the trees. Fish bask in the ponds. And those who flock here in fear of evil will always be welcome. But unless Zanack is stopped, not even our magic will be strong enough to protect this place. The land will be plunged into an age of war, and in the end, I fear no Wizard nor army will be able to resist the might of Zanack. The world will be painted with blood, and in the place of good, all will become evil."

As you come to the edge of the walled gardens, Pelanthius hands you a map. It is far more detailed than the one you received a few days ago. It shows the Wizard's castle, Zanack's fortress and all the land in-between. "Keep this with you," he says, "and remember, Zanack might be expecting an attempt on his life. There could be spies on the road ahead, so be wary!"

NOW TURN TO **1**.

W
E
S
W
S
The Enchanted Forest
The WIZARD'S CASTLE
The Vast Plains
BlackThorn Wood
GRIMBREE Village
The Arid Foothills
Green Water Stream
Dark Marsh Inn
Harrowmoor
STORM WATER
SHELL-HAVEN

1
Illustration Opposite

You study the map before putting it in your backpack. (You may return to this page at any time to look at it.) After all that you have heard, you decide that there is no time to delay. After many thanks and farewells from the Wizards, you set off from their castle in search of the shield. It is midday and the sky is scattered with white clouds. You march south for a few hours along a lonely trail that is surrounded by fields, and a cool wind whispers through the long grass. Eventually you see a line of trees ahead, with a signpost that reads *Black Thorn Wood*. Just as you are about to follow the trail inside, you hear a deep rumbling. You look around to see a horse-drawn cart storming after you along the road. A tall figure, clad in black robes, is steering the horse at full speed towards you. The rider's face is concealed beneath the shadow of a large hood.

If you wish to move out of the way, turn to page **352**.

If you choose to hail the rider, turn to page **327**.

2

You tug on the lever, but nothing happens. You have chosen poorly. The door remains sealed and the water begins to rise even faster. In a panic, you reach for one of the other levers, but they suddenly withdraw into the wall, vanishing into narrow slots! There is now nothing you can do. In a few minutes the water will have filled the sealed chamber. You are condemned to death by drowning.

3

You open the door and step through into a windowless, empty hall. Candles line the walls, but their flames do little to expel the gloom. At the far end, barely visible in the dim light, are three arched doors. As you head towards them, a hunched figure, swathed in hooded robes, melts out of the shadows. It pauses and looks you up and down with an air of amusement. "So," it chuckles, "a fly has crawled willingly into the spider's web. Welcome to the Dark Castle, stranger." Its demonic voice is deep and sinister, and an aura of powerful magic flickers around him. "I am the Games Master," it hisses. "You have chosen passage by the sword, so you must prove yourself worthy of passing through my arena. Let us see if you have the courage to pass my test."

If you wish to listen to the Games Master's challenge, turn to **44**.

If you wish to attack him, turn to **190**.

4

The robed figure shakes its head. "No," it hisses, pointing its staff at you. "I sense your lie. You are the one we seek." With a swift movement, it turns to its huge mount. "There is your enemy," it screeches. "Kill!"

The huge beast obeys its master and leaps forward, raking the air with its terrible claws.

You must fight this awesome opponent.

TERRASAUR

LIFE FORCE 12   STRIKING SPEED 9

Focus	Move	Damage
1	Tail Slam	1
2-3	Slashing Claws	2
4-5	Monstrous Bite	2
6	Burning Breath	3

If you win, turn to **102**.

5

You fumble around for some time in the gloom of the pit. At length you find a metal grille in the wall, which is sealed with a rusty padlock. Behind the bars is a narrow tunnel which is sloping gently upwards. It looks like a ventilation shaft, though it is impossible to be sure.

If you possess **Picklock** (or a **Skeleton Key**), you may enter the cylindrical shaft by turning to **176**.

If you want to shatter the padlock with your sword, turn to **54**.

Alternatively, you can brave the wall, turn to **173**.

6

(Deduct **three Crimson Coins** from your belongings.)
Childeer gives you the potion, then without another word
he skips out of sight into the ferns. The sweet tasting drink
is not half as potent as the Valley Elf boasted, but
nevertheless, it has a wonderous effect. (Increase your **Life
Force** by three points.) As soon as you have finished, the
empty bottle dissolves into a sparkling dust which drifts
away into the sky.

You continue along the trail. Roll one dice to determine
what random events lay ahead of you.

If you roll a one, a two or a three, turn to **280**.

If you roll a four, a five or a six, turn to **157**.

7

You are suddenly struck by a feeling of grave danger.
Many an unwary adventurer has perished in this room.

If you explore the chamber, turn to **78**.

Otherwise, you may step back into the corridor and
open a door that you have not yet tried. If you head
through the red door, turn to **61**. If you head through the
door with the symbols, turn to **22**.

8

You are about to fill your hands with water when the
ground rumbles behind you. You spin around and see a
hill on the west side of the valley, shaking violently. With
a gasp, you realise that the slope is actually a long mossy
coat, and what looked like a heap of dead twigs is really
a set of great, bushy eyebrows. You are face to face with

a monstrous Hill Giant. Its huge shoulders are hunched, and its ugly face is brimming with fury. It looks much like an oversized human, with massive arms and gnarled features. With a series of savage grunts, the brute rips a small tree from the earth and starts to swing it around like a club. The creature stomps towards you, hoping to make a soup from your flesh.

UTHGAR THE GIANT

LIFE FORCE 13   STRIKING SPEED 8

Focus	Move	Damage
1	**Wind-Blast Roar**	1
2-3	**Mighty Punch**	3
4-5	**Giant's Kick**	3
6	**Sweeping Club**	4

If you defeat your opponent, the Giant collapses by the bank and his green blood flows down into the pool. The water suddenly begins to bubble and turn very dark. The enchanted pond has been poisoned by his evil blood, and the water is now undrinkable. You slump by the bank to catch your breath, wishing you had never stopped here. Before you leave, you search the Giant's clothing. His left pocket is filled with human bones, which you toss aside with a grisly look, but in his right pocket you find **four Crimson Coins**, which you may take if you wish. You return to the path and continue your journey.

Turn to **137**.

You are almost at the top when your hand slips and you topple backwards. You crash back onto the bone littered floor, gashing your shoulder on the pointed shard of a mouldy ribcage.

(Reduce your **Life Force** by two points.)

If you are lucky enough to have survived the fall, you pick yourself up and attempt to climb the wall again. Your second endeavour proves more successful, and you reach the lip of the doorway and pull yourself back into the square chamber. Relieved to be out of the pit, you investigate the other door. Turn to **148**.

10

You stumble through the blackened, sooty haze, then fling open the door to a rush of fresh air. Springing forward, you escape the burning structure just as it collapses into a mess of blazing timbers. You look to the sky and see the fleet swooping into the distance. They must have thought that you were burnt alive in the ruined house. Not wishing to point out their mistake, you keep low until they have gone.

You had a close call. Your lungs are filled with smoke and your body is singed, but at least you are alive. You congratulate yourself for outwitting the enemy, but you cannot rest easy yet. The fleet might return, so you keep low and hurry away from the burning debris. Turn to **97**.

The arched door is twelve feet in height. It slowly opens, revealing a yawning darkness, then you steady your nerves as a huge beast emerges through the opening. It is a colossal humanoid, clad in dark furs. The Green Giant is eleven feet tall, with arms that are thick with muscle. Greasy black hair hangs about its mighty shoulders, and its nose is upturned like a pig's. It opens its mouth, which is lined with sharp fangs, then it releases a thunderous roar. Considering its massive size, you doubt that your opponent will be very agile, but its incredible power is sure to make up for any lack of speed.

(If you possess a **Crossbow**, you have time to fire one **Bolt** before the beast is upon you. If you wish to do this, erase the **Bolt** from your inventory and reduce your enemy's **Life Force** by two points, then draw your sword to finish the fight!)

GREEN SKINNED GIANT

LIFE FORCE 18   STRIKING SPEED 7

Focus	Move	Damage
1	Ear Splitting Roar	1
2-3	Crushing Grapple	3
4-5	Giant's Punch	4
6	Giant's Kick	4

If you win, turn to **200**.

12

You step through the door, hacking your way through the tangled mass of webs. Tiny black spiders are prevalent here, but they seem more frightened of you than you are of them, and they scurry out of your way and take shelter in the lightless cracks in the walls. After a while your sword arm begins to ache, so you pause for a moments rest. Suddenly, an enormous shape melts up out of the passage floor in front of you. It is humanoid, but it is made from solid rock. The Earth Elemental is at least eight feet tall, with huge shoulders that fill the width of the corridor. Its features are grim, with callous black pits for eyes. It stalks towards you, parting the cobwebs like a veil.

"I am the guardian of the Secret Passage. To pass, you must answer my question," it booms in a deep and terrible voice. "Who be thy master? Be it day or night?"

If you wish to respond, you had better do so quickly!

Will you say;

"Day", turn to **36**.

"Night" turn to **425**.

Or will you skip the pleasantries and launch a sudden attack, turn to **386**.

13

Your search reveals nothing: you have taken the wrong turn.

If you run back to the junction and explore in the opposite direction, turn to **356**.

If you give up on the hunt and return to the safety of Mok's house, turn to **66**.

You follow the man inside and he quickly bolts the door behind you.

"What were you doing out there? Trying to get yourself killed?" he snaps.

You explain that you are just a traveller passing through and have no idea of the goings on here.

After apologising for his sharpness he introduces himself as Mok, a farmer. You sit down at a table while he tells his story.

"Every night for two weeks now," he explains, "a strange figure, swathed in black robes, has ridden into the village and terrorized the folk 'ere. Just last week it killed poor ol' Torren while 'e was workin' on his crops. Other folk 'ave simply vanished during the night. Rumour has it they were stolen from their very beds, and were carried away by the robed phantom. A few days ago we tried to scare off the menace with our pitchforks, but we were no match for it, and we barely escaped with our lives." You can see the burden of fear upon him as he talks. "We are a simple people," he says, "farmers and hard workin' folk of the land. We are not warriors. These recent events 'ave left a cloak of fear over the whole village. I couldn't ask you to leave with that cursed thing runnin' round out there, you can sleep 'ere the night if you wish."

Will you:

Take up Mok's kind offer and spend the night at his place, turn to **66**.

Or set off to kill the beast in the village, turn to **41**.

Not long after you have begun your search, you hear a deep rumbling somewhere in the castle. You go to investigate, and you soon realise that there has been a cave in on the upper levels. The only stairwell leading to that area is now filled with dust and rubble. If you have not already searched the upper rooms, it will be too dangerous, if not impossible, for you to do so now, so you resolve yourself to exploring the ground floor.

You wander through the cold corridors for some time, finding nothing but an air of abandonment among the decrepit and empty rooms. After a while you come to a heavy door with a rusty padlock. The door is made from a mysterious dark wood, which is remarkably sturdy considering its age.

If you possess the special ability of **Picklock**, and want to open the door, turn to **55**.

If you do not have this ability, you may attempt to barge down the door, turn to **150**.

If you do not want to open this door, there is nothing else of interest here, so you decide to continue with your quest, turn to **42**.

The Games Master mutters with disappointment, and you know that you have chosen well. He utters a spell, then the door swings open.

A Giant Rat leaps from the opening and rushes towards you. Its body is five feet long, with a thick tail swinging behind it. Its jet black hair is slick and greasy, and it stinks of filth and disease. Its razor sharp claws click and screech against the stone-flagged floor, while strings of saliva flail from its bloodthirsty jaws. It suddenly launches itself into the air and dives towards you! (If you possess a **Crossbow**, you have just enough time to fire one **Bolt** before the beast is upon you. If you wish to do this, erase the **Bolt** from your inventory and reduce your enemy's **Life Force** by two points, then draw your sword to finish the fight!)

GIANT BLACK RAT

LIFE FORCE 6   STRIKING SPEED 8

Focus	Move	Damage
1	**Speeding Ram**	1
2-3	**Tumbling Embrace**	1
4-5	**Slicing Claws**	2
6	**Mauling Frenzy**	2

If you win, turn to **200**.

17

A flash of light suddenly erupts from the ring, causing your enemy to reel backwards with an expression of pain. Its skin and eyes burn and hiss in the white glow, and its jaws fall open with a roar of agony. The creature turns and retreats into the throng, clutching at its smoking face. Turn to **50**.

18

Wasting no time, you quickly leave the rise and follow the footprints. It is not long before you hear the sounds of a ferocious battle, somewhere in the mist ahead. The Werewolves must have caught up with their unfortunate prey, so you quicken your pace. You soon come to the edge of a vast, deep pool. There, on the far bank, is the man you saw earlier. The body of a Werewolf lies dead at his feet, where he has run it through with his sword, but three more are still alive. They have surrounded him, and you doubt that he will survive the next assault!

If you are going to save him you will have to be quick!

If you have a **Crossbow**, you may fire on the Werewolves from where you stand, turn to **321**.

Alternatively you may dive into the water and swim towards him, turn to **38**.

Or abandon the man to his fate, and sneak back to the trail before you are spotted, turn to **330**.

You give the lever a hard tug. Suddenly there is a loud crash. You spin around and see that a hidden doorway has slid open, revealing a dark and secret room beyond. You walk through the opening and find yourself in a large burial chamber. The candles on the walls have been extinguished for many years.

In the centre of the room, resting on a plinth, is a huge stone sarcophagus, surrounded by skeletal remains. As you peer around the gloomy space, the candles suddenly flicker to life by themselves. The eerie firelight dances across the old coffin, and you see an inscription on the stone lid which reads:

'Here lies Lord Elendrik,
Dreaded owner of this castle.
Put to death by his servants
for crimes of torture and murder.
May he rot forever in the Land of Shadows.'

Do you possess the special ability of **Sixth Sense**?
If you do, turn to **96**.
If you do not, turn to **90**.

20

Do you possess the special ability of **Greater Wisdom?**
If so, turn to **31**.
If you do not possess this ability, turn to **79**.

21

You trudge down the road, leaving the village of Grimbree far behind. The rooftops of the little settlement slowly shrink into the distance, before vanishing altogether. At length, the morning clouds are swept away on a refreshing breeze, then a sweltering heat beats down. Come midday, you reach a split in the road. To the east the trail rises into the barren foothills. To the southwest it twists through fields and meadows.

Will you:

Take the eastern road, turn to **48**.

Or the southwest road, turn to **87**.

22

You find yourself standing in a vast hall. Rows of boxes have been stacked up to the ceiling, creating narrow walkways that lead around the room. You explore the area, but no enemies seem to be present. At the farthest end of the hall, you discover one box sitting alone in the center of an aisle. The air around it is full of strange scents, and you can hear the faint rustle of movement within.

If you wish, you can use your sword to break the padlock on the lid, turn to **162**.

Otherwise you may retrace your steps and leave via the door through which you entered. Having returned to the corridor, you may now open:

The red door, turn to **61**.

Or the blue door, turn to **46**.

As you walk, you survey the destruction. Several houses have been torn down and you see bodies sprawled on the earth; local people, mowed down by Zanack's thugs. You try not to look at them, as it causes a weight of sadness to fall upon you. Not long ago, this place was thriving with life. Children had played near the buildings while fishermen prepared their nets for the day's toil. Now all that is left is stillness... an unnatural quiet that haunts the shadows.

You feel determined to slay Zanack more than ever. The Demon Sorcerer must be stopped, before his reign of terror spreads further.

The track grows steeper, then it opens onto a green field at the top of the hill, which is encircled by houses. You have reached the centre of the village. Wild flowers grow here, as high as your waist, and a fountain dances amidst the undergrowth. You also notice a hole in the earth nearby.

As you are looking around, a shadow falls across the scene. You look up and are startled by a fleet of huge bat-like creatures, gliding through the gloomy clouds. They are mounted by dark figures swathed in black robes. These foul creatures are Zanack's Sky Guards, and they are patrolling this area. There are too many to fight, so you jump down the hole to avoid being spotted. You fall only a short distance before landing expertly on your feet. Turn to **67**.

As you step towards the door you are struck by a sudden feeling of impending doom. A cold sweat comes over you and you have to pause to regain your composure. Never yet on your adventure have you been struck by such a fierce sense of danger. Something terrible lurks beyond the closed door, of that you are certain. But what horror could send your senses into such a frenzy?

If curiosity has the better of you, and you still wish to open the door, turn to **288**.

If you would rather head towards the stairs, turn to **277**.

The beast you are facing used to be small. But Zanack's followers recently dumped their magical potions into the water, deliberately warping the lake's inhabitants into bloated horrors! You must fight!

IMMENSE ABOMINATION

LIFE FORCE 20   STRIKING SPEED 8

Focus	Move	Damage
1	**Sweeping Clout**	2
2-3	**Thrashing Strike**	3
4-5	**Bone Breaking Grip**	4
6	**Crushing Embrace**	5

If you win, you clamber into the dinghy and row out towards the dark castle. Turn to **324**.

26

Your grassy bed is soft and comfortable, and it does not take long for you to fall into a deep slumber.

You sleep well for several hours, but late in the night you are woken by a strange, harsh cry. The sound is coming from behind a large boulder on the far side of the path.

If you wish to investigate, turn to **88**.

If you would rather ignore it and go back to sleep, turn to **123**.

27

Sword raised, you charge forward with a battle cry. As the enemy try to flood in through the broken window, you vent your fury and send several heads rolling across the floor. Burlybe is momentarily frozen in awe, stunned by your awesome display of swordsmanship, but then he leaps to your aid, putting his own sword to use.

You both fight valiantly, but your combined efforts are not enough to hold back the throng. At length, they begin to force their way in through the broken window and you find yourself surrounded.

You stand back-to-back with your comrade, hacking and slashing at the sea of snapping jaws.

"We cannot hold out against this attack for much longer!" cries Burlybe, who is beginning to tire from the fierce battle. "Our enemies are too many!"

Despite your courageous nature, you know that he is right. The situation is becoming desperate. And if you do not think of something quickly, you will surely be overwhelmed!

You grab Burlybe and drag him over to the bar area. Here, at least, you are less exposed to attacks from all sides, and the Demons can only come at you one at a time. The creatures surge and thrash, fighting to be the first to attack you. A huge Demon, the largest you have seen this night, forces its way to the front of the queue.

If you have a **Magic Ring**, turn to **17**.

If you do not possess this item, you must fight!

GIANT NIGHT DEMON

LIFE FORCE 11   STRIKING SPEED 9

Focus	Move	Damage
1	**Monstrous Punch**	2
2-3	**Stabbing Horns**	3
4-5	**Crushing Grapple**	3
6	**Mauling Frenzy**	3

If you win, turn to **50**.

28

The stallion suddenly surges out of the darkness, spurred forward by the crack of its rider's whip. The horseman glares at you from beneath the shadows of his hood, and you see his demonic eyes gleaming brightly. He tugs abruptly on the reigns, intent on crushing you beneath the galloping steed!

If you have the special ability of **Haste**, you dive and roll to the left, narrowly avoiding the attack.

If you do not possess **Haste**, the horse slams into you and you must roll one dice.

If you roll a three or less, the animal thunders directly over the top of you, bludgeoning you with its hooves: reduce your **Life Force** by four points!

If you roll four or higher, you are flung to the left and the hooves narrowly miss you: you are dazed but uninjured.

If you are still alive, turn to **421**.

29

You move with the reflexes of a wild tiger, and the bolt misses you by the narrowest of margins, skimming past your cheek. But luck is not on your side this day. The projectile ricochets off the wall and spins to the left. Your teeth grind in pain as it thuds into your shoulder and buries into your flesh. Worse still, the bolt's tip has been laced with poison. With a grunt you quickly pull it free, but the toxins are already pushing through your bloodstream and causing your vision to blur.

Ragroda's eyes narrow. She can see that you are

wounded, and with an eager look she rushes in with her knife. You duck the swish of her blade, then your fist slams into her stomach, knocking her back. Winded, your enemy retreats, watching from a safe distance. Suddenly your muscles stiffen, then sounds and sights fade into a blur. You stagger sideways and collapse onto the floor, the life ebbing from your body. You can see Ragroda's fiendish eyes, watching with devilish anticipation. A wicked smile, etched with triumphant glee, begins to spread across her face. Moments later, you pass out, never to wake again.

Your quest has failed.

30

You are bewildered by the events that you have just witnessed. After regaining your composure, you find yourself being led into the depths of the mire. Eventually you come to a halt by a deep stream, where a small dinghy is lashed to the muddy bank. The woman skirts the area to ensure that the danger has passed, then you sit together by the water's edge.

"My name is Avion," she says. "I know all about you and your quest. The Wizards sent me to find you. New information has been uncovered. There is only one way into Zanack's fortress, and that is via the castle's main gate. However, the entrance is barred by an impassable force, and only those who know the secret password can gain access to the inner halls. Rumours have surfaced that Zanack has named the password after an old Demon of legend, whose tomb can be located on one of the islands that scatter Merkwater Lake. We must head there without delay, to find out the name and hence the password. We must take this dinghy down Green Water Stream, which flows deep into the marsh and then out onto the Merkwater. Once we have uncovered the password, we can carry on to the Demon's castle. I will lead the way, if you will follow."

Will you:

Agree to travel with Avion, turn to **159**.

Or refuse to travel with her, turn to **127**.

31

The carvings on the box are written in the language of the Orcs. The message reads:

WARNING!
Property of Our Lord Zanack.
Contents: The Flesh Devourer

Will you:

Move away from the box and head towards the dinghy, turn to **58**.

Or open the box, turn to **91**.

Illustration Opposite

The body of the Witch lies crumpled on the floor, lifeless and still. You decide to search the room, and you soon turn your attention to the large desk. In the left drawer you find scrolls regarding black magic. There are similar scriptures in the book she was reading. You dare not risk toying around with dark sorcery, so you move your search to the desk's right hand drawer. Here you have better luck. On a yellowing parchment is a roughly sketched map, revealing every part of the labyrinth! On it, the Witch has marked the position of her study with a scribbled note. Now that you have your bearings, you should be able to find your way out of the labyrinth! You take the maze map, along with a twisted green key which you also find in the drawer.

As you turn to leave, a gruesome sight catches your attention. The countless little spiders that live on the ceiling have swarmed down the walls, completely covering the Witch's body. They appear to be making a meal of her, and by the look of it she will soon be nothing more than a pile of bones. You shudder at the grisly spectacle and quickly leave the study.

Following the directions on the map, you eventually find your way into a secret passage which ends at a locked door. This is the exit to the labyrinth. The green key is a perfect fit, so you open the door and step through into the room beyond. Turn to **109**.

You walk around the pond and halt by the large boulder. You part the ferns and wipe away the moss. Each symbol on the rock represents a separate word. This is the language of the ancient Giants, a fierce race of primitive beasts who still stalk the wild regions of the world. The message reads:

Like a mountain of old I watch night and day,
unseen in the valley whilst folk go their way.
The wanderers mistake me for a large grassy hill,
but I've no interest in them, I just lay still.
Pity the fool though, who drinks from my pool,
for I am the Giant, Uthgar The Cruel.

You look around. If indeed a Giant is sitting nearby, he must be very well camouflaged, for there is no sign of him. Will you:

Drink from the pond, turn to **8**.

Or heed the warning and press on through the valley, turn to **137**.

The woman stirs and sits up. Her eyes are dark and striking, filled with sultry evil, and her perfect white skin and blood-red lips give the impression that she is not human after all! With a hiss, she snatches a dagger from under her pillow and slides from the bed. You notice that her teeth are long and pointed like the fangs of a carnivorous killer, but that is not the worst of it. Instead of legs, she has the lower body of a large, writhing snake, with a scorpion-like stinger at its end. She immediately moves forward to attack you, forcing you to defend yourself!

MUTANT WOMAN

LIFE FORCE 6   STRIKING SPEED 10

Focus	Move	Damage
1	Slashing Nails	1
2-3	Bite For The Throat	2
4-5	Swiping Dagger	2
6	Venomous Stinger	3

If you win, you may quickly search the room by turning to **74**.

Or you may leave the room by turning to **185**.

As you are clambering along the rain washed path, something makes you freeze in your tracks. Away to your left, a massive guttural roar suddenly shakes the night, mingling with a boom of thunder. You catch sight of a four-legged animal, nearly the size of a horse, standing on a rise in the sheet of rain, a quarter of a mile away. Lightning sears around it, silhouetting its muscular build and stocky frame. A wild mane frames its huge head, and its teeth look like those of a Saber-Toothed Tiger. It is one of the great Mountain Lions of this region, and it is clearly out on the prowl, looking for a late dinner. The beast does not yet appear to have noticed you.

This is one fight you could do with avoiding. Thinking quickly, you duck behind a large boulder and stay very still and quiet. After a while your patience is rewarded and the big animal wanders off towards the east, disappearing from sight. Avoiding the battle was a good tactic, as Mountain Lions are notoriously powerful. But sitting motionless in the freezing wet has left you blue lipped from the cold.

Shivering uncontrollably, you hurry on up the trail, eager to find a place of shelter and warmth.

Turn to **278**.

"Then you must die!" roars the creature. The beast steps forward, its huge hand reaching towards you. You grasp your sword and swing with all your might, causing splints of stone to shatter from your opponent's body... but your enemy seems unfazed. With a vice-like grip it grabs you by the scruff of the neck and lifts you off your feet. Your foe is incredibly strong, and there is no escape from its grasp. It smashes your face against the side of the corridor, crushing your head into the wall.

Your quest is over...

37

The concoction tastes delicious and you quickly empty the bottle. You have drunk a potion of healing.

(Increase your **Life Force** by five points!)

Finding nothing else of interest, you exit the room. Turn to **185**.

You dive into the water and swim as fast as you can. In a few moments you are clambering up the far bank and drawing your sword. You have burst into the middle of the battle. The young man is surprised by your appearance, but before he can say a word, his ambushers begin to advance. The beasts do not seem dispirited by your unexpected arrival, on the contrary, their eyes gleam with excitement, and saliva drools from their fierce jaws. You have arrived not a moment too soon, for a second later they pounce. Gripping his sword, the young man leaps forward, attacking two beasts simultaneously. You take on the third Werewolf. It springs towards you and almost catches you off guard, but you duck just in time to avoid the snap of its jaws. You then wield your sword into the fray!

WEREWOLF

LIFE FORCE 6   STRIKING SPEED 9

Focus	Move	Damage
1	Speeding Ram	1
2-3	Slashing Claws	2
4-5	Life Draining Howl	2
6	Bite Of The Lycan	2

If you win without being bitten, turn to **340**.
If you win but were bitten, turn to **336**.

You halt by the entrance and peek inside. You can see two empty cages hanging from the ceiling, each one big enough to hold a person, but you have arrived too late to save the prisoners. The big brute has already made a stew of them.

You have stumbled upon the lair of Bagross the Hideous and, unfortunately for you, he has a keen sense of smell.

The ugly creature grunts and sniffs the air with his pig-like nose. He has caught your scent above the aroma of his repulsive brew, and before you can act he turns and fixes you with a hungry look. His face is a revolting sight, with countless eyes, sharp pointed ears and a lopsided, salivating mouth. The mutant tears his stirring staff from the pot and lumbers towards you, clearly delighted by your appearance. He is looking forward to adding you to his recipe, and with a grunt he swipes at your head with his stick. Fortunately, you are far too quick for him. You dodge the blow and strike your enemy, sending him toppling backwards towards his huge pot. A roar of horror escapes him as he trips on the uneven floor, then there is a loud splash as he vanishes forever into the steaming contents of his own, boiling brew.

Shivering with revulsion, you search the interior and find **two Skeleton Keys**. (They are very rare items that can open any lock, but they are brittle and will break after one use. You may take them if you wish.)

The intense heat from the stew is making the room unbearably hot, so you return to the ledge and continue your climb towards the grim fortress. Turn to **440**.

You are unsure how many enemies are approaching, so you hide behind a large pile of books at the back of the room. A moment later, the door swings wide and a tall figure strides through. He looks almost human, but he is not. The creature is a Markun, an evil being from the cold, distant lands of Rowtunda. His face is blue, with red markings, and his eyes are completely black. His long dark robes are adorned with menacing symbols, and they sweep across the floor in his wake. At his side is a short, fat Goblin, who is clad in battle-scarred armour. The Markun slams the door behind them and turns towards the little monster. The language they speak is sinister and strange, but your honed skill allows you to make sense of it.

"You pathetic wretch!" snarls the Markun. "Your order was to crush Shellhaven. Fifty War-Bringers were in your ambush party, with you commanding. This should have been a simple task even for you!"

"It was the guards," says the Goblin. "The archers-"

"Excuses will not save you," interrupts the Markun, his eyes narrowing. "When the Demon King hears the news of your failure he will tear the flesh from your bones and hang your corpse from the castle walls."

The Goblin looks suddenly nervous, and the blood drains from his green face. "I beg you, do not tell Zanack of this. The fate of Shellhaven has been delayed, but not for long. I will travel back there tonight! You must give me a second chance!"

Somewhere, in a distant part of the castle, a bell tolls. You can hear the sinister ring echoing through the dark corridors. The two figures pause to listen, and after a short time the ringing stops. "The bell of torment has been struck," says the Markun. "We have been summoned." He turns to leave the room, and the trembling Goblin scurries after him.

Will you:

Leap from your hiding place and attack them while their backs are turned, turn to **167**.

Or stay hidden and allow them to leave, turn to **199**.

41

Disturbed by what you have heard, you tell Mok that you intend to purge the village of the terror that is plaguing it. He seems startled, as if he did not expect your response, then he bravely offers to come with you. You tell him that you work alone. You arrange to meet him back at his house at the stroke of midnight, by which time you hope to have dealt with the troublesome quarry. Wasting no time, you leave the building and set off on your hunt. In your mind, you picture the cloaked phantom that was described to you. The image is suspiciously similar to the hooded rider who tried to run you down on the road outside Black Thorn Wood, and you suspect the two antagonists are one and the same.

If this menace has been terrorizing the folk of Grimbree for the past few weeks, you gather that it is probably somewhere nearby right now. It may even be creeping about the village at this very moment.

If you wish to start your search among the quiet, moon soaked streets, turn to **378**.

If you would rather start by looking around the outskirts of the village, turn to **393**.

Wasting no time, you leave the old castle behind you. It is cold and dreary and, for most of the day, rain patters in muddy puddles along the trail. Thunder rolls out of the distance, but it is too far away to sound threatening now. As you walk along, you cannot help but wonder what terrors await you in the depths of the Demon's fortress.

After an hour of peaceable travel, you notice a flock of birds flying east over the foothills towards the distant, Great Ocean. As you watch, you realise that they are flying in a frantic hurry, as though something has startled them. A second later, an ear-piercing screech fills the air, then a huge black beast, with great leathery wings, bursts out of the clouds. A tall figure, swathed in dark robes, is seated upon its back. The rider sights you upon the trail, then at his command, the winged terror dives towards you. You draw your sword in a flash, but the beast does not attack. It swoops over the road and lands on the muddy track a few metres ahead.

With slow, lurching movements, the rider comes down from its mount. His face is hidden beneath the shadows of a dark hood, but you can tell by his sinister motion that he is not human. He holds up a long staff and, as if in response, lightning flickers across the grey clouds.

"Are you the Shield Searcher?" hisses the figure, in a low and haunting voice.

Will you answer:

Yes, turn to **85**.

No, turn to **4**.

Or say nothing, and launch a swift attack, turn to **47**.

43

As you are climbing the stairs, you hear a terrible, inhuman scream from above. It is twisted by pain and anguish, and it fills your heart with dread. You listen warily as it echoes into the distance.

Will you:

Carry on up the stairs, turn to **168**.

Or descend the winding staircase instead, turn to **118**.

44

With a slow, sinister movement, the Games Master points his staff towards the arched doors in the far wall. "Behind each door is a creature. One beast is powerful, one is weak, and the other is of average might, but none lack fierceness and savage determination," it hisses. "I have chosen these barbaric creatures to fight in this hall for the amusement of Zanack. As you have come unwittingly into my domain, I see an opportunity to test their aggression before they do battle for the entertainment of my master. Choose a door. I do not expect you to defeat what lurks beyond it, but if you do, I will allow you to continue on your way. The choice… is yours."

If you wish to go along with his 'game,' which door will you choose?

The smallest one, turn to **196**.

The largest one, turn to **11**.

The medium sized one, turn to **16**.

Or would you rather attack the Games Master, turn to **190**.

45

As her mouth issues no sound, you try to read her lips. This is what you can make out:

"Stormwater attacked... many dead... please, avenge us... if you go to the village, seek the golden fountain... the water gives life... there is danger in the sky... avoid the tunnels... maybe Harn could have helped... but he is in Shellh... too late for that now... too late?"

She says much more, but that is all the information you can comprehend. After delivering her mysterious message, the spirit turns sorrowfully and fades into the darkness, as if she had never been.

The distant howl of a Werewolf suddenly echoes through the night, snapping you back to reality. The night is still dangerous, and you cannot afford to linger here any longer.

Will you:

Continue along the trail towards Stormwater, turn to **84**.

Or retrace your steps to the fork and turn west, turn to **197**.

46

You open the door and step into a gloomy, sparse chamber. The first things you notice are the circular openings in the walls, each about a foot in diameter, set at midpoint between the ground and the ceiling. There are claw marks on the walls and several human bones are scattered on the floor.

Do you possess the special ability of **Sixth Sense**?

If so, turn to **7**.

If not, turn to **78**.

You know a Demon when you see one. This foul rider is probably a servant of Zanack, a wretched assassin who has been sent to hunt heroes in the barren hills. You decide to waste no time on conversation. You spring foward with your blade raised, but the winged terror leaps forward to protect its master. You duck the snap of its jaws, then thrust your blade into its shoulder. It reels backwards with a monstrous roar, before lunging at you again!

(Because you struck first, reduce the Terrasaur's **Life Force** immediately by two points, then resolve the battle as normal. You will have to deal with the Terrasaur first, before you can reach the dark rider.)

TERRASAUR

LIFE FORCE 12   STRIKING SPEED 9

Focus	Move	Damage
1	Tail Slam	1
2-3	Slashing Claws	2
4-5	Crushing Bite	2
6	Burning Breath	3

If you win, turn to **102**.

Illustration Opposite

The trail winds slowly higher and higher, up into the grey hills. The grassy lowlands are left far behind and the terrain grows lifeless and barren. You occasionally sight a withered and ashen tree that is struggling to survive on the steep, rocky slopes, whilst overhead, a scavenging bird circles watchfully. It follows you for a few hours, as if hoping you might be struck down by an untimely death, but you are pleased to disappoint it, and it eventually swoops off into the distance. After several more hours of crossing steep rises and rocky ledges, you hear the sound of footfalls somewhere on the path ahead. You reach for your sword, but your nerves relax when you see that it is only an old man, apparently alone and unarmed. He is dressed in dusty clothes, and he appears to be blind. Apparently unaware of your presence, he comes slowly down the trail towards you, holding his walking stick in front of him. As you watch, he suddenly slips on the uneven ground and tumbles to the earth. You hurry forward and help him to his feet. Apart from a few scrapes, the man is uninjured. He is grateful for your kind gesture and he bows to you in thanks.

You decide to talk to him.

Turn to **297**.

You wake suddenly, shaken from your sleep by the dream. Beads of sweat glisten upon your forehead. It is still dark, and the hour is very late.

Having woken so abruptly, it takes a little while for you to get back to sleep. You gaze up at the distant galaxies that swirl and glimmer in the clear night. As your eyes grow heavier, you imagine that the stars are falling slowly from the sky, until they swirl and dance about you like tiny orbs of magical light.

Suddenly your eyes blink and you shake your head. Quite to your amazement, it becomes apparent that you are not imagining things at all. All around you, little lights are shimmering and dancing beautifully through the air, bathing you in a gentle blue aura. As you marvel at the spectacle, you recall an old tale that seems to explain the sight. You heard stories from a traveller many years ago, who said that Hill Fairies had come upon him late one night, sparkling like little stars.

As you watch, some of the lights flitter close to your ears, and you are aware of the delicate whisper of their faint, beautiful voices.

If you possess the special ability of **Greater Wisdom**, you may try to communicate with them, turn to **152**.

If you do not possess this ability, you watch the shimmering lights for a while longer, then they flitter into the darkness and vanish. Turn to **56**.

The other Demons seem undeterred by your victory. They smash the bar to pieces with their claws, destroying the last cover you had. Besieged, you watch in horror as the demonic mass rushes in like a wave of darkness.

In a desperate move, Burlybe suddenly grabs a candle from the wall. The wooden floor is soaked in alcohol from the smashed bar area, and he swiftly sets light to it. As the fighting continues, the flames spread to a tapestry on the wall, then up to the ceiling beams. The air becomes thick with smoke, but the Demons are possessed by an insane battle fury, and they show no sign of retreating. You attempt to defend yourself, but you will have to fight hard to avoid the frenzy of incoming blows.

Roll two dice and add the numbers together.

If the total is three or less, you take a heavy battering from the horde: reduce your **Life Force** by six points.

If the total is four or five, you sever six groping arms, but two swift Demons still manage to strike you: reduce your **Life Force** by four points.

If the total is six or higher, your brutal sword work keeps the enemy at bay and you take no damage.

If you are still alive after this onslaught, turn to **438**.

As you follow the trail into Black Thorn Wood, you notice a patch of grey clouds in the far distance. An hour later they have been blown overhead, and water patters and drips through the leafy canopy which arches over the path. The rain is soon gone, but the trail has been left wet and sludgy, and your progress is slowed. As the day draws late and the shadows start to lengthen, the twisting trees take on an ominous look. You march on, but it is not long before you hear a strange and sinister voice echoing through the moonlit wood. Up ahead, you see the hooded rider once again. The cart is parked on the trail, and the robed figure is standing next to it, chanting at the trees. Before you can act, he jumps back into the cart and gallops off, leaving behind the echo of sinister laughter.

Suddenly, the woodland vines begin to twitch and writhe. They wrap themselves around your ankles and try to pull you to the ground. You draw your sword and hack them away, but more are soon slithering from the shadows. The rider has put a curse upon this area. He is obviously intent on killing you, but before you can wonder why, you must first fight your way through to the far side of the wood.

If you possess the special ability of **Haste**, turn immediately to **240**.

If you do not possess this ability, you must fight!

ENCHANTED VINES

LIFE FORCE 10   STRIKING SPEED 7

Focus	Move	Damage
1	Lashing Vine	1
2-3	Strangling Grip	1
4-5	Entangling Crush	1
6	Thorny Grasp	2

If you win, turn to **240**.

52

To your surprise, a pulse of dark energy leaps out of the bracelet and strikes the plinth, pushing it aside to reveal a secret flight of steps. You decide to investigate and you walk down into a tiny dark chamber, where you are forced to stoop to avoid bashing your head on the ceiling. The room is empty, except for a bloodstained treasure chest.

If you have **Picklock**, (or a **Skeleton Key,**) you may open the chest if you wish, turn to **306**.

If you do not have **Picklock**, or if you do not want to open the box, you may climb back out of the chamber and investigate the unexplored passage, turn to **276**.

A clawed hand suddenly sweeps in through the entrance and strikes you with such force that you are knocked to the floor.

(Reduce your **Life Force** by three points!)

If you are still alive, you look up and are greeted by a horrendous sight. Turn to **394.**

It takes only three swipes of your blade to break the lock. But the clanging has disturbed the broken remnants that have been sleeping near your feet. The skeletal remains suddenly come to life, and several dismembered hands claw at your legs with jagged bone fingers! (Reduce your **Life Force** by two points.) If you are still alive, you quickly leap into the dark opening. As you do so, the bones cease their juddering, and they collapse to the floor and lay still once more. Eager to get away from the wretched pit, you scramble up the tunnel. Turn to **176.**

You fiddle with the lock and after a few minutes you hear a faint click. The door creaks open and you step through into a dingy room. The only light comes through the opening behind you, and it is evident from the musty smell that nobody has been in here for a long age. Cobwebs are everywhere, draping from the ceiling, and everything is covered in a blanket of dust that is at least an inch thick. As you look around, you see that luck has befallen you. You are standing in an armoury. Many of the weapons have rusted with age and are now useless, but there are a few items that have escaped the ravages of time. You find an excellent crossbow, crafted from a flawless material that you have never seen before, and you also discover two golden crossbow bolts to accompany it. In addition, there is a heavy, immaculate looking broadsword leaning in the corner of the chamber. Blowing the dust from it, you discover that its fearsome blade is etched with ancient symbols and it looks superior to your other sword. (Make a note that you now have a **Crossbow, two Golden Crossbow Bolts** and a **Rune Broadsword**.)

Feeling pleased with your find, you decide to leave. Turn to **82**.

As you are trying to get back to sleep, you become aware of the crunch of footfalls in the darkness nearby. You stand up and cautiously draw your sword. A moment later you see a young woman walking across the rocky terrain. She is fierce looking, with long blonde hair and studded leather armour. A black sword, which is sheathed at her side, marks her as a warrior. When she sees you, she quickly draws her weapon, but does not attack. "Are you a thief?" she says sharply. You shake your head. She seems wary, but after questioning you for a few minutes she decides to believe you. She sheathes her sword and apologises for the inquisition. Her face is pretty, but it looks weary and burdened, and she asks if she can sit with you for a while. You sense no evil from the newcomer, so you agree to her request. As you talk, you learn that the woman has travelled from the distant east, from a little known region called Rovencia. Her accent is heavy, and you have to listen carefully to make out her words. "My father lies ill," she explains, "so I am travelling to the Wizard's castle to ask for their aid. My quest was going well, but three days ago I became lost in the foothills. I had strayed from the path in an attempt to avoid a group of bandits." You tell her that the thieves should no longer be a problem, as you dispatched them a couple of days ago.

The woman seems impressed, and also somewhat relieved by this news. She informs you that she has spent all her money on her travels, so she offers you a trade.

If you wish to buy some of her rejuvenating herbs, she will sell them to you at a cost of two crimson coins.

She explains that their usefulness diminishes with time, so you must use them now if you want to benefit from their effects. (If you choose to buy them, you eat them immediately: increase your **Life Force** by two points and adjust your money.)

The woman sits with you for only a short while. She is eager to press on, so you show her your map of the area. Now that she has her bearings, her quest is far more likely to succeed. With a grateful wave, she takes to the road once more, vanishing into the night. Tiredness now weighs heavily on you. As you drift back to sleep, your thoughts dwell on the young woman. The roads in this region are dangerous. You can only hope that she reaches the Wizard's castle safely. Turn to **93**.

57

As you follow the path towards the village, you see a bunch of toadstools growing at the side of the trail. They are shimmering with a mysterious green light.

If you wish to eat one of the toadstools, turn to **442**.

If you would rather continue on your way, turn to **75**.

58

You are heading towards the dinghy when the water begins to bubble all around the pontoon. Huge tentacles suddenly burst from the depths and reach towards you! You glance a massive, eyeless head, with a gaping mouth and pointed teeth, lurking just below the surface!

A horrific ambush predator has set up home in the waters by the ruined harbour, and you have just wandered into its domain! Turn to **25**.

59

As you strike the final blow, the Demon lets out a terrible cry that fills the air. Your vanquished foe collapses backwards and, as it does so, its body crumbles into dust before your very eyes. You watch as the grey ash swirls away into the surrounding darkness. You sense an aura of evil magic lifting from this place, causing you to breathe a sigh of relief. You wipe the blood from your sword and are about to sheathe your weapon when something catches your eye. On the floor is a small ring, surrounded by a faint glow.

If you have met **Torin RavenSword**, turn to **449**.

Otherwise, you may take a closer look at the ring, turn to **341**.

Or leave the ring be, turn to **320**.

60

You strike out with your weapon, but your blade passes harmlessly through your foe. Your enemy is a creature of mist and miasma, and it can only be harmed by magical weapons. The taunting horror grasps you by the neck, then a freezing pain tears into you! You will not win this battle. Your adventure ends here, on the dark waters of the ghostly lake.

Leaving the passage, you follow a flight of red steps up to a wooden door. You try the handle and it opens with a soft click. You find yourself looking into a lavishly decorated bedroom. The room is obviously catered for a person of some importance. A candle flickers upon a black desk against the right wall, casting shadows about the room. In the dim light you see a black iron bed, draped in blood-red silk covers. A red rug lies on the stone floor. The room looks strangely lavish in contrast to the dark and winding corridors that you have seen in the rest of the fortress. As you look around, you notice a more sinister aspect to the room. Upon the walls, several paintings portray screaming faces in twisted positions. As you watch, the tortured, painted eyes glimmer and move with an eerie realism, as if they are watching you. You decide to investigate the closed door at the far side of the room, but as you head towards it, your heart suddenly jumps when you notice a beautiful woman with flowing dark hair asleep among the ruffled covers of the bed. You gather that she must have an evil heart, for why else would she be here in this wicked place? Or maybe all is not as it seems... could she be a prisoner in this grim fortress?

If you wake her, to find out what she is doing here, turn to **34**.

If you choose not to wake her, you may quietly tiptoe towards the door at the far side of the room, turn to **149**.

62

You throw open the door, but to your horror it merely leads into another room which is utterly consumed by fire. Waves of heat push you back, and the temperature is unbearable. You can hear creaking sounds where the building is about to crumble in on itself. You have seconds to escape! You realise that the green door must be the exit, so you turn to face it. Suddenly, the ceiling starts to collapse in a shower of burning embers.

If you possess the special ability of **Haste**, turn to **10.**

If you do not have **Haste**, you are not fast enough to escape the deluge. The rafters and fiery wreckage smash into you, burying you and knocking you unconscious. Your body will be burnt to ashes in the flaming house.

63

You rummage around in the study for some time. There are many books and scrolls that cram the overburdened shelves, all of which contain notes on dark sorcery. You are no expert in the art of black magic, so you wisely shut the books and leave them be.

The burning fireplace crackles warmly as you move to the untidy desk. Paper is scattered across the table, but beneath the strewn mess is an object which draws your interest. You have discovered a glass bottle filled with black liquid. As you hold it up to the light, you see that it is shimmering with strange lights, as though you are looking at dim stars glowing in a night sky.

If you wish to drink the contents of the bottle, turn to **37.**

Otherwise, you exit the room via the door, turn to **185.**

You have a sudden feeling that you should not turn right. A terrible fate will befall you if you take that tunnel.

"Left," you exclaim. "We should turn left!"

He obeys your command and races into the gloom.

Turn to **335**.

If you possess the special ability of **Sixth Sense,** you are struck by a sudden urge to move away from the box: you wisely listen to your instincts, turn to **58**.

If you do not possess this ability, read on. Cupping your hands, you dip them into the ooze to scoop up the slime. Too late you realise that the slime is actually acidic, designed to react only with human flesh.

Screaming, you tear your hands out of the liquid, but the flesh has already been eaten away, leaving two skeletal hands. You stagger around for a brief moment before passing out from the unbearable agony. Unfortunately, when you lose consciousness, you fall forward, headlong into the contents of the box. In a few, brief seconds, your body melts away.

Nobody will ever know what happened to you.

Mok is a kind host, and you are given a small room and a comfortable bed for the night. You lay down and rest your head on the thick pillow. Beyond the window, the night grows blacker than you have ever known it. No moon can be seen through the heavy weight of cloud that gathers over the rooftops of Grimbree. You close your eyes, wrapped in the warmth of your covers as you fall into a shallow slumber. All through the night you twist and turn in your sleep. From the edge of the village, an eerie screech carries on the cold wind and invades your dreams. Only when the sun begins to rise do the strange sounds stop, and a deathly quiet settles over the area.

Due to your disturbed sleep, you wake feeling little more refreshed than the day before. When you see Mok, he also looks weary and drained. His stance is burdened and his eyes are dark with worry. "I was awake before you," he says. "I've been out in the village, talking to some of the locals. There were plenty of sightings of an ominous figure moving through the streets last night, but fortunately none of the villagers were assaulted. It seems we 'ad a lucky night… let us pray such luck continues." Despite his hopeful words, he does not look optimistic.

Your host invites you to join him for breakfast, and you are treated to a bowl of thick stew. (Increase your **Life Force** by one point.) When you have finished, you thank Mok for his hospitality. You cannot afford to stay any longer in Grimbree; time is pressing and you must get back to your quest. After saying your farewells, you set off from the village. Turn to **21**.

You are in a dark and gloomy place, surrounded by shadows. As your eyes adjust, you find that you have landed in a long tunnel which snakes down, then south towards the lake. The tunnel appears to have been made recently, possibly by Zanack's minions, to allow swift crossing from the fortress to the mainland. Peering up through the opening, you watch the fleet flying north over the hill. They soon disappear into the distance. With the danger passed, you ponder over your next course of action.

If you follow the tunnel, turn to **182**.

If you would rather climb back into the open, turn to **116**.

68

The figure fades into the gloom behind you, then you drift onwards down the dark stream. After a short while you notice the remains of a rotting dinghy, wedged against the bank.

If you wish to investigate the wreck, turn to **178**.

If you drift onwards, turn to **143**.

Illustration Opposite

As you approach the bar, you notice that the woman's eyes are red, as though she has been crying. Her skin is pale and her face pretty, and you discover that she is the owner of the inn.

Her voice sounds solemn when she greets you. "I can see by your look that you are after a bed for the night," she says, "but I'm afraid I can't help. We used to rent rooms here, but not any more. Not since the death of my father. It was he who owned this place. I just open the bar now, as this inn is too big for me to run on my own." Her voice lowers to a whisper, and she leans forward so that only you can hear her. "Have a drink if you wish," she says, "but do not stay for long. It is not safe in Grimbree; the rider comes when the hour grows late, and you do not want to be here when he arrives." Her nerves grow more visible as she talks, and her hand is trembling as she offers you a mug of local ale, named The Ferret's Brew. (If you wish to purchase the drink, deduct **one Crimson Coin** from your belongings now.)

You notice that it is growing darker outside.

Will you:

Ask the young lady some more questions about the mysterious rider, turn to **219**.

Sit by the fireplace, to listen to the conversations of the other customers, turn to **300**.

Or immediately leave the inn, and exit Grimbree via the southerly road, turn to **72**.

You pull a blanket from your rucksack and make yourself as comfortable as you can on the hard earth. You have not long been asleep when you are woken by a roll of thunder. It is so loud, it sounds as if the sky has been ripped apart. You open your eyes and see that the stars have vanished, blotted out by heavy storm clouds. Rain patters about you and a cold wind begins to blow across the hill, chilling you to the bone. You bury yourself under your blanket, but it is not long before the rain soaks it through and you are shivering with the cold. You had hoped for a better rest than this!

Will you:

Ignore the weather and go back to sleep, hoping that the clouds will soon pass, turn to **317**.

Or gather up your rucksack and trudge off down the road after all, in the hope of finding a drier place to spend the night, turn to **98**.

As you lift the cover, you are greeted by a gruesome sight. The cart is filled with the remains of local villagers, and they have not long been dead. Their faces are pale and their lifeless eyes are staring up at you.

Suddenly, a bestial shriek pierces the sky, echoing through the shadowy streets.

"What are you doing?" says the young man. "Come inside. Hurry! Have you lost your mind?"

You are intrigued by the grim events that have beset this place, so you decide to do as he says. Turn to **14**.

72

You leave the village and trudge south for several miles. Before long the rooftops of Grimbree are out of sight and the moon is dipping in and out of scattered clouds. The hour is now very late. Your legs are drained from the long day's walk, and a deep tiredness weighs upon you. Eventually you are forced to settle down at the roadside to get some sleep.

You find a soft spot in a wild meadow, and for a while you sleep well. However, deep in the night you are woken by a rustling in the long grass.

Your eyes flicker open, and you catch sight of several lithe shadows, stalking through the field towards you. A pack of green haired Wolves have caught your scent, and they have surrounded you. You have awoken not a moment too soon! You leap to your feet, and in a flash you draw your sword. There is a famished look in your enemies' eyes, and for several minutes there is a tense standoff as you attempt to scare them away with your thrashing sword. Despite your best efforts, you eventually hear a fierce snarl to your left, then one of the animals makes a daring leap towards you. The rest quickly follow, and you suddenly find yourself fighting for your life.

(As soon as you have reduced their **Life Force** to 6 or below, turn to **415**.)

WOLF PACK

LIFE FORCE 14   STRIKING SPEED 9

Focus	Move	Damage
1	**Slashing Claws**	1
2-3	**Snapping Jaws**	2
4-5	**Savage Bite**	2
6	**Unified Attack**	4

You hurry off the track, but by the time you reach the foggy hill where you last saw him, the young man is nowhere to be seen. The sounds of battle have ceased and all is unnaturally quiet. Down on the ground you notice footprints in the wet earth, revealing that the man has fled the hill in a bid to escape his attackers, but you do not fancy his chances. You can see the imprints of the Werewolves' paws, pursuing him with hellish speed.

Will you:

Abandon the rescue attempt and head back to the road, turn to **330**.

Or follow the footprints deeper into the marsh, in the hope that you can still save him, turn to **18**.

74

On a desk, you find a potion of healing which you drink immediately. (Increase your **Life Force** by four points.) You also find a single **Golden Bolt** (if you have a crossbow, add the **Bolt** to your belongings, otherwise leave it.) The eyes of the paintings are now staring at you with greater intensity, and their mouths have turned into silent snarls. You are unsettled by the oddity. Having found everything of use, you quickly leave through the door at the far side of the room. Turn to **185**.

By the time you reach Stormwater, the settlement is deserted and quiet. The tall wooden buildings are clustered on a hill which rises up out of the marsh. It is encircled by a wooden wall, but the main gate is open, so you look inside. It is clear that a battle has taken place here at some point in the last few days. Scanning the dwellings, you see that the doors have been kicked in and blood fills the heavy footprints that mark the earth. A small army has rampaged through this place, that much is clear, but there is no one about now. The marauders have left, and the locals have either fled or been killed. The place has been left with a ghostly air of abandonment.

You know that Stormwater rests on the banks of a great lake, at the centre of which sits Zanack's Island fortress. This massacre was surely the work of Zanack's minions, of that you are in little doubt. The villagers have paid a costly price for living so close to the dreaded castle of the Demon Sorcerer.

As you survey the scene, anger swells within you. You control your temper, knowing that you must keep a clear head to determine your options.

If you are going to face Zanack, you must first find a way to reach his island.

If you cut through the village along Dock Street, to see if any boats are in the fishing harbour, turn to **145**.

If you walk up Fountain Lane, towards the top of the hill, to explore the centre of the village, turn to **23**.

After your recent battle, you are on full alert over the next few hours. You march onwards, and by the time that dusk is falling you are weary from the long day's hike. The rain has now stopped and the clouds have blown away. Across the late evening sky, the darkness is speckled with the glint of stars. With the promise of a dry night, and with no danger in view, you settle down by the roadside to get some well-earned sleep…

For a while you dream peacefully, but it is not long before you are beset by a sinister nightmare. You dream that you are standing in the high tower of a haunted castle. The shadows writhe and come to life, clawing at you with their black hands. Though you strike out mercilessly with your sword, your weapon merely sweeps through their ghostly bodies, doing them no harm.

Roll one dice.

If you roll a four or less, turn to **49**.

If you roll a five or a six, turn to **348**.

"Wrong!" leers the Fire Demon. Without warning it breathes out, blasting you with the intense heat of its breath. Your body bursts into flames, your flesh bubbles and melts, and in a few seconds you are reduced to a puddle of boiling sludge. For the next hour you hiss and pop, then slowly drip down the rocks, back towards the dark lake.

As you step forward, the door behind you suddenly springs shut. To your dismay, there is no keyhole or lock for you to pick, and it will not open. You have walked into a trap! You look around for a means of escape, and you notice three levers in the wall. There is a red lever which is marked with the number 100, a yellow lever marked 104, and an orange lever marked 106. You also discover numbers on the floor beneath a skeleton. The deceased man has left a message, etched in the moments before his death. It reads:

36, 25, 49, 16, 64, 9, 81, 4...

Suddenly, a mechanical clunk emanates from the ceiling, then waterfalls gush out of the holes in the walls. This chamber of death has been sealed by magic, and there is only one way to escape. You must work out the next number in the above sequence, as it will give you a clue as to which lever you must pull. You must think quickly though, before the water fills the chamber!

If you wish to pull the red lever, turn to **100**.

If you wish to pull the orange lever, turn to **2**.

If you wish to pull the yellow lever, turn to **170**.

79

The writing on the box seems to be a warning of some kind, but that is as much as you can deduce.

If you wish to open the lid, turn to **91**.

If you squeeze past the box and head for the dinghy, turn to **58**.

With the threat dispersed, you head over to the young man. At first all you can get from him is endless appreciation. After more thanks than your ego can handle, the stranger finally introduces himself as Bayek. "There are not enough words to express my gratitude," he says. "If you had not appeared so unexpectedly to help me… well, I would surely have been slain!" You soon learn that Bayek is not local to these parts. He had set out from his homeland in the west in search of adventure, after hearing about some lost ruins that had sunk into the marsh long ago. "The tale says that he who finds the fabled ruins will also find its ancient treasure. Maybe it was a fool's errand," he tells you, "but I had thought it worth a look. However, since I arrived in this land two days ago, I have found nothing but evil upon this marsh. These lands are more dangerous than I had bargained for. I fear a dark power is rising in the south. I cannot explain quite why, but for a shivering feeling in my bones. Tell me stranger, what brings you out along the marshland trail after dark?"

Will you:

Tell him the truth about why you are here, and explain about your quest, turn to **361**.

Or will you keep the nature of your mission a secret, and simply inform him that you are a traveller heading south, turn to **331**.

You continue along the trail and soon come to the body of a young man lying amongst the rocks. He has been murdered and his pockets have been emptied. This is the work of Bandits, and footprints near the scene inform you that the criminals were here very recently. A letter in the dead man's pocket reveals that he was a trader from a distant port town in the east, and he had come travelling this way in search of a new place to set up business. You bury the man under some rubble and are about to say a few words for his departed soul, when you hear the crunch of footfalls. You spin around and see a bearded man springing at you from behind a rock. You dodge his attack and kick him in the chest, knocking him backwards to the ground. With a snarl, he leaps up and jumps at you again!

SAVAGE BANDIT

LIFE FORCE 7   STRIKING SPEED 9

Focus	Move	Damage
1	**Elbow To The Face**	1
2-3	**Eye Gouge**	2
4-5	**Sweeping Blade**	2
6	**Stabbing Blade**	3

If you win, the man sags to the floor. With his dying breaths, he utters a vile warning. "My brothers live in these hills. They will cut your heart out for this!"

Then he lays still, and his eyes close.

You press on and soon come to the base of a large hill. If you climb it, turn to **434**.

If you stay on the path, which is now bending southward, turn to **205**.

82

You are about to leave the weapons room when you notice a dusty lever in the wall.

If you wish to pull the lever, turn to **19**.

If you would rather leave the ruins, turn to **42**.

83

Suddenly your sword begins to glow. As your enemy sweeps towards you, you thrust your blade straight into the snarling phantom. A shriek of horror tears through the gloom. The Mist Demon is particularly vulnerable to your magical weapon. There is a flash of light, then the scream is silenced, and darkness returns to the lake. You look around, but there is no sign of your foe. With one strike from your enchanted blade, the creature has been completely obliterated.

Your weapon now ceases to glow, so you return it to its scabbard. You sit back in the dinghy and row onwards. It is not long before you see a huge, rocky island emerging through the mist at the centre of the lake. Upon the rise sits Zanack's forbidding castle.

Feeling bold after your recent victory, you row towards it.

Turn to **324**.

You have only been walking for a short while when you hear a strange noise behind you. You turn around and see that a mossy mound with a door in it has appeared not ten feet from where you stand. It was not there a second ago, and you have to rub your eyes to make sure that you are not dreaming. On a boulder by the door sits a hunched little woman, whose long mossy hair completely covers her face. "Do not be alarmed," she croaks. "I am Haggadus the Witch. Normally I like to trick travellers, for I am quite fond of human stew, but I am not here to cast a spell on you this night." As she speaks, she strokes a black crystal ball, which is resting on her lap. "You are on a quest to kill the Demon Sorcerer, so says my magic sphere. Zanack is also my enemy, for this marsh is my home, and yet he has dared to lay claim to it. His servants run amok here like they own it, and I fear that things will only get worse. If anyone should be eating travellers it should be me, not his mindless thugs." She throws you a vial of black liquid. "Drink it," she orders, "for this is the only chance I may get to help you. It will give you luck, and that is something you will need lots of on the journey ahead. Now be off with you, and do not dally!" She waves her hand, and suddenly the mound and the Witch are both gone, leaving you alone once more.

You look at the vial of black ooze in your hand.

You now have a choice.

If you drink the contents, turn to **412**.

Otherwise, you may throw the vial into the marsh and continue on your way, turn to **408**.

The robed figure lets out a shuddering breath, which makes your skin crawl with revulsion. "Good," it hisses. "I have been looking for you. It will please my master Zanack, when I return to him with your head on a spike!" Beneath the darkness of its hood, it grins evilly. "You should have fled these lands when you had the chance," it cackles. With a wave of its hand, it orders the Terrasaur to destroy you.

The winged beast immediately leaps forward, raking the air with its terrible claws. You must fight this awesome opponent!

TERRASAUR

LIFE FORCE 12   STRIKING SPEED 9

Focus	Move	Damage
1	Tail Slam	1
2-3	Slashing Claws	2
4-5	Crushing Bite	2
6	Scorching Breath	3

If you win, turn to **102**.

86

Badly wounded, Avion backs towards the dinghy. You leap after her, but she suddenly raises her hand and a flash of flickering blue energy springs towards you!

If you possess the special ability of **Haste**, turn to **124**.

If not, will you:

Leap to the left, turn to **110**.

Or leap to the right, turn to **135**.

87

You follow the track through beautiful fields and wild meadows. To the east you can see distant hills rising, but your path veers away from them, and soon all that you can see is miles of lush grassland. Wild horses graze near the footpath and rabbits leap about in the sweeping meadows.

After a few hours the trail starts sloping gently downward and you find yourself walking through a wild and beautiful valley that is deep in ferns. The air here is fresh and humming with life, and strange birds with bright and striking colours wheel and flitter under the blue sky.

Before long you hear the faint sound of bubbling water. Looking around, you see a pond not far from the path. The cool water is sparkling as if with an aura of magic.

If you wish to investigate this find, turn to **333**.

If you would rather ignore the pond and carry on through the valley, turn to **137**.

88

Cautiously, you draw your sword and creep towards the rock. Standing behind it is a small purple bird. It has a little pouch clasped in its beak, which it promptly drops to the ground before fluttering into the night.

The bird looked similar to the ones in the garden at the Wizard's castle. Could it have been a messenger?

You look in the pouch and find a small **Golden Key**. Wondering what significance it might have, you drop it into your pocket before going back to sleep.

Make a note of this new possession, then turn to **123**.

89

You swing your sword, but it sweeps harmlessly through the Demon's fiery essence. When your weapon reappears from the flames, you find that the blade has melted!

For a brief moment the Demon seems puzzled by your curious actions, then, suddenly realising that you are attempting to kill it, it bursts into uncontrollable, roaring laughter. When it has regained its composure, it exhales forcefully. You are blasted by the intense heat of its breath. Your flesh is liquefied, and in a few seconds you are reduced to a bubbling pulp. Your quest is over.

Illustration Opposite

Suddenly there is a rumbling in the crypt. Sensing danger, you step back and grip your weapon. The heavy lid bursts from the coffin and the Skeleton within rises up to look at you. It is clad in tattered armour and a tarnished crown, with a rusty broadsword clutched in both hands. Withered strips of flesh hang from its body in long drapes, and its eyes are filled with black fire. It suddenly chuckles in a wicked tone, and its spectral laughter echoes eerily around the room.

For a brief moment you are frozen in alarm by the grisly sight. In the flickering light you watch as the undead horror steps from its death bed. Slowly, it descends towards you, gripping its ancient sword. You regain your senses as the sardonic terror lunges forward!

VAMPIRIC SKELETON

LIFE FORCE 10   STRIKING SPEED 8

Focus	Move	Damage
1	Life Draining Stare	1
2-3	Breath of Death	2
4-5	Rending Blade	3
6	Glacial Curse	See Below*

(*Special Move: If you are blighted by your enemy's Glacial Curse, a freezing pain stiffens your muscles, reducing your Striking Speed by one point.)

If you win, turn to **328**.

91

It is a struggle to open the lid, but with the use of your sword you finally prize it free. You look down and find that the container is filled with black slime. The ooze is odorless, and its surface glistens strangely. Will you:

Scoop the substance into your hands, to examine it more closely, turn to **65**.

Or lay the lid back on the box and head for the dinghy, turn to **58**.

92

The footsteps halt just beyond the door and you hear a furious voice shouting and bellowing. Spying through the keyhole, you see a tall and angry looking figure. He looks almost human, but he is not. The creature is a Markun, an evil being from the cold, distant lands of Rowtunda. His face is blue, with strange red markings, and his eyes are completely black. His long dark robes hang down to the floor, and they are adorned with menacing symbols. He is talking to a short, fat Goblin, who is clad in battle-scarred armour. They are having a heated discussion, but due to their strange language, you are unable to decipher what they are saying.

Suddenly, the Markun kicks the door, causing it to fly open. The tall figure strides through, but he has barely put a foot into the room when he sees you. You are standing with your sword like a vanquisher of evil, and he leaps backwards in shock. With a swift movement, he grabs a knife from beneath his robes, but you kick the weapon from his hand and slam the pommel of your sword into his jaw. He staggers sideways with a dazed expression, grabbing the door frame to stop himself from falling. Before you can do anything else, the fierce little Goblin springs forward, stabbing and thrusting with his short-sword. You must fight!

GOBLIN

LIFE FORCE 5   STRIKING SPEED 8

Focus	Move	Damage
1	Shoulder Barge	1
2-3	Vicious Punch	1
4-5	Sweeping Blade	2
6	Stabbing Blade	2

If you win, turn to **167**.

93

The next morning you rise early. You feel refreshed after your good sleep, and you are eager to get back to your quest. The sky is grey and cloudy, but you are thankful that it is not raining. The rolling foothills lead on for several miles, and at length the trail begins to slope gradually downwards. Small, withered trees begin to dot the landscape, and their bitter fruits suffice to suppress your hunger.

By the time that dusk is setting, the path has left the hills and meandered to the border of Harrowmoor, the shadowy marshes of the southern realm. After spending the last few days in the rolling highlands, the land ahead now seems distinctly flat and shapeless. The ground soon turns boggy and soft, and the spongy terrain squelches underfoot. As twilight turns to darkness, a break in the clouds reveals a full moon. It is an unwelcome sight, for you have heard tales that lycanthropy is rife in this area, which means that Werewolves may be out on the prowl. As you head deeper into the marshes, a terrible howl soon shatters the eerie silence and you decide that it would be wise to keep on the move. As the hours of darkness draw on, a creeping mist rolls in from the west, crawling across the mire with ghostly hands.

Suddenly you pause. Away to the east, not far from the path, you see the silhouette of a young man. He is standing on the rise of a small, lone hill, and he is surrounded by a number of terrible creatures, most likely the foul Werewolves you heard howling earlier. The man is armed with a sword, but he is clearly outnumbered. The mist is continuing to gather across the mire, and in the next instant he vanishes from your sight behind the curtain of fog. Although you can no longer see him, you can hear the start of a desperate fight.

Will you:

Leave the path and rush towards the sounds, in a bid to help him, turn to **73**.

Or stay on the path and carry on your way, turn to **330**.

As you row forward, the indistinct shape becomes clearer, and you find yourself looking at a small white bird. Its little wings sparkle with a magical aura and, when it sees you, it sweeps gracefully towards you and lands on the edge of the dinghy. It is holding a small, rolled up parchment in its beak, which it promptly drops at your feet. It seems pleased with itself, and with a little chirp it beats its wings and flutters away. Curious, you pick up the parchment. And when you see that it bears the seal of the Council of The Wizards, your heart beats faster with excitement!

The parchment reads simply this: "I only hope that our messenger finds you in time. Good luck!"

It is signed by Pelanthius, the head of the Wizard's Council. As you unroll the parchment fully, you find a key inside. (Make a note that you now have a **Blue Marble Key**.)

You look around, but the little bird has vanished. It seemed in quite a hurry to get out of this place. Tucking the key safely into your pocket, and wondering what importance it may have, you row onwards.

Time passes, yet there is still no sign of the castle. It becomes evident you have rowed off course, so you decide to explore in a different direction.

If you wish to veer to the right, where the mist hangs deepest, turn to **299**.

If you veer to the left, where the mist is less dense, turn to **401**.

95

You find yourself standing in a long, wide entrance hall, whose floor, walls and ceiling are made of dark stone. A flickering black candle is mounted on the wall several metres in front of you, forcing the shadows into an eerie dance. The ominous quiet causes your nerves to tingle. You follow the passage until it opens into a vast square chamber. Directly ahead is a huge set of open, iron doors, leading into what looks like a throne room. In the west wall is an average sized door which is closed and made of black stained wood.

Will you:

Head into the throne room, turn to **318**.

Or try the door in the west wall, turn to **195**.

96

As you continue to scan the chamber, an icy chill enters your bones. You have a strong feeling that if you linger here any longer, you are going to find yourself in grave danger. You sense an aura of evil in this room. At the moment it lays dormant, but you have a feeling that your continued presence would be unwise. You take a step backwards and, as you move away from the coffin, your premonition of doom begins to fade.

Will you:

Continue to search the chamber for anything useful, turn to **90**.

Or listen to your instincts and immediately leave the ruins, turn to **42**.

The village grows ever more dishevelled as you make your way along the lane. You keep to the shadows, wary of your ominous surroundings, and your discretion is rewarded. In the following minutes you see two more fleets passing overhead, looking for trespassers in the ruined landscape. Thanks to your wary movements, they do not see you and they fly out of sight.

Before long, you find yourself down at the small fishing harbour, which is situated in the shadow of a large warehouse. The structure is unstable, having been damaged by the marauders. It looks ready to come crashing down at any moment, so you keep an eye on it as you head towards the pontoons.

The area is still and silent. A deep mist hovers over the lake, but you can vaguely see Zanack's island fortress out in the murk. As you scan the area, you notice a small dinghy tied to a nearby pontoon. You head towards it, but blocking the walkway is a box bearing strange markings.

If you wish to investigate the container, turn to **20**.

If you would rather not linger here, you may squeeze around it and head straight for the dinghy, turn to **58**.

98

As you set off along the trail, the night grows deeper and colder. Storm clouds thicken overhead, lashing you with rain. You trudge on, keeping watch for a suitable place of shelter. After crossing a couple of steep rises you see a large cave not too far from the path. At first your spirits are lifted, but on closer inspection you do not think it would be wise to go in there. Animal bones are scattered all around the entrance, leading you to suspect that the cave is already occupied by a large beast. You decide not to venture into the lair, so you set off again in the hope of finding a safer place further down the track.

Roll one dice to determine what random events lay ahead of you.

If you roll a five or a six, turn to **35**.

If you roll a three or a four, turn to **243**.

If you roll a one or a two, turn to **264**.

99

You politely decline and continue on your way. After a few seconds the little Elf suddenly leaps in front of you, holding the potion right in front of your face.

"Are you sure you don't want it? Are you certain?" he pesters. "You may regret missing this opportunity. It's very good you know. Are you sure you don't want it?"

Will you:

Change your mind and purchase his potion, turn to **6**.

Or make yourself absolutely clear that you have no intention of buying it, turn to **184**.

100

You tug on the lever and the influx of water ceases. A small, barred opening appears in the chamber floor, causing the water to drain away, then the door opens. You step back into the passage, relieved to be alive. You decide to investigate the red door. Turn to **61**.

101

"There is no way I can persuade you?"

You shake your head.

"Your funeral," she says, and her booted foot slams into your stomach! You fall back, winded by the blow. With a snarl Avion suddenly springs on top of you, raining wild punches at your head, (reduce your **Life Force** by one point.) You bring your knee up between her legs, throwing her off of you, but you have barely recovered from her first onslaught when she leaps at you again, thrusting her dagger towards your throat!

You must fight!

(As soon as you have reduced Avion's **Life Force** to 3 or below, turn to **86**.)

AVION

LIFE FORCE 7	STRIKING SPEED 10	

Focus	Move	Damage
1	**Uppercut Punch**	1
2-3	**Spinning Kick**	1
4-5	**Thrusting Blade**	2
6	**Slashing Dagger**	2

102

You spring over the body of the fallen beast, ready to face the ominous rider, but your cunning opponent has other plans. Before you can reach him, he draws a black sword from beneath his cloak and hurls it towards you. You are forced to leap to the ground, then the blade whistles overhead and slams into the earth behind you. With a curse, your foe takes a step backwards. "We will meet again, Shield Searcher," he hisses in a furious voice, then with a wave of his staff he vanishes. An eerie tingling of magic hangs momentarily in the air where the figure has disappeared. You sense that your enemy's sorcery has transported him far away from here, and you do not have the feeling that he will be back anytime soon. When you have regained your breath, you turn to examine your enemy's sword, which is still impaled in the earth nearby. The long blade is flickering with a dark and magical fire.

If you wish to pick up the sword and take it with you, turn to **112**.

If you would rather leave it behind, turn to **76**.

103

With a beat of its powerful wings, Snowfire speeds away from the scene, carrying you to safety. You look back, clinging to the flowing white mane. The fortress is crumbling away, sinking beneath the surface of the lake. Clouds of dust and smoke billow into the sky as the building crumbles into ruin.

However, as you glide away, you see a huge shape escape from the castle. The beast soars up out of the dust cloud, chasing after you on enormous leathery wings. As it comes closer, your blood goes suddenly cold. It is a huge fire-breathing monster, covered in red scales, with a long neck and a terrible, horned head. It seems that Zanack was keeping a Red Dragon as a pet, and the cursed thing is out for vengeance after the death of its master. The beast is probably a hundred years old – young for a Dragon – which means that it is not fully grown. But that is of little comfort to you, as the creature's head is already as large as a barn. Snowfire is flying as quickly as he can, but the enormous beast is gaining fast.

You can hardly believe your foul luck, for it seems that you will have one last fight on your hands after all!

The intelligent horse banks into a low cloud, hoping to elude its pursuer. For a moment you lose sight of the monster, then you hear a sudden roar which rips through the sky with an almighty fury. You look up, in time to see the predator hurtling through the cloud.

Because you lost all of your weapons in the lake, you will not be able to help Snowfire to fight off the beast. But maybe there is still something in your possession that could prove useful?

If you have a **Magic Ring**, turn to **242**.

If not, turn to **271**.

"I am a weary traveller from afar," you call. "I request that you open the gate and let me in."

There is a long silence, but you know they have heard you, for you see the dim silhouettes turn and look down towards your position.

"I have travelled long and far," you implore. "I ask again, will you not open the gate? I seek only to rent a boat from the town's harbour."

Suddenly you hear a whine, and an arrow thuds into the soft earth near your foot. It was a mere warning shot, not intended to hit you.

A voice calls out, and its tone is less friendly than you would have liked. "Menace has besieged this land!" exclaims one of the guards sternly. "Nothing now but evil lurks in the marshes after dark. A traveller from afar you say? No good folk come this way any more, only foul things drift down on the northerly road; dark spies who work for Zanack! We can ill afford to trust anyone these days. Turn back while you can, stranger, or the next arrow will find itself imbedded in your heart."

The folk here may once have been a friendly and welcoming sort, but the threat of evil in this land has clearly made them suspicious of outsiders.

If you try to convince the guards to let you in, by telling them that you are no friend of that foul hearted Demon, Zanack, turn to **339**.

Otherwise, you retreat into the night, fooling the guards into thinking that you have fled, then you look for another way into the town, turn to **193**.

105

You grasp your weapon and hack through a tentacle as it tries to snare you by the throat. But more are coming, groping towards you in large numbers. You deduce that there are too many to kill, so you dash along the walkway towards the open door. A giant tentacle, as thick as a tree trunk, surges after you, but you are too quick to be caught. You hurl yourself through the open doorway and into the corridor beyond. From here, you are out of the Pool Beast's reach, but your troubles are not over yet. To your dismay, the castle guards suddenly break through the door at the far end of the chamber. You grasp your sword, ready for a battle, but luck is on your side. As the horde rush into the room, they are ambushed and immediately dragged into the water by the writhing tentacles. The chamber is suddenly filled with screams and raised voices, as they attempt to defend themselves from the slithering arms of the Pool Beast. The ravenous monster is one of Zanack's favourite pets, and although it has recently been fed, it seems all too happy at the prospect of a second meal. You quickly turn and run off down the corridor, while the mob are preoccupied with the monstrous abomination. Turn to **446**.

106
Illustration Opposite

…a huge cyclone of fire erupts from within the ring of stones, forming a raging tornado of flames. You leap back in surprise as the entire sky is lit in a blaze of red. To your horror, the upper part of the spinning vortex takes the form of an enormous red Demon, whilst the lower part remains a blazing twister. A huge and muscular chest appears from the fiery chaos, along with hulking, powerful arms. Clawed hands then form, followed by a giant head with two curved horns. The beast glowers down at you with nightmarish eyes, wearing a grin of dagger-like teeth. The Elemental Fire Demon towers to eighty feet in height. Without doubt this is one of the most powerful beings you have ever encountered. It is not of this realm; it is one of the horrors born in the Elemental Plane of Darkness.

A forked, snake like tongue hisses out at you. "I am the servant of chaos and sin, and guardian of the entrance to the black fortress! Speak now the password, or you will suffer the agony of a thousand deaths!" Its booming voice shakes the ground and echoes about the shadowy turrets.

You may attack the guardian by turning to **89**, or respond with one of the following answers:

Rakmar, turn to **183**.
Doomroth, turn to **77**.
Banrok, turn to **132**.
Gorath, turn to **161**.
Canaz, turn to **441**.
Valanor, turn to **407**.

107

After several attempts, you succeed at picking the lock. You hear a faint click, then the door rumbles open. A group of bats flutter out from the gaping blackness that is revealed.

Breathing deeply, you move inside. Turn to **174**.

108

Complying with your wishes, Avion brings you to a halt and waits in the dinghy for your return. You make your way through the deepening mist. The ground is soft and marshy and you have to watch your footing. After a short while you come to the figure, only to find the remains of a human skeleton propped up against a lone tree. Fumes belch out of a nearby bog, flapping the skeleton's coat and making it look as though its arm is waving. Peculiar trinkets have been scattered over the figure, and you realize that you are looking at the scene of a sacrifice. You wonder who this offering was intended for, then you notice a plaque hanging around the dead man's neck, which seems to give you an answer. It reads, *To Makazen, The Tree God*.

You stare at the tree, whose leafless arms are sagging towards the ground. As you watch, a cavernous mouth opens in the bark, and wooden stake-like teeth are clearly visible! With a gasp of surprise you stagger backwards, but a thick branch suddenly wraps around your leg and drags you towards the gaping cavity. (Your leg is being crushed by the powerful grasp, and your bones are close to shattering. Reduce your **Life Force** by three points.) If you are still alive, you manage to hack through the branch and scramble out of your enemy's reach. Limping with pain, you hurry back to the safety of the dinghy. Turn to **143**.

109

You are now standing in a large, circular chamber. A spiral staircase hugs the walls, ascending into shadows and darkness. On the far side of the room there is a sturdy black door, which has been stained with a bloody handprint.

If you wish to open the door that is marked with the red hand, turn to **304**.

If you would rather head up the stairs, turn to **277**.

110

You land face down in the mud, narrowly avoiding the energy blast. It explodes into the ground behind you, causing lumps of earth to rain from the sky. You look up and see Avion sitting in the dinghy, rowing away into the darkness. As you pull yourself to your feet, you catch a last glimpse of her as she vanishes downstream.

As you walk back to the trail, you wonder why Avion attacked you. Maybe she did not want you to succeed in your mission, but then why did she save you from your captors?

Maybe you will never know… Turn to **417**.

Having recovered the Doom Shield, you are filled with a well-earned sense of achievement. The only downside to this moment is that you do not have much time to bask in it. Your presence here has not gone unnoticed! You hear footfalls coming from the room where you discovered the Golden Guardian. By the sound of it, at least ten angry brutes are closing in on your position, and they will be crashing through the door at any moment! You realise that you must have tripped a silent alarm when you deactivated the magical barrier.

You must act quickly, before the guards arrive.

Will you:

Swiftly make your exit through the door at the other side of the room, in the hope of eluding the approaching mob, turn to **290**.

Or draw your sword and attack them as they come through the door, turn to **236**.

112

As soon as you grasp the sword hilt, you realise that you have made a terrible mistake. The black flames suddenly rush up the hilt and ignite your arm, burning you with a dreadful heat! (Reduce your **Life Force** by two points.) You quickly drop the weapon and it crumbles into ash as it hits the ground. The sword must have been cursed, so that only its wicked owner could touch it!

If you are still alive, you move away from the scene and continue down the track. Turn to **76**.

113

Do you possess the special ability of **Scale**?
If so, turn to **153**.
If not, turn to **140**.

114

Do you possess the special ability of **Stealth**?
If so, turn to **147**.
If not, turn to **166**.

115

You have only been rowing for a few minutes when you notice a gigantic, evil shape swooping and soaring, far, far above you. Your hand tightens upon the hilt of your blade, but luckily the enormous, bat-winged creature does not see you through the green vapour. You see wild flames spewing from its monstrous jaws, as if it is trying to set fire to the clouds in some furious and futile rage, then it banks sharply and flies out of sight.

Relieved that it has gone, you dip your oars back into the water and row onwards.

Before long, the fog shifts and thickens around you once again. You row blindly in circles for about an hour, but at length, by pure chance, you come upon the centre of the lake. You see a huge rocky island emerging through the haze, and upon its summit sits Zanack's forbidding castle.

Steadying your nerves, you row towards it. Turn to **324**.

116

You clamber back into the daylight. The sky, for the moment at least, is clear of enemies.

Looking around, you notice something that previously escaped your attention. The water in the nearby fountain is the colour of gold. It splashes and gurgles lethargically, glimmering as if with an aura of magic.

Although your enemies are out of sight, the dark fleet could return at any time, and with that in mind you decide what to do.

Will you:

Investigate the fountain, turn to **208**.

Or head straight for the harbour, turn to **145**.

117

From the shadows of its hood, you hear a fiendish chuckle that seethes with dark intentions. "We will see… we will see..." it hisses.

You suddenly have a strange feeling that someone, or something, is sneaking up on you from behind. Before you can spin on your heel to look, you are struck by a heavy blow across the back of the head. Darkness fills your mind, and your unconscious body hits the earth with a dull thud… turn to **220**.

After a while you reach the bottom of the stairs and enter a short passage that ends in two closed doors. Carved into the stone above one door is the image of a curved sword. Over the other door is an ancient symbol which signifies knowledge.

Which door will you open?

The door with the sword, turn to **3**.

Or the other door, turn to **364**.

"Excellent!" cries Burlybe. "Then we will be leaving early morning?"

You nod.

Suddenly the rain begins to fall even harder, and the heavy droplets shake the windowpane. The storm is growing continually worse, and you are glad to be out of it. The fireplace crackles warmly, but outside, beyond the safety of the tavern walls, the night is unnaturally deep. The wind is howling like a wolf and lightning scars the bellies of the dark, boiling storm clouds.

"This is no normal storm," mutters Burlybe, with an air of superstition. He sits quietly for a moment, then his expression grows deep and thoughtful. "These are dark days my friend... I fear a great evil is abroad." He rubs tiredly at his eyes, then bids you goodnight and heads up to his room.

Looking around, you see that all of the customers have now gone to bed. You decide to approach the barman and ask for a room for the night. Turn to **156**.

The door is not locked, but it is very old and stiff. With a little force you decide you can get it open, so you take a short run up and barge into it with your shoulder. The door does not open; instead, the old timber gives way with unexpected ease, causing you to crash straight through it. To your horror, there is no floor on the far side, and you are unable to stop yourself from tumbling into the yawning darkness. You plummet downwards with a cry of alarm, and a few moments later you see the ground rushing up to meet you. There is a loud crack as you slam into the floor - reduce your **Life Force** by two points – and the jarring impact knocks you unconscious. If you are still alive, turn to **413**.

After lashing the dinghy to the bank, you both scale the rocky shore. It is not long before you reach the square building. The structure is made of thick, grey stone, and is around ten feet in height.

Somewhere over the mist shrouded lake, you hear the distant call of a nightmarish creature. You cautiously grip the hilt of your sword. Looming not far away is the second, larger island, upon which sits the dark form of Zanack's forbidding fortress. You have to crane your neck to look up at it. The evil cry echoes once more, drifting from one of the towering spires of that dreaded castle. For a moment you wonder if you have been spotted by some sharp-eyed lookout. But you have not. The sound fades, and all goes quiet.

"We must hurry," whispers Avion anxiously. "We should not linger here any longer than we have to."

Nodding in agreement, you turn your attention back to the small building. The walls are very smooth, and the only entrance is a heavy, stone door that is set into the west wall, facing away from Zanack's fortress. In the smooth surface of the door is a tiny keyhole.

Will you:

Use a **Golden Key** (if you possess one), turn to **163**.

Use your strength to force the door open, turn to **139**.

Suggest Avion uses her magic to break in, turn to **186**.

Or, if you possess the special ability of **Picklock** (and want to use it), turn to **107**.

122

Your veins are still burning from the effects of the snakebite and you are overcome by a feeling of exhaustion. (Reduce your **Life Force** by one more point.) You need to rest, so you lay down by the side of the trail. Your dreams are strange and disjointed, and sweat rolls from your forehead as you twitch in a feverish slumber. When you wake, it is late in the night. Your skin is still puffy around the area where you were bitten, but you are relieved to discover that the symptoms are fading. (You are feeling much better. Remove the word **Venom** from your Character Sheet.) The stars are gleaming, but in the faraway sky a fierce thunderstorm is raging. You can see that the distant lightning is heading your way.

Will you:

Look for a place of shelter, turn to **98**.

Or stay where you are and go back to sleep, turn to **70**.

The next morning you wake early, feeling refreshed after your rest. Eager to get on with your quest, you set off again down the valley.

The sky is clear and the air humid, and you soon begin to sweat vigorously. It is around midday when you see a small Valley Elf child sitting by the path in the shade of a lonely tree. He looks almost invisible amongst the ferns in his leaf-green clothes. His ears are pointed and his overly large eyes are gazing up through the branches at the sky. He looks like he is enjoying the peaceful day, but it is not long before your footfalls gain his attention. He turns his head to see who is coming, then he jumps nimbly to his feet.

"Well well, what have we here?" says the magical creature, peering at you with his emerald eyes. "My name is Childeer, and I do not see many of your kind down here in the valley. Are you on a quest?" he asks, looking at your sword and rucksack. "Or maybe you are a wanderer, looking for adventure?" He rubs at his chin as if trying to decide for himself. "Either way, you will not get far without some good provisions. Maybe I could interest you in a potion of healing, which I made myself? It may look small, but do not let that fool you. It could make you twice as healthy as you are now. If you want it, it can be yours for only three crimson coins." He pulls a small bottle from his pocket which is filled with a sparkling green liquid.

Will you:

Agree to buy the Elf's potion, turn to **6**.

Or decline his offer and be on your way, turn to **99**.

124

With lightning reactions you dodge the spell. A second comes hurtling towards you, but you dive onto the ground and it explodes into the earth behind you. Mud rains from the sky, then you see Avion floating away in the dinghy. As you pull yourself to your feet, you catch one last glimpse of her as she vanishes downstream.

As you walk back to the path you wonder why she attacked you? Maybe she did not want you to succeed in your mission, but then why did she save you from your captors?

Maybe you will never know… turn to **417**.

125

A pile of books, stacked four feet high and wide, offers a perfect hiding place. You dive behind it as the door swings wide, then a tall, angry figure strides in. He looks almost human, but he is not. The creature is a Markun, an evil being from the cold, distant lands of Rowtunda. His face is blue with red markings, and his eyes are completely black. His long dark robes are adorned with menacing symbols, and they sweep across the floor in his wake. A short, fat Goblin eventually joins him, then they start to talk in hushed voices. The conversation soon turns into an argument, but their language is strange and you cannot understand the cause of their dispute.

Several minutes later, they turn and head for the exit. Will you:

Attack them while their backs are turned, turn to **167**.

Or stay hidden and let them leave, turn to **199**.

The barman takes your money. Out of curiosity, he asks if you are heading south. You tell him that you are. "I'd be careful heading that way," he says. "I've been hearing rumours of late, from travellers who have passed through here. If the tales are to be believed, a foul Demon has settled in the castle on Lake Merkwater, and his servants haunt the marsh trails to the south. They have been attacking anyone who travels that way. If I were you, I'd be wary of heading in that direction."

You tell him that you have no choice in the matter, as you have important business to attend to.

The barman nods. "Very well then, but if it's Shellhaven you're heading for, just be aware that the town's guards live their lives by a code of honesty. If you meet them, don't lie to them about anything, or you'll end up in trouble for sure. I hope you reach your destination safely, stranger."

You thank the barman for his advice. Turn to **188**.

"But you *must* come with me!" says Avion as you turn to leave. "The mission will fail if you do not trust me and the world will fall into the hands of Zanack! If you do not believe me, then answer me this: if I had not wanted your mission to be a success, then why would I have saved you from Zanack's assassins? I could have left you to die, I did not have to endanger my own life to help you. Surely you can see reason in that." She stares at you hopefully, placing a gentle hand on your shoulder. "I will not stop you if you want to go your own way, but please try to believe me." She tries to ease your doubts with her soft tones, whilst looking at you with her gleaming, blue eyes.

After hearing her words, will you:

Agree to travel with Avion after all, turn to **159**.

Or tell her that you work alone, and nothing she can say will change your mind, turn to **101**.

128

The Snake pauses, watching you with glassy eyes. Had you reached for your sword, or made any other aggressive movement, it would almost definitely have struck you. Now it seems indecisive. You are too big for it to eat, but it is clearly angry at having been disturbed.

Its tongue licks the air with an ominous hiss.

You are faced with an unpredictable creature. Roll one dice to determine the Snake's action.

If you roll a one, a two or a three, turn to **437**.

If you roll a four or higher, the Snake decides not to strike and you continue on your way, turn to **81**.

The building is vast. The upper levels consist of many small rooms, which you assume to have been servant's quarters. They are now empty, save for cobwebs and lingering shadows. At length, at the end of a long corridor, you come to a bedroom which is distinctly larger than the rest. This is where the castle's owner would have slept. Tapestries hang from the walls, but they are torn and decayed, and their images have faded beyond recognition. Above a broken and decaying bed, an ornate, tarnished frame hangs at an angle. The portrait has been torn out and is nowhere to be found.

The chamber has an ominous feel, and you have the impression that many terrible events occurred here long ago. As you walk around the room, an inexplicable shiver runs the length of your spine. You have an urge to leave this level, but before you do, you decide to search the chamber. After a while, you discover a loose stone in the wall near the head of the bed. You pull it out and find a hidden compartment. The hole is filled with shadows.

If you reach into the black hole, turn to **435**.

If not, you find nothing else of interest, so you head back along the corridor to the top of the stairs.

If you wish to explore the ground floor, turn to **15**.

If you want to leave the castle, turn to **42**.

As soon as you step into the strange barrier, your vision blurs and you lose consciousness. A moment later, you awake to find yourself floating in an expanse of inky darkness. You feel completely weightless. All around you, everything is totally black. And a strange, dead quiet looms.

Where are you?

Something brushes your shoulder and you spin around to see what it is, but you can see nothing. It is as though you have lost your sight! You hang in the void, feeling as if you are adrift in some strange dream. Your nerves are tingling with alarm, and it is not long before you sense a terrible evil in this place. You hear a frightening roar booming through the darkness, then you feel a rush of wind all around you. Something is in this strange place with you; it is big, and it is about to attack!

THE THING

LIFE FORCE 10   STRIKING SPEED 8

Focus	Move	Damage
1	**Aura of Pain**	1
2-3	**Suffocating Darkness**	1
4-5	**Inexplicable Agony**	2
6	**Claws of Shadow**	3

If you win, an eerie moan fills your ears, then silence returns to the dark. Turn to **192**.

The well-rounded fellow shakes your hand as you sit down beside him. "Hello! Hello! How do you do?" he says. "My name's Greenwood, Burlybe Greenwood." He then lowers his voice so that only you can hear him. "I should thank you for coming over. I have found the other folk in this inn, well, not too friendly, one might say. It is good to have someone to talk to at last."

Grateful for your company, the talkative Burlybe soon lightens the mood, and you find that he makes good conversation. Apparently he arrived at the unwelcoming inn some hours ago whilst on route to Shellhaven, where he is going to visit some relatives. He is a jolly enough man and it is not long before you discover that he used to be an adventurer, much like yourself. He has not been on any quests for some years though, as nowadays he prefers a good tankard of ale and a merry night by the fire. For some time you sit and exchange tales of past adventures, but as the night wears on you start to feel very weary. As you talk, you unwittingly mention that you too are heading south, in the direction of Shellhaven. With a sudden, beaming smile, Burlybe says, "excellent, then we can travel together! Is it not always more pleasant to travel in the company of friends?"

If you wish to agree to travel with Burlybe, turn to **119**.

If you would rather politely decline his offer, and tell him that you prefer to travel alone, turn to **187**.

"Wrong!" leers the Fire Demon. Without warning it breathes out, and you are blasted by the intense heat of its breath. Your whole body suddenly bursts into flames, your flesh bubbles and melts, and in a few seconds you are nothing more than a puddle of mush on the ground.

Your adventure is over.

Down through a field you follow, across a lonely meadow bathed in the pale light of the moon. Always the spirit remains ahead of you, never looking back. Grimbree shrinks into the distance, and at length you see an old watchtower up ahead, that looks rickety and sinister. A dead tree looms at its base and the moon is painting it in a beam of sallow light. The ghost halts and fixes you with a cold stare.

(Make a note that you have made an **Alliance With The Vengeful Dead**. You should also write down that you have met **Torin RavenSword**, the old innkeeper of Grimbree.)

The spirit points to the tower. A great tangle of undergrowth appears to block your approach, but with a wave of the ghost's hand, the foliage parts. You can now see a door ajar at the foot of the building, and you sense a sinister presence within. Sword drawn, you approach the entrance. Just before you step inside, you look back and see that the ghost has vanished. You are alone once more. Taking a deep breath, you step through the opening. Turn to **420**.

In the heat of the battle, you suddenly notice several guards rushing out of a nearby alley. The new arrivals are none other than the night watchmen who gave chase to you earlier. You can afford to waste no more time on swordplay! You leap forward and kick the harbour guard in the chest, knocking him off the jetty and into the water. Due to his heavy armour, the man begins to sink fast, and while the other guards are forced to stop and help him, you make your escape. Leaping into the dinghy you row off into the shadows, leaving the pontoon and the guards' angry curses behind in the gloom. In a few moments, the mist on the lake swirls around you, and a silence descends of the like you have never known.

You have escaped, but your recent exertions have left you weary. Your heavy eyes cannot stay open any longer, and you are forced to lay down in the dinghy to sleep. When you wake, the world is still dark and swathed in breathless shadows. The rest has partially revived you. (Increase your **Life Force** by one point.)

As you sit up, you find yourself drifting aimlessly through a deep, impenetrable fog. You grasp the oars, but you cannot see anything through the deep murk, and you are unsure which way to go. As you are considering your predicament, you suddenly notice a small white shape, no bigger than a clenched fist, hovering in the miasma a short distance ahead of you. It seems to glow with a faint light, but you cannot make out what it is through the fog. The little shape darts through the air, first to the left, then to the right, as if it is seeking something. Whatever it is, it has not seen you, as you are shrouded in a particularly dense pocket of mist.

If you want to row forward to investigate the mysterious shape, turn to **94**.

If you remain still, turn to **424**.

135

You avoid being struck, but only by a mere inch, and you feel the burning heat radiating from the spell as it whooshes past.

Your body is singed by the close proximity, (reduce your **Life Force** by one point.) The spell then explodes into the ground behind you, sending blue sparks and lumps of mud into the air. You turn to see Avion floating away in the dinghy, born aloft on the swift moving current, then she vanishes downstream into the night.

As you walk back to the road, you wonder why Avion attacked you. Maybe she did not want your quest to succeed, but then, why did she save you from your captors?

Maybe you will never know… turn to **417**.

136

Along the passage, burning candles line the walls at every step. Before long you see two arched doors to your right; one has been painted blue, the other red. A third door looms directly ahead where the passage comes to an end, and strange symbols have been scratched into the brickwork above it.

If you possess the special ability of **Greater Wisdom**, turn to **194**.

If you do not possess this skill, you may open:

The red door, turn to **61**.

The blue door, turn to **46**.

Or the door with the symbols, turn to **22**.

137

Leaving the pond behind, you strike out deeper into the lush valley. You march on for the rest of the day, but as night begins to creep in, you grow very tired. The stars have already begun to shine and the land is soon cast under the bright blue light of the moon. A short walk away, you notice a small group of trees clustered together near the slope of the valley.

If you want to climb one of the trees and spend the night under the leafy canopy, turn to **123**.

If you would rather sleep in the long grass by the side of the trail, turn to **26**.

You kick your way through a burning door and stumble blindly down a smoke filled corridor into a room at the back of the structure. Timbers fall around you as the ceiling starts to sag, and burning ash sears your lungs. Frantically you look around. You know that there must be a back door to this residence close by, but the heavy smoke is obscuring your vision. Your senses are bewildered by the blazing chaos. For a few tense moments you stagger aimlessly through the scene, then you catch sight of two doors, one blue, the other green. Flames leap about you. With no time to think, you run forward, but which door will you head for?

The green one, turn to **10**.

Or the blue one, turn to **62**.

139

Long and hard you push, but the stone door is immensely heavy. It refuses to budge, so you decide to try a different course of action.

You may now:

Suggest Avion uses her magic break down the door, turn to **186**.

Use a **Golden Key** (if you possess one), turn to **163**.

Or, if you possess the special ability of **Picklock** (and want to use it), turn to **107**.

140

The climb is difficult and your skills are pushed to their limit. When you are someway up, your hand slips and you fall with a heavy thud onto the ground below. (Reduce your **Life Force** by one point.)

You are not one to be dissuaded by a challenge, so you clamber to your feet and try again. This time your perseverance wins through. You scale the wall and drop into a straw stacked cart on the far side. You have landed in a dark and quiet street. Looking around, you see that nobody is about. Dusting the hay from your clothes, you set off into the town. Turn to **303**.

141

As you gaze into the gathering darkness, you are struck by an ominous premonition. Crossing the marsh would be especially risky at this current time, as something extremely dangerous lurks out in the gloom. You sense that it would be wiser to seek shelter for the night and continue your trek at dawn.

If you wish to follow your instincts and head for the inn, turn to **172**.

If you would rather take a gamble and try to cross the marsh tonight, turn to **349**.

You haul up your equipment and quickly leave the room, using a chair to wedge the bedroom door shut behind you.

Down in the main bar area you find the two men who you saw last night. One, the man in black, is boarding up windows as fast as he can. The other, the plump man named Burlybe, is trying to drag a heavy table towards the front entrance.

"Quickly!" Burlybe shouts to you, his voice fraught with tension. "The night outside is crawling with Demons. There are too many to fight! Help me wedge this table against the door, to stop them from breaking in!"

The door is indeed trembling. A heavy assault is being launched against it, and cracks are already appearing in the heavy timber frame.

"The door is holding for the moment," snaps the man in black. "We can blockade it in a minute. We must finish boarding these windows first. I have done most of them already, but there are still some gaps where the enemy might squeeze through!" He looks towards you. "Quickly," he demands, "make yourself useful and help us!"

Will you:

Help Burlybe to fortify the front door, turn to **326**.

Help the man in black to finish boarding the windows, turn to **369**.

Or will you leave the inn via the rear exit, and try to escape the building, turn to **414**.

You scan the darkness as the gurgling current takes you onwards. As you watch, you see pale eyes staring back at you from the misty reeds by the riverbank. A low moan rises over the mire and soon the eerie sound is taken up all around you, filling the air with grief and despair.

"Do not look into their eyes," warns Avion.

"What are they?" you ask.

"They are the tortured souls of the dead," she says, "the lost spirits of all those who have been killed upon the marsh. Do not look into their grief ridden eyes, or you will be cast under a spell of sadness. You will become like them, a pitiful soul doomed to an eternity of darkness, cursed to roam the marshes forever. They were human once, long ago… but not any more. Not all spirits are evil, but these ones have been twisted and embittered by their untimely deaths. We had best keep away from the banks from now on."

Taking heed of Avion's warning, you look away from the spectral eyes. After a while, the unsettling moaning fades away and the sounds become distant.

If you wish to lay back in the dinghy and use this time to sleep, turn to **447**.

If you think it would be wiser to stay awake and alert, turn to **179**.

You have been climbing for some time, and are more than halfway up the incline when your foot slips on the uneven terrain. You are thrown off balance, and a second later you are tumbling downwards. Unable to stop your descent, you eventually roll off of a precipice and crash-land ten feet below onto a jutting outcrop. (Reduce your **Life Force** by two points.) Your head is dazed and the world is spinning, but at least you did not impale yourself on one of the up-thrusting claws of rock.

As you take a moment to compose yourself, you notice that you have tumbled slightly to the east. You can now see a small light gleaming amidst the rocks not far away, and there is a strange smell in the air. You creep along the narrow outcrop to investigate, and you soon find yourself peering into the mouth of a cave. Firelight is illuminating the interior, where you can see a large looking humanoid with a broad, hunched back, stirring a giant pot of boiling brew. The beast is dressed in grey rags and its back is facing you, hence it is not aware of your presence. Some kind of contraption is hanging from the roof, but from your current position you cannot see what it is.

If you wish to creep away from the cave and resume your climb towards the black fortress, turn to **440**.

If you wish to creep towards the doorway, to get a better look at the scene, turn to **39**.

145
Illustration Opposite

You follow the track between the buildings around the base of the hill, but you soon find your way blocked by a mound of smashed wood that has been piled at least twenty feet high. As you clamber to the top, a dark and ominous shadow falls across the area. You look up and see a huge fleet of gigantic bat-like creatures, mounted by Zanack's Sky Guards. The evil beasts have been completing rotations over the area. You have avoided their roaming eyes thus far, but if you do not think fast you will soon be spotted.

Will you:

Scramble down the wreckage and duck into a derelict house, turn to **281**.

Or lay down and remain still, in the hope that they do not spot you amongst the mess and disorder, turn to **202**.

146

You follow the lonely trail for some hours, your legs wading through the mist that settles over the boggy terrain. The day is hot and humid, and the clouds slowly give way to a clear blue sky. Flies and other strange insects buzz around you, and you are forever brushing them away from your face. After a while a warm breeze scatters the mist into thin wisps, allowing you to gaze across the bleak expanse of land. You think that you can see dreary hills rising and falling in the heat hazed distance, but the fog soon thickens again, and the terrain becomes murky and indistinct once more.

As dusk starts to fall, strange and bestial sounds begin to echo across the land. The nocturnal beasts of the marsh are slowly waking, and their eerie calls are ominous indeed. A short while later, you see a sign by the roadside stating that you are a few hours walk from the town of Shellhaven. As you are looking at the sign, you suddenly hear thundering hooves approaching. A huge black stallion emerges from the swirling mist, mounted by a tall and ghostly figure. The horseman is swathed in dark robes and a concealing hood. He drags on the reigns, halting twenty feet in front of you. With slow, shuddering movements, the sinister figure points his hand towards you.

"Are you the Shield Searcher?" he hisses.

The rider's sudden appearance has caught you off guard, but you quickly gather your wits and decide what to do.

Will you answer:

Yes, turn to **402**.

No, turn to **117**.

Or say nothing and draw your sword, turn to **28**.

You creep silently down the pontoon and step into the dinghy. The guard snores softly in his sleep. With a grin you untie the ropes and row into the mist.

The harbour is soon out of sight and all you can see is swirling fog. There is a deep silence over the lake, and it is not long before an overpowering tiredness comes upon you. You have not slept for some time and your exertions have left you weary. Your heavy eyes cannot stay open any longer, so you lay down in the dinghy to rest. When you wake, the world is still dark and swathed in breathless shadows. The rest has slightly revived you. (Increase your **Life Force** by one point.)

As you sit up, you find yourself drifting aimlessly through a deep, impenetrable fog. You grasp the oars, but you cannot see anything through the murk, and you are unsure which way to go. As you are considering your predicament, you notice a small white shape, no bigger than a clenched fist, hovering in the miasma ahead of you. It glows with a faint light, but you cannot make out what it is through the fog. As you watch, the little shape darts through the air, first to the left, then to the right, as if it is seeking something. Whatever it is, it has not seen you, as you are shrouded in a particularly dense pocket of mist.

If you want to investigate, turn to **94**.

If you want to remain hidden, turn to **424**.

148

The door is unlocked. Beyond it you find a flight of roughly hewn steps leading up to another closed door. As you begin to ascend the stairs, the door at the top suddenly opens and an ugly looking Orc, clad in heavy armour, comes blundering through. He is a powerful, broad looking monster, probably the night watch guard. The startled Orc jumps when he sees you and reaches swiftly for his axe!

The beast is about to attack. If you have a **Crossbow** and any remaining **Bolts**, you may shoot at him before he can descend the stairs, turn to **175**.

If you do not have these items, or if you would rather defend yourself with your sword, turn to **189**.

149

Silently you creep across the room, your footsteps muffled by the soft rug. Just in time you see the small, blood-red cat curled up asleep in front of you, almost invisible on the rug. Breathing quietly, you step over it.

If you possess the special ability of **Stealth**, you make it to the door and open it with a soft click, turn to **185**.

If you do not possess **Stealth**, you reach out to open the door, but the sound of rustling covers catches your ear. You glance back over your shoulder. Turn to **34**.

The door is old and the hinges look rusted and weak, so you might have a chance of ramming it down. You rush forward and hurl yourself against it. It shudders, but it takes another three attempts before you finally crash through into the room beyond. (The effort of breaking the door has injured your shoulder. Reduce your **Life Force** by two points.) You have entered a dingy room, where the only light comes through the wrecked doorway behind you. From the musty smell it is evident that nobody has been in here for a long age. Cobwebs are everywhere, draping from the ceiling, and everything is covered in a blanket of dust that is at least an inch thick. As you look around, you see that fortune has befallen you. You are standing in an old armoury. Many of the weapons have rusted with age, but a few items have escaped the ravages of time. You find an excellent crossbow, crafted from a flawless material that you have never seen before, and two golden crossbow bolts. In addition, there is a formidable, immaculate looking broadsword leaning in the corner of the chamber. Blowing the dust from it, you discover that its fearsome blade is etched with ancient symbols. It looks superior to your current sword, so you decide to take it. (Make a note that you now have a **Crossbow**, **two Golden Crossbow Bolts** and a **Rune Broadsword**.)

Breaking through the door did not leave you unscathed, but it was worth the effort. Pleased with your new belongings, you decide to leave. Turn to **82**.

151

As Ragroda topples backwards, you unleash a final blow, disemboweling your enemy. A terrible shriek escapes her, which echoes around the chamber as she collapses upon the floor. As you watch in disgust, her corpse begins to melt and dissolve. A few moments later, all that is left of her is a stinking puddle of bubbling green slime. Evil smelling fumes rise from the muck, polluting the already stagnant air in the chamber. You glance at her crossbow, but it is of no use to you: it lies broken upon the floor where she threw it down with great force, and her other belongings have been melted by her acidic remains. There is little left of interest here, and the grotesque smell is quickly becoming unbearable.

If you wish to investigate the sarcophagus, turn to **419**.

If you would rather leave the stinking chamber, turn to **181**.

152

As you listen, their childlike demeanor quickly becomes apparent. They seem to have no understanding of the complexities of the world; they are merely benevolent little creatures who want nothing more from life than to flitter around singing and dancing. You try to talk to them, but they are too busy harmonising to engage in any meaningful conversation. However, your effort to focus their attention is not completely in vain. They are fascinated by anything that glimmers, and it is not long before they offer you a trade.

(They will use their magic to increase your **Life Force** by one point for every **five Crimson Coins** that you give to them. If you want to do this, make the necessary deductions to your money and increase your **Life Force** accordingly. Even though the Fairies are barely the size of a single coin, they have no problem picking them up and darting around with them.)

Eventually they all flitter off into the darkness, but not before singing you a song and wishing you farewell. The surreal meeting has left you feeling strangely relaxed, and their final song has induced a state of indescribable calmness. Feeling light-headed, you cannot help but drift into a peaceful dream.

Turn to **93**.

153

You make short work of the wall. You clamber unseen over the defences and skillfully drop into a hay laden cart on the far side. You roll off the back of the cart, brush yourself down, then stroll into the shadows of the town. Turn to **303**.

You burst through the entrance, slam it shut behind you, and quickly lock it using a central deadbolt. A second later, the door shudders violently. Wild voices echo on the far side, then you hear the sound of a weapon chopping into the wood. Cracks appear in the shuddering timber as the enemy try to smash their way through.

The door will not hold for long, but you have bought yourself a few, valuable minutes.

You have come into a vast circular chamber. The room is dominated by a large round pool of stagnant smelling water, and you are standing on the narrow walkway that encircles it. You can see an open door at the far side of the room, leading to a well-lit passage.

You rush towards the door, but you are barely halfway around the walkway when the pool begins to bubble and froth. A second later, you are blinded by spray as several green tentacles erupt from the foaming water. They flail towards you, blocking your route of escape. You can scarcely afford this delay! You must get past this beast as swiftly as possible.

If you possess the special ability of **Haste**, turn to **105**.
If not, turn to **160**.

You are on full alert over the next few hours. Night thickens over the plains, and after putting several miles between yourself and the river, you begin to grow tired. You lay down by the path but you are too wary to sleep, so you decide to walk on through the night.

For the rest of the darkling hours the moonlit path grows quiet and lonely, the tranquil silence broken only by the trudging of your feet. You march on through a fiery dawn, watching as the sun climbs into a clear sky. The day grows warm and the air is at first scented with the fragrance of wild flowers, but the land soon begins to change; the grassland turns wet and boggy and the track feels soft underfoot. You have crossed into the southern marsh known as Harrowmoor, and the environment grows less pleasant the further you go. The colourful valley birds have been replaced by buzzing gnats, and you have to constantly watch your footing so as not to lose the indistinct marsh trail. Withered trees, bearing black fruits, occasionally dot the landscape. The food tastes grim, and the scant pickings barely suppress your hunger. When evening creeps in, you notice a patch of threatening storm clouds racing in from the north.

The lack of sleep is weighing heavily on you, but as the stars begin to twinkle, you see the faint lights of an inn in the distance.

If you have the special ability of **Sixth Sense,** turn to **141** immediately.

Otherwise, you may:

Head towards the inn, to escape the oncoming storm, turn to **172**.

Or force yourself to stay awake, and march on through another night, turn to **349**.

156

The innkeeper is a bear of a man. He must be close to seven feet tall, and almost the same around! He glowers down at you with hard eyes. "Welcome stranger," he says gruffly, "glad you dropped in."

Far away, out on the marshes, you suddenly hear a strange baying, mingled with the rumbling of the storm. The innkeeper pauses and listens for a moment, then the distant sound dies away and is heard no more. "No need to worry yourself," he says, "many strange things haunt the marshes after dark, but spend the night here and you'll be safe enough." He holds out the palm of his huge, gnarled hand. "Five crimson coins is the price for a room."

If you wish to pay his fee (and can afford it) deduct **five Crimson Coins** from your belongings and turn to **126**.

If you do not have enough money, or simply do not want to pay that much, you may haggle: turn to **180**.

157

It is getting late by the time you come up out of the valley onto the open meadows again. Throughout the wild grassland, you notice several small bushes packed with berries. You are not fond of their taste, and the food seems to have little nutritional value, but at least you are not left feeling hungry. The sun soon falls low on the horizon, painting the sky in deep hues of red, and the land looks particularly beautiful under the dusky light. As you march on, you see that the path is heading towards a deep stream which is spanned by an old bridge. As you step onto the arched crossing, you are greeted by an ominous sight. A trail of blood is smeared across the stonework, and a severed hand lies nearby. There is no sign of the rest of the body.

If you possess the special ability of **Sixth Sense**, turn to **416**.

If you do not possess this ability, turn to **169**.

158

Heading through the shadows, you slip into the back of the moving cart. You pull the cover forward to conceal yourself, then you lay still and quiet. Luckily the driver does not notice you. Before long, you jolt to a halt and the man at the reigns calls out to the guards. From the conversation that ensues, it appears that the driver is a local man who knows the watchmen. "You should not have stayed out so late, Throm," you hear the guards saying. "These are dark times! Demons stalk the marshes after sundown, if you are not careful you will end up dead!" You hear the driver call something back, but his accent is heavy and his voice muffled, so you cannot quite make out what he says. "Truly?" responds a guard, with an edge of alarm. "Well, you had best come through, Throm, and be swift about it! We will bar the gates for the night once you're inside, don't you worry!"

Hidden beneath the cover, you hear the main entrance creak open as the cart rumbles forward. If seems that your plan has paid off! Once you are safely through the gates, you slide out and sneak into the back lanes of the town. Turn to **303**.

159

Avion seems relieved by your decision. She is eager to get underway, so you both board the dinghy and push off from the bank. A slow moving current soon takes hold, pulling you downstream, and you sit back and rest your weary muscles. Because of the fog, you can see little or nothing beyond the banks of the river. Now and then, a dead tree branch floats lazily past, as the dinghy pushes its way through the long reeds that poke from the water. The enduring fog continues to curl around you, and it soon feels as though you are drifting through a cloud. Turn to **171**.

You grasp your weapon and hack through a tentacle as it tries to snare you by the throat. But more are coming, groping towards you in heavy numbers. There are too many to kill, so you make a dash towards the open door. However, you have only gone a few paces when a huge tentacle, as thick as a tree trunk, writhes forward to block your path. You try to dodge past it, and for a second it looks as though your attempt will succeed… but then you feel an icy grip upon your ankle. With terrifying force, you are pulled off your feet and dragged towards the edge of the pool.

You must hack your way through the slimy thing before it drags you into its underwater realm!

(As soon as you have reduced its **Life Force** to 3 or less, turn to **406**.)

TENTACLE

LIFE FORCE 7   STRIKING SPEED 8

Focus	Move	Damage
1	Tightening Grip	1
2-3	Crushing Grapple	2
4-5	Constricting Embrace	2
6	Strangling Grasp	3

161

The tornado of fire accelerates, consuming the Demon, then there is a sudden gust of wind which makes you blink. When you open your eyes, the beast and the flames have vanished, leaving an eerie quiet over the cold, dark ledge. You are alone once more, and not a trace or a sign of the creature remains.

Your answer was correct.

Breathing deeply, you walk through the open gates, into the looming darkness... Turn to **95**.

162

It takes only a second for you to regret your action.

A dog-like beast instantly pounces from the box, its curving claws slashing towards your throat. You jump back in surprise, barely avoiding its attack, then it leaps at you again with a ferocious snarl. A red mist surrounds its body, and its wild eyes are pits of flame.

FIRE HOUND

LIFE FORCE 7   STRIKING SPEED 9

Focus	Move	Damage
1	Scorching Aura	1
2-3	Blazing Breath	2
4-5	Lava Claws	2
6	Burning Fangs	2

If you win, the dead beast bursts into flames, then the fire almost instantly goes out, leaving only a scattering of ash on the floor. It would be foolish to open any more of the boxes, for you now know what lies within them. You can hear the other Fire Hounds trying to claw their way out, eager to get a piece of you. The only exit from the room is through the door by which you entered, so you return to the passage.

You can now try:

The red door, turn to **61**.

Or the blue door, turn to **46**.

163

To your relief, the key is a perfect fit. When you turn it in the lock, there is a deep rumbling and the door starts to move.

The door is being pushed open by an ancient mechanism, and a series of rusty cogs creak and groan within the building. A gaping darkness is eventually revealed, then you hear the beating of many wings. You duck as a bat colony swoops out, scratching at you with their tiny claws. Spiteful they may be, but they cause you no significant harm, and a moment later they are gone into the mist.

Breathing deeply, you move inside. Turn to **174**.

164

The Games Master stares into your eyes, and you feel his vision piercing deep into your soul. His hypnotic gaze overcomes you, and a swirling darkness consumes your mind. Now that he has you under his control, your enemy raises his hand and orders you to follow him. Under the grip of his magic, you have no choice but to obey. Your new master leads you through the dark corridors and up the winding stairwells. At a lofty summit, he orders you to throw yourself from the highest tower. Again, you have no choice but to comply. The last thing you hear is the rushing wind and the Games Master's delighted laughter, as he watches your body hurtling towards the rocks below.

165

The man's gaze stays transfixed on his mug of ale as you pull up a chair alongside him. You notice that his somber eyes are extremely dark in colour, so that you can barely distinguish his pupils.

Without looking away from his drink, he says in a deep, solemn voice, "I am not looking for company, stranger. Leave me alone."

Will you:

Try to make conversation, turn to **338**.

Leave him be and join the plump man, turn to **131**.

Or approach the barman and ask for the price of a room, turn to **156**.

Although you move as quietly as you can, a pontoon plank creaks as you step on it. The guard wakes with a startled snort and sees you sneaking towards the dinghy. He grabs his heavy axe and leaps to his feet.

"You there! Halt!" he cries. He peers across at you, and when he does not recognize you, his eyes light up with immediate suspicions. "Grakhul!" he snarls. He rushes forward, and you are suddenly forced to duck the sweep of his weapon. You slam the pommel of your sword into his armoured body, causing him to stagger backwards, then you adopt a defensive stance. You open your mouth to speak, but he rushes forward once again, giving you no time to protest your innocence.

You must defend yourself! (As soon as you have reduced his **Life Force** to three or less, turn to **134**.)

HARBOUR GUARD

LIFE FORCE 8   STRIKING SPEED 8

Focus	Move	Damage
1	**Elbow To The Face**	1
2-3	**Gauntlet Smash**	2
4-5	**Axe Hilt Slam**	2
6	**Sweeping Blade**	3

You leap forward and deliver a death-dealing strike, catching the Goblin off guard with your well timed attack. The alarmed Markun springs sideways into the corner of the room. He lifts his hand, then a beam of blue energy leaps from his fingertips. You duck the attack and the magical blast slams into a bookshelf behind you, completely incinerating it! You surge forward, dodging a second beam of light, then you leap into the air and send your blade slashing downwards. Your enemy's robes are no substitute for armour, and his body suddenly falls to the left (and to the right) as you cleave through him.

Having put an end to his murderous spell casting, you sheathe your weapon and search the bodies. The Goblin owns nothing of interest, but the Markun is carrying three glowing gems. (Add **Three Emerald Gems** to your belongings.) The gems are priceless - if sold they could make you incredibly rich - and you could buy yourself a regal castle, or use the money to travel the Far Lands of the world. The possibilities are broad, but you will have to escape this fortress first, after killing its dreaded owner.

If you wish to search the study, turn to **63**.

Otherwise, you may exit the room by turning to **185**.

168

Human skulls are mounted on the walls every ten feet or so, with burning candles perched on top of them. Shadows dance and move, giving life to the thick cobwebs that cover the ceiling. After a few minutes a small dark shape drops out of the shadows and lands on your shoulder. To your alarm, you see that it is a jet black Spider. It has a furry body about the size of your fist, with large glistening fangs.

If you wish to brush it off with your hand, turn to **391**.

If you would rather stand absolutely still, turn to **357**.

169

You suddenly feel a tug on your leg, and you look down to see a thick, scaly tentacle curling around your ankle. Before you can act, you are suddenly dragged off the bridge and into the bubbling stream. Down under the water you go, until you hit the river bed with a bump. It is hard to see anything in the shadowy depths, but you manage to determine that you are in the clutches of a Giant River Snake. Its body is as thick as a tree trunk, and unless you are mistaken, the beast has not one, but two savage heads. In a thrashing panic, you somehow manage to break free. Fighting the strong undercurrents, you swim back to the surface, but you have barely caught your breath when you are pulled back under. The serpent has once again curled itself around you, and for a second time it tries to crush and drown you in the murky depths. You do not want to end up like the Snake's last victim, whose remains you saw strewn across the bridge, so you draw your weapon and strike out at the ravenous beast.

TWO-HEADED GIANT SNAKE

LIFE FORCE 10   STRIKING SPEED 8

Focus	Move	Damage
1	**Drowning Embrace**	1
2-3	**Right Headed Bite**	2
4-5	**Left Headed Bite**	3
6	**Crushing Grasp**	4

If you win, the serpent releases its grip and you swim to shore. You drag yourself up the bank and stagger away down the grassland trail. Turn to **155**.

You tug on the lever, but nothing happens. You have chosen poorly, and the door remains sealed. The water begins to rise even faster. In a panic, you reach for one of the other levers, but they suddenly withdraw into the wall, vanishing into narrow slots! There is now nothing you can do. In a few minutes the water will have filled the sealed chamber. You are condemned to death by drowning.

After a short time, a gust of wind temporarily breaks up the fog. As it begins to grow thicker again you see the silhouette of a man standing out on the mist shrouded marsh. As you watch, he begins to wave to you. He is alone and probably lost. He is wearing a long coat that hangs down to his ankles.

Avion is staring vacantly away from the figure. She does not seem to have noticed him.

Will you:

Ask Avion to stop the dinghy so that you can investigate, turn to **108**.

Or ignore him, turn to **68**.

You reach the inn on the eve of a great downpour. The old place stands alone by the side of the trail with a creaking sign that reads *Dark Marsh Inn*. You pause near the entrance to marvel at the large moon, which is soon consumed by clouds. You also spot a **Crimson Coin** on the doorstep, which you add to your belongings.

You step into the tavern just as the rain begins to pour. The small bar area has wooden beams on the walls and ceiling, and is lit by an old fireplace and flickering candles. The room is occupied by three people, the innkeeper among them. He is a burly man, with dark hair in a ponytail and a hard face. He stares at you from behind the bar as you enter, but says nothing. The other two men are sitting quietly at separate tables. One is a plump fellow in traveller's boots and well-worn clothes. He looks up and waves at you, as if hoping that you will join him. The other, a broad shouldered, strong looking individual, sits motionless, clad in black clothes and boots. A golden locket hangs around his neck and his face is stern and unshaven. He stares austerely into his drink, as though unaware of your entrance. (If you want to purchase a mug of ale, delete **one Crimson Coin** from your inventory and increase your **Life Force** by one point, then choose what to do.)

If you join the plump man at his table, turn to **131**.

If you sit with the man in black, turn to **165**.

If you ask the barman about a room for the night, turn to **156**.

Even though you are a skilled adventurer, the climb proves very difficult. The walls are smothered with slimy moss, making your ascent incredibly treacherous.

If you do *not* possess the special ability of **Scale**, turn immediately to **9**.

If you do possess **Scale**, you eventually pull yourself back into the light of the square chamber. Glad to be out of the pit, you cross the room to investigate the other door. Turn to **148**.

174

Avion keeps close behind as you descend a flight of dark and slippery steps. Water drips from the ceiling and a foul smell like ancient decay hangs in the air. As you head further down, the temperature continues to drop. It becomes icy cold, and you can hear the sound of your shivering footsteps echoing back at you.

Before long you reach the foot of the stairs, where you pass beneath a stone archway into a deep, underground crypt. In the gloom you can just make out a rectangular plinth in the centre of the room, upon which sits a large sarcophagus made of jet black stone. The outside mist has drifted down the stairs and is now flowing slowly about your feet. As you look around, you see that cobwebs drape from the ceiling in a tangled mess, the dust on the floor is inches thick, and the wall-mounted candles look as if they have been extinguished for many years.

"This place has probably been untouched for centuries," whispers Avion.

As you step towards the plinth, the candles in the room flicker eerily to life by themselves.

Under the firelight, you can now see that the stone sarcophagus is engraved with a single inscription. Chiseled into the centre of the lid, is the word *Gorath*. (Make a note of the password to Zanack's fortress.)

Suddenly, Avion coughs to draw your attention. She is standing at the foot of the stairs, grasping a loaded crossbow which is aimed at your head. Her friendly eyes have changed, replaced by two sinister orbs, and her delicate lips have stretched to form a chilling smile. Turn to **431**.

175

You load your crossbow and fire up at the Orc. The bolt spins with pinpoint accuracy and slams into the beast's armoured chest, puncturing the breastplate. With a look of agony, the guard tears out the bolt and snaps it in half with its monstrously powerful hands!

(Delete one **Bolt** from your belongings.)

The beast storms towards you, foaming at the mouth with fury! If you have any more bolts, you have no time to load them, so you quickly raise your sword. Turn to **189** to fight your enemy, but reduce its **Life Force** instantly by two points due to the damage from the bolt.

176

(If you just used a brittle **Skeleton Key**, you must remove it from your belongings.)

You are at first blinded by utter darkness as you wriggle along the narrow shaft, and you can hear and feel the bustling of rats all around you. After a few minutes you turn a bend and see a beam of light coming up through a hole in the floor. You are disconcerted by the number of vermin that are clambering around, so you drop down through the gap.

You have emerged into the corner of a warm study, lit by a roaring fireplace. The walls are flanked with shelves that are bent under the weight of old books, and a nearby desk is covered with papers and scrolls. There is a grim smell in here, and you comprehend that the shaft is allowing the stench of decay to drift up from the pit and spread around the fortress, for the pleasure of the castle's inhabitants.

You move across the room, to a barred window which offers a view of the surrounding lake. The air smells slightly less foul here, so you pause to scan the rest of the study. You appear to be alone, but you can hear footsteps behind a closed door at the far end of the room.

If you possess the special ability of **Greater Wisdom**, turn immediately to **40.**

If you do not possess this ability, you must either:

Find a place to hide, turn to **125**.

Or head towards the door with your sword drawn, to catch the newcomers by surprise if they enter, turn to **92.**

Suddenly, the Witch leaps backwards into the corner of the room, her eyes bulging with terror. "Mogroth's Idol!" she shrieks, glaring at the carving in your hand. "Where did you find that thing? Get it away from me!" She is shaking from head to toe, and even her black cat has scurried away in horror. "That is an artifact of destruction!" she snaps. "Only Zanack can control it! Quickly, throw it into the fire, before it kills us all!" Before you can act, the idol suddenly comes to life and springs out of your hand. In an instant, it swells and grows until it is so large that it has to bend over to fit in the room. Its expression is one of murderous rage. Bolts of blue light shoot from its eyes, incinerating the nearby desk and blasting a hole through the back wall of the chamber. By chance, the collapsed wall has revealed the entrance to a secret passage, and you wonder if this could be your way out of the labyrinth. The rampaging idol now turns to attack the Witch, who retaliates with a barrage of powerful spells. The walls and ceiling crack under the battering of sparks and explosions, and the whole room looks ready to collapse! You decide to make a swift exit, so you leap through the hole in the wall and race off down the passage. A deep boom shakes the ground, then silence descends.

Curiosity grips you. Who won the battle? Or did they both kill each other?

You look back, only to find the passage blocked by dust and rubble. You press on and soon come to a narrow door. A human skull hangs above it, housing a green flamed candle. Your senses tell you that this is the exit from the labyrinth. With an expression of triumph, you step through onto a winding staircase. Turn to **277**.

178

Having halted alongside the vessel, you can now see the body of a man inside. He has been deceased for some time and is all but a skeleton. A pale sword is clutched in his bony fingers, and the blade glimmers with traces of old magic. You gently remove it from his hand. Add the **Sword of the Fallen** to your list of weapons and increase the **Damage** of your **Sweeping Blade** and **Heavy Sword Strike** by one point each.

You keep searching, and you soon discover a small diary in his decaying breast pocket. Most of the pages have been rotted by the water, but a few lines are readable. This is what you can make out:

*I hope to return to Shellhaven as soon as I can.
Harn warned me not to come by boat. I should have
listened! The watchers in the water have been
following me for some time, but I think that they have
given up and decided to leave me be… the rowing has
left me tired… I shall rest a while by the river bank,
but not for long…*

A faint breath of murky wind blows eerily against your face.

"We should not linger here," says Avion nervously. She is about to say more, when your boat suddenly rocks violently. You look down, and to your horror you see a mass of spectral shapes moving in the reeds beneath the water. Ghostly arms reach from the black depths and grip the sides of your boat, in an attempt to overturn the vessel. You hack downwards, but your sword has no effect on the demented apparitions! Avion tugs wildly on the oars and the boat suddenly surges free of their grasp. The spectral beings seem unwilling to leave the tangled reeds by the bank, so she rows swiftly into the safety of the deep water. Turn to **143**.

179

For a while the boat meanders onwards. The banks of the river grow wider apart until they eventually peter out altogether. You have come at last onto the vast lake known as Merkwater. The green mist is even thicker here, choking the air with its ghostly fingers.

Avion draws the oars quietly through the dark water, watching her surroundings warily.

It is an hour before an island emerges from the mist. As you move closer, you see that it has a steep rocky shoreline, and upon its summit is a vast and terrible castle. It is Zanack's fortress, and it is an ominous sight indeed. You can see its great spires and pointed summits of black stone, stabbing up into the night sky.

Avion veers away from it, and a second, smaller island soon comes into view. In the light of the wandering moon, you can see a little building on its peak.

"There! There it is!" Says Avion excitedly, and with a stroke of the oars she steers towards it. Turn to **121**.

180

"Agh! Three crimson coins and your sword then. And that is my last offer!" says the innkeeper.

"Three crimson coins and nothing more," you insist, "or I will sleep on the doorstep and you will have nothing from me!"

The huge man rubs at the rough stubble on his chin. "Aye," he says at last," these are hard times, stranger… three crimson coins it is then," he grumbles.

Mumbling with dissatisfaction, he takes your money.

(Subtract **three Crimson Coins** from your inventory.)

You decide to engage the barman in some light conversation, so you ask if he has heard any rumours of late. He shrugs his shoulders. You gather that he is no longer in the mood for talking. Turn to **188**.

181

You head down to the water's edge and peer out over the lake. The mist has deepened greatly, and you can no longer see Zanack's castle through the murk. All around, the deep fog encompasses you like an impenetrable veil. You find the dinghy and push off from the bank. You know that the island fortress is not far away, so you begin rowing in the direction where you last saw it.

Suddenly, you notice a small white shape, no bigger than a clenched fist, hovering in the gloom a short distance ahead of you. It seems to glow with a faint light, but you cannot make out what it is through the fog. As you watch, the little shape darts through the air, first to the left, then to the right, as if it is seeking something.

Whatever it is, it has not seen you in the dense blanket of mist.

If you row forward to investigate the mysterious shape, turn to **94**.

If you remain still, turn to **424**.

182

You walk for some time, eventually coming to a flight of roughly hewn steps which lead deep under the lake. Water is dripping from the ceiling, and strange purple mosses cling to the walls, glowing faintly. For ten minutes you follow the eerie staircase. When at last you come to the foot of the steps, you hear a crackling sound ahead. As you edge forward, you discover that the passage is blocked by a vertical wall of black liquid. The dull crackling seems to emanate from this strange barrier.

There is obviously some curious magic at work here. Will you:

Strike the barrier with your sword, in the hope of destroying it, turn to **343**.

Try to step through the liquid wall, turn to **130**.

Or head back the way you came and climb into the open, turn to **116**.

183

"Wrong!" leers the Fire Demon. The giant beast suddenly exhales and you are blasted by the intense heat of its breath. Your whole body bursts into flames. Your flesh bubbles and melts, and in a few seconds you are reduced to a puddle of boiling slush. For a while you pop and hiss, steaming in the cracks in the ground, then your remains drip slowly down the rocks, back towards the dark lake. Your quest is over...

184

"Very well," says the Elf at last. He looks almost sorry for you, as if convinced that you have made the wrong decision. He clicks his fingers and melts away into the green surroundings, vanishing as if he was never there. You press on along the trail and you do not see him again.

Roll one dice to determine what random events the rest of the day has in store for you.

If you roll a one, a two or a three, turn to **280**.

If you roll a four, a five or a six, turn to **157**.

185

The door has opened directly onto a winding stairwell of black stone.

If you head upwards, turn to **43**.

If you head down, turn to **118**.

186

"I will try my best," says Avion. Taking a deep breath, she approaches the door and places both hands on the rock. She closes her eyes, then her face becomes a picture of concentration. A stream of light begins to pulse from her hands into the stone, but the door fails to move, so she halts and shakes her head. "I cannot do this alone," she says. "Come, let us work together."

Once again she puts her hands on the door and casts her spell, but this time you assist her. You dig your heels in and shove as hard as you can. The door starts to rumble, and after a few minutes you eventually manage to push it open.

You are about to congratulate yourselves when you hear an ominous click. By forcing the door ajar, you have activated an ancient mechanism within the building. It suddenly fires a spear out of the dark opening, and Avion narrowly dodges the projectile.

If you have **Sixth Sense** or **Haste**, you also manage to avoid injury. But if you do not have **Haste** or **Sixth Sense**, the spear gashes your arm as you leap for cover, and you must reduce your **Life Force** by two points.

If you are still alive, you check the door for more traps, then you cautiously move inside. Turn to **174**.

Burlybe tries to look unbothered by your decision, but you can tell that he is disappointed.

Suddenly the rain falls harder and the heavy droplets shake the windowpane. The storm has grown worse and you are glad to be out of it. The fireplace crackles warmly but, beyond the safety of the tavern walls, the wind is howling like a wolf. You watch as lightning scars the bellies of the dark, boiling storm clouds.

"I am glad to be in the warm and dry, I will tell you that for nothing," mutters Burlybe. "This is no normal storm." He sits quietly for a moment, and his eyes grow serious and thoughtful. "These are dark days my friend... I have a strange feeling that dangerous times lay ahead." With that, he pushes himself to his feet and bids you goodnight.

All of the customers have now gone to bed, so you approach the barman to ask about lodgings. Turn to **156**.

As the innkeeper hands you your keys, a deep tiredness settles over you.

(You cannot stay awake for much longer, but before you head to your room, you may order a quick meal from the bar. If you want to do this, hand over **two Crimson Coins** – if you can afford it - then eat the food to increase your **Life Force** by two points.)

Heavy eyed, you make your way up the stairs and open the door to your room. It is rather small inside, and sparsely furnished, but it has a comfortable enough bed. You head over to the room's west facing window, which points away from the road into the deep, shadow haunted mire. Rain splatters furiously against the pane, as if the heavy droplets are trying to beat their way in.

You climb under the warm covers and settle down to sleep, listening to the inn sign creaking back and forth; to the pounding water on the roof; to the wind whistling across the ghostly mire. Slowly you drift into a deep slumber. For a while your rest is peaceful and undisturbed, until you are woken with a start late in the night by the sound of fists hammering on your bedroom door. You recognize the voice of the innkeeper yelling for you to let him in.

If you wish to unlock the door, turn to **201**.

If you would rather ignore him and go back to sleep, turn to **444**.

With a deep roar the Orc charges at you, wildly brandishing his axe!

ORC GUARD

LIFE FORCE 10   STRIKING SPEED 8

Focus	Move	Damage
1	**Brutish Headbutt**	2
2-3	**Elbow To The Face**	2
4-5	**Axe Hilt Slam**	2
6	**Downward Axe Strike**	3

If you win, you find **four Crimson Coins** among the Orc's possessions. (You may take them if you wish.) Leaving the night guard slumped on the floor, you head through the door at the top of the stairs and into the corridor beyond. Turn to **136**.

190

Sword drawn, you advance swiftly on the Games Master. The hunched figure does not stir in fear. It stands motionless, chuckling eerily at your approach. "I admire your confidence if you think that you can defeat *me*," it hisses. "Very well, I will dispose of you myself." Suddenly, your opponent's eyes shine red beneath the darkness of its hood. You are instantly transfixed by the glowing orbs, and you find yourself rooted to the spot. The hypnotic stare grows more intense, and you feel a darkness closing in on your mind. Thinking quickly, you try to break eye contact, but it is easier said than done: you have already become as stiff as stone and you cannot turn your head to look away, nor even can you shut your eyes!

If you are wearing **Gorath's Savage Helm**, the enchanted armour offers you some protection from your enemy's Mind Grasp spell, so turn to **354**.

If you are not wearing **Gorath's Helm**, you will need to be lucky to break free from this crippling magic.

Can you summon enough willpower to resist the spell? Roll one dice four times to find out.

If you roll a six on at least one occasion, turn to **354**.

If you fail to roll a six, turn to **164**.

191

You regain your balance, reaffirm your grip on the wall, then resume your descent. After a short while you drop out of the shaft and land in a gloomy, stone walled passage. As you look up at the opening in the ceiling, it closes with a sickening, rasping sound. You are not certain what you have just climbed down, and you are unsure if you want to find out.

You are now in a much lower part of the fortress. The air is far colder here and the smell is musty and stale. You can head north or south along this passage. As you are deciding which way to go, you hear the sound of footfalls approaching from the north.

Will you:

Hold your ground, turn to **247**.

Or hurry southward, away from the footfalls, turn to **256**.

A moment later, you sense the approach of another entity. A growling voice booms around you. You spin in a full circle, but you cannot see what is speaking. "Who dares enter the Realm of Darkness? Only those with hearts of pure evil may pass beyond the Black Door. Be gone with you!" You feel a sudden, cold wind dragging at your body, and you realize that you are being pulled backwards. The gale becomes stronger and wilder, and you are soon spinning through the darkness at a tremendous pace. You blink against the tempest, but when you open your eyes again, you find that the wind has abruptly halted. You look around and discover that you are standing back in the passage in front of the liquid wall. Your efforts have merely led you back to where you started!

A fiery heat is now radiating from the barrier, and you are unable to get close to it. You will have to return to the village after all, and look for another way to cross the lake. Turn to **116**.

You survey the town's defences. If you are not going in through the main entrance, your only alternative is to scale the outer wall. You put some distance between yourself and the gate, then you sneak through the darkness to the foot of the barricade. As you are deciding the best way to tackle the obstacle, you notice a horse-drawn cart rumbling up the marsh trail toward the town.

If you want to slip unnoticed into the back of the cart, and hide there in the hope that the guards let the cart into the town, turn to **158**.

If you would rather climb the wall, turn to **113**.

194

The strange symbols above the door read:

Warning! Do not handle crates without the
permission of Braargg the Beast Trainer.
The creatures must be kept contained.
This order shall be enforced under pain of death!

If you wish to open this door, turn to **22**.
Otherwise, you may try the red door, turn to **61**.
Or the blue door, turn to **46**.

195

You head through the stained wooden door into a twisting passage. It leads to an empty square chamber where small, iron bowls are mounted on the walls. The bowls are filled with glowing mosses that paint everything in an eerie green light. There are two doors exiting the green room. Upon one door, the small symbol of an upward pointing arrow has been carved into the wood. Upon closer inspection, you see that the other door also has a small arrow carving, this time pointing down. Which door will you choose?

The door with the arrow pointing up, turn to **148**.

The door with the arrow pointing down, turn to **120**.

The Games Master releases a sardonic chuckle of pleasure, and you know that you have chosen badly. The hooded figure waves his hand and the smallest door opens as if by magic. Out of the blackness bounds a fierce, rapidly moving shape. It is on all fours, a panther-like beast with purple fur. To your alarm you see that it has not one, but two heads, and its savage eyes are snarling and fierce. It rushes across the chamber and leaps towards you, claws outstretched!

(If you possess a **Crossbow**, you may fire one **Bolt** before the beast is upon you. If you do this, erase the **Bolt** and reduce the beast's **Life Force** by two points, then use your sword to finish the fight.)

BICATHIAN

LIFE FORCE 9   STRIKING SPEED 10

Focus	Move	Damage
1	Ram	1
2-3	Left Headed Bite	2
4-5	Right Headed Bite	2
6	Slicing Claws	2

If you win, turn to **200**.

197

You hurry off down the winding, westerly trail. The track is narrow and sodden, and you are continually getting your feet stuck in the waterlogged earth. Deep in the night, you come to a fetid stream that is running south across your path. A dead tree leans over the water, arching forward so that its branches touch the bank on the far side. You treat it like a bridge and clamber over to the far shore. As you continue, the land becomes very quiet. No longer can you hear the howl of the Werewolves, and a short while later the onset of dawn breaks over the lonely horizon.

The dangers of the night have now passed, and you are forced to rest by the trail to recover your energy. The earth is cold and wet, but you manage to get a few hours of broken sleep.

Feeling slightly more refreshed, you push on down the trail.

The land feels strangely peaceful and calm under the light of the day, which is a welcome contrast to the night before. However, peril is never far away, as you have to keep watch for sinkholes and mud traps. Some hours later, you pass a large boulder with an inscription carved into it. It informs you that you are heading towards the town of Shellhaven. Unenthused at the idea of spending another night on the marsh, you push on quickly. You make good progress, but evening draws in early, like a portent of doom, and there is still no sign of the town. As night settles, the trail begins to bend to the south, then you hear a rider's voice and thundering hooves on the track ahead. The horseman is not yet visible through the thickening gloom, but he is approaching swiftly.

Will you:

Stand your ground and hail the rider, turn to **28**.

Or hide in the darkness near the trail, turn to **432**.

The weather remains pleasant for the rest of the day. As you trudge through the wood, beams of light slope lazily through the leaves and the mottled shade on the path is cool and welcoming. Birdsong fills the canopy and the woodland berries are rich in pickings. You make good progress, and you reach the edge of the forest just before sundown. In the distance you can now see the rooftops of Grimbree, nestled under a reddening sky.

As you wander into the village, you are surprised to find that the streets are deserted. Through the lengthening shadows, you stroll along a lane until you come to the market square. No one stirs, but the local inn is open and you can hear voices within. A painted sign above the door reads: *The Thirsty Ferret*. Yellow firelight glitters against the windows, making the dwelling look warm and inviting, so you head inside.

As you enter the small inn, you see three men drinking at a round table in the corner. They pause and turn to see who has entered, before returning to their quiet discussion. You cannot hear what they are saying, but you notice a nervous look in their eyes. Across the room, a young woman is standing behind the bar. It is warm in here and your legs are aching after the long day's walk, so you decide to rest for a while.

If you wish to speak to the lady at the bar, to enquire about a drink or a room for the night, turn to **69**.

If you would rather sit near the men at the round table, to listen in on their conversation, turn to **300**.

199

With the danger passed, you take a moment to rummage around in the study. There are many books and scrolls that cram the overburdened shelves, and as you thumb through the pages you find that they all contain cryptic notes on dark sorcery. You are no expert in the art of black magic, and nothing good would result from meddling with it. You wisely shut the books and leave them be.

The burning fireplace crackles wildly as you move to the untidy desk. A pile of papers are scattered across the table, revealing more scribblings about evil spells, but beneath the strewn notes you find something which draws your interest. You have discovered a glass bottle filled with black liquid. As you hold it up to the light, you see that the fluid is shimmering with strange lights, as though you are looking at dim stars in a night sky.

If you wish to drink the contents, turn to **37**.

Otherwise, you find nothing else of interest, so you exit the room. Turn to **185**.

200

A hiss of disbelief escapes from the Games Master. He mutters a spell, causing every door in the hall to slam shut. He is clearly disappointed that you slew his hideous pet and, despite his earlier promises, he has no intention of letting you leave this chamber alive. He points his hand towards you, whilst muttering the words to a murderous spell.

Will you:

Run towards him with your sword raised, turn to **363**.

Throw your sword at him, in the hope that it impales him before he can cast his spell, turn to **334**.

Or, if you have a **Crossbow** and any remaining **Bolts**, you may fire at him from where you stand, turn to **422**.

201
Illustration Opposite

The innkeeper bursts into your room. He is dressed in his night robes, which are soaked in blood, and his face is pale with shock. His whole body is trembling and his eyes are alight with horror. "We're being attacked! Demons! Hundreds of them!" he yells. "Grab your sword! There's no time to waste!"

You rush to the window and look outside. For a few seconds you can see nothing through the storm soaked darkness. Then you hear a deep rumble of thunder and a fork of blue lightning flickers against the heavy clouds, illuminating the haunted marshes. In that moment of eerie light, you see them: a horde of giant winged Demons, swooping out of the blackness towards the inn. The lightning then passes, and the shadows roll back in.

"We killed some of them already," stammers the innkeeper, "but we need help to barricade the windows and doors downstairs. We must hurry! Or they will get inside and tear us apart!"

Before you have time to think, the bedroom window shatters and the huge silhouette of a Demon bursts through into your room. The beast slams straight into you, and you are flung violently against the far wall. (Reduce your **Life Force** by two points.) As you stumble to your feet, you hear the innkeeper let out a cry of horror. Before he can defend himself, the Demon rakes its talons across his throat, killing him instantly.

You grab your sword and turn to face your adversary. The beast is well over seven feet tall, with deep purple skin, hideous features and curving red horns. It rakes the air with its bloodied claws, beckoning you to approach it.

You look at the crumpled form of the innkeeper, then with a vengeful shout you rush forward to slay your enemy!

WINGED NIGHT DEMON

LIFE FORCE 9   STRIKING SPEED 9

Focus	Move	Damage
1	Crushing Headbutt	1
2-3	Slashing Claws	2
4-5	Savage Bite	2
6	Frenzied Attack	3

If you win, turn to **142**.

202

Hoping to avoid the gaze of your enemies, you quickly fall onto your back and drag some of the wreckage over your body, partially burying yourself. You remain as still as stone, watching the dark fleet swooping north over the settlement. For a moment it looks as though your plan might work. However, the winged terrors have advanced eyesight, and they are not easily deceived. Far above you, the pack suddenly changes direction, creating an aggressive spearhead formation. You have been spotted!

Before you can act, the largest beast opens its blazing jaws, then a ball of fire streaks downwards and hits the mound to your left. There is a huge explosion, and you are momentarily deafened by the sound. In the next instant, a surge of heat rushes over you, then the blast wave lifts you into the air and hurls you through the window of a nearby house!

You crash to the floor amidst a shower of glass and debris. (Reduce your **Life Force** by four points!)

If you are still alive, turn to **226**.

203

With the invisible creature dead, you move over to the ravaged body of the prisoner. As you approach, his eyes suddenly flicker open.

He is alive!

As you kneel beside him, you see that he is close to death. Sadly, there is little you can do to help him.

"Thank you," he says weakly, "for trying to… save me. My name is Thrain. My wounds are grim, but do not look sadly upon me… my time has come, and I do not intend to meet it with fear." You respect his bravery, and you listen intently as he speaks. You learn that Thrain was taken prisoner along with many other people, after Zanack's servants captured the lakeside village of Stormwater. "The people who died in the carnage were the lucky ones," he tells you. "Zanack has been experimenting on those he took prisoner. He has used his dark magic to turn them into twisted, blood crazed mutants. His experiments have not gone entirely to plan though, as they are too frenzied to be controlled. He has locked them for the moment in the lower cellars of the castle. When the time is right, he intends to release them into the towns and villages that are scattered across the lands. They are mindless, wild things, who will kill anything that they can lay their hands on. Whatever you do, don't go down into those cellars. Stay away from any doors marked with the red hand, that's where he keeps his mutant creations."

You tell Thrain that you are on a quest to destroy the Demon Sorcerer, to put an end to his reign of terror. At this revelation, Thrain's eyes abruptly widen with a newfound energy. He finds the strength to grip your hand, and he fixes you with a serious look. "By the gods! You are brave indeed adventurer! Life fades from me, but I may be able to help you yet! Continue down this passage," he says, "through a cavern and up the left staircase. Cross the battlements at the top. There is a door. You will find Zanack through there, in the high tower." Thrain continues to speak, but he is struggling to remain conscious, so you listen carefully as his words grow fainter. "Be careful," he says, "Zanack is a powerful Demon, heartless and terrible and filled with cunning plans, but I wish you luck adventurer! May your heart steer you on the path to success. In the cave… drink the water… eat afterwards, but avoid the red ones… and remember… remember… the black ones bring death…" His voice ebbs away, then he sags limply into your arms.

In his last moments, Thrain gave you many important clues. Remember his warnings and his advice, for it may serve you well in the near future. After whispering some words of empathy for his departed soul, you set off down the corridor. After a short while you come to a flight of stairs that leads downward for a long time. At length, you come to an open archway at the bottom.

Turn to **229**.

204

The passage bends to the left, then ends at a heavy, closed door!

You try the handle and find that it is locked! The pursuing footfalls are growing ominously loud.

If you have the special ability of **Picklock** (or a **Skeleton Key**), you may open the door and keep running, turn to **291**.

Otherwise, you will have to flee back to the previous door, turn to **154**.

As you continue, the track grows ever more arduous, with large rocks blocking your way. You slowly clamber over the debris. (If you have the word **Venom** written on your Character Sheet, you begin to feel hot and ill, and you must reduce your **Life Force** by another point.) Just when you are thinking that the terrain can get no more gruelling, the path dips into a valley. As you enter the gorge you see a young man sitting on a boulder by the side of the path. He is dressed in dark clothes and his face is long and narrow, with a hawk-like nose and beady little eyes. Your hand tightens on the hilt of your blade, for you can tell by the look on his face that he is up to no good. You watch as he casually walks onto the narrow trail in front of you.

"You had best stop where you are," he says with an arrogant smirk. "This valley belongs to me, so if you want to pass safely through here, you'll have to pay me for the privilege."

Your eyes narrow. You have stumbled upon another Bandit, and his wicked grin is repulsively sinister. He is slight of build, armed only with a dagger. His weapon is currently tucked into his belt, and his hand is rested on the hilt. He would be no contest for you in a fair fight, but his confident swagger tells you that he is not alone. You suspect that several of his villainous comrades are lurking behind nearby boulders, ready to ambush you if you do not agree to his terms.

"Unless you want to get yourself killed, you'd best hand over all of your coins," he says with a nasty look.

Will you:

Do as he says and hand over all of your money, in the hope that he will let you pass safely through the valley, turn to **283**.

Or will you draw your sword and teach this little thug a lesson, turn to **307**.

206

The twisting passage takes you into a small circular chamber. The space is lit by a single wall-mounted candle that is glowing with a purple light. There is another plinth in the centre of this room, with a strange inscription etched into its surface. It reads:

In evil it dwells,
In hatred it lays,
You will find what you seek,
At the end of the maze.

There are four exits from this room. Which way will you go now?

North, turn to **302**.
East, turn to **217**.
South, turn to **239**.
West, turn to **314**.

You spring from the shadows, hoping to behead the Orc with a surprise attack. But this one is a battle hardened monster. It senses your presence and spins towards you, just in time to see your blade sweeping for its head. In a flash, it draws its sword and parries your attack.

Zanack steps back, surprised by your appearance, then he orders his servant to rip the head from your shoulders.

As the battle commences, you can see the Demon Sorcerer looming at the back of the room, awaiting the outcome of the fight.

ORC, LEGION COMMANDER

LIFE FORCE 12   STRIKING SPEED 8

Focus	Move	Damage
1	Powerful Headbutt	2
2-3	Jaw Shaking Punch	2
4-5	Pommel To The Face	2
6	Massive Sword Strike	4

If you win, turn to **216**.

208

You walk to the centre of the clearing and pause by the fountain. The bubbling water is indeed glittering with magic, and a dead Orc is sprawled in the flowers at your feet. The beast's expression suggests that it died in agony, probably after drinking the water. Your eyes narrow and you wonder if the fountain has been poisoned.

Suddenly you are distracted by a rumbling sound, so you turn and see dust coming up out of the hole. One of the tunnel's supports has given way, causing a cave in, and the entrance is now completely blocked.

If you want to drink from the fountain before moving on, turn to **261**.

Otherwise, you decide that time is pressing, so you start to make your way towards the harbour, turn to **145**.

209

By feeling your way around the walls, you discover that the room is circular. You also bump into a plinth at the heart of the chamber. Lastly, you ascertain that there are three exits, each leading to more passageways. But in the total darkness, which one should you take?

Will you head:

North, turn to **217**.

East, turn to **227**.

West, turn to **267**.

"It's in the tower," he says, his eyes fixated upon the sharp edge of your sword.

"Where is the tower?" you demand.

"There is a labyrinth," he hisses, pointing down the passage. "Go north, east, south, east, south. In the small room, head down the warm passage and knock twice at Padayat's door. She knows the way out - yes yes! When you've escaped the labyrinth, you'll reach the cold stairwell. Winding steps. Up, up to secret place. Secret guarded place. Shield there. Horrible shield. All light." He shudders and squirms at the thought of it, his ugly face contorted with revulsion. "Don't kills me now. Rog has told you all he knows."

You know that Rog could be lying, but you have a feeling that this hideous creature is telling the truth.

You suddenly hear the echo of footfalls. Unless you are mistaken, it sounds like ten guards are marching along a nearby corridor. You cannot afford to get into a brawl with that many enemies, so you knock Rog unconscious with the pommel of your sword. You hurry away and soon come to a tall, open archway. Remembering Rog's words, you step through the opening. Turn to **239**.

211

With a final, almighty effort, you manage to drive your sword through the gleaming scales of your powerful enemy. The Golden Guardian crashes to the floor, exhaling its last breath as it does so, and there it lies, still at last. You wipe the sweat from your brow, pausing for a moment by the body of the slain beast. When you have caught your breath, you approach the door to see what the beast was guarding. Turn to **265**.

212

You speed on, driving your legs as hard as you can. A short distance ahead you see a flight of steps. You leap off the top, land expertly at the bottom, then race into another candlelit corridor. You can hear a chilling chorus of voices behind you now, calling to you like the phantom breath of a shrieking wind. You look back. To your dismay, there is already movement at the top of the stairs. Dark bodies are sweeping down the steps after you, their shadowy, nightmarish forms moving with unnatural haste. Your pursuers are swifter than you had thought! Sweat is now pouring from your forehead, your legs are tiring and your lungs are burning.

You hurtle around a sharp twist in the passage, then you see an open door to your left.

Will you:

Leap through the door, turn to **154**.

Or run past it, turn to **204**

The Witch suddenly snatches a bottle from her desk and slings it to the floor. The glass shatters and a cloud of smoke pours out, filling the room in an instant. As the mist clears, you find yourself face to face with a mighty looking Demon. It is at least eight feet tall, with frosty white skin that glistens like cold crystal. Its eyes are the striking colour of azure, and its twisted horns, that are frozen blue at their tips, protrude from the sides of its head. With a roar like thunder, it steps forward, positioning itself defensively between you and the grinning crone. This is a truly powerful looking adversary. Its icy form is thick with gleaming muscle, and it radiates a freezing aura.

If you wish to flee from the room, turn to **426**.

If you stand your ground and fight, turn to **235**.

214

Two humanoid forms sweep towards you. Both are around six feet tall, dressed in grey and tattered rags. You glance at their hideous, blue skinned faces, black horns and red eyes. They are Demon Spell Weavers, and their veins are surging with destructive power! Their hands crackle with magical energy, and their mere touch will fill you with pain. (If you have a **Crossbow** and any remaining **Bolts**, you may shoot at your enemies while they are charging towards you. Reduce their **Life Force** now by two points for every shot fired, then resolve the fight as normal.)

DEMON SPELL WEAVERS

LIFE FORCE 12   STRIKING SPEED 9

Focus	Move	Damage
1	Spell of Wounding	1
2-3	Freezing Grasp	2
4-5	Burning Touch	2
6	Curse of the Damned	3

If you win, turn to **255**.

215

The black ones are oddly tasteless, but they feel cold and icy when you swallow them. Suddenly you start to cough. Your stomach churns and your vision blurs, then you collapse to the floor. Strange hallucinations pass before your eyes, making you delirious. You stumble to your feet and run back through the dark corridors, laughing manically. Due to the noise you are making, it does not take long for the castle guards to find you. Possessed by a crazed delirium, you do not have the wits to fight off your attackers. Your hands are bound and shackled, then you find yourself being hauled towards a torture chamber. Fortunately you pass out on the way, never to wake again. The deadly mushroom has done its work.

216

The Orc tumbles to the floor in a pool of green blood.

Zanack is momentarily silent. Then he grins and claps his hands. "Very impressive," he growls, "You fight well, worm. It is almost a shame that I have to destroy you." He sighs, then spreads his arms, "but such is life. Do think of me in the void." His deep voice is rich with mockery and arrogance, and you sense no fear in him.

"HUSHNUCK!" He roars.

Before you can act, the gloom in the chamber abruptly deepens. On the floor, the shadows rise up. Growing. Shivering. Transforming into terrible black creatures.

"If you came seeking death, fool, then you have found it," Zanack laughs. With a vile cry, he orders his spectral servants to tear you apart! Turn to **254**.

217

You follow a snaking passage which curves and bends in a disorientating manner. At length you come to a circular room that is lit by a solitary candle. At the centre of the chamber is a large plinth with no etchings on it.

There are four exits.

Will you take:

The north passage, turn to **206**.

The east passage, turn to **289**.

The south passage, turn to **259**.

The west passage, turn to **267**.

Or will you sit on the plinth and briefly rest your legs, turn to **389**.

As you head up the stairway, you hear the howl of distant wind. The only other sound is that of your footfalls, echoing in the narrow space. Suddenly, the stone walls begin to move on either side of you. For a fleeting second you think that your eyes are deceiving you, but they are not. Arms of solid rock suddenly melt out of the walls and attempt to grab you!

Will you:

Draw your sword and defend yourself, turn to **284**.

Or surge past them and make a run for the top of the stairs, turn to **270**.

"It was the robed horseman that killed my father," she informs you. "His body now lies buried on the hill by the edge of Grimbree. No one is safe here these days, especially not in the darkling hours." She grows very upset, then tears roll down her pale cheeks. A customer comes to console her. He is a young man with a kind face, and he introduces himself to you. "My name is Mok," he says. "You picked a bad time to come to Grimbree, friend." He points out of the window to a cottage across the street. "That's my home. It used to be a nice place to live, but not anymore. Every night for two weeks now, the robed figure has ridden into this village and terrorized the folk here. Several people have vanished after dusk, and their bodies have been found the next day out on the fields. It is not safe for you to leave at this hour. You can spend the night in my cottage, if you like."

(If you paid for a mug of ale at the bar, you drink the brew whilst considering Mok's offer: increase your **Life Force** by one point.)

What will you do now?

Agree to spend the night at Mok's place, turn to **66**.

Leave Grimbree via the southerly road and continue with your main quest, turn to **72**.

Or set off to kill the beast in the village, turn to **41**.

220
Illustration Opposite

You wake with a start.

It is dark. The night is cold and curiously calm, and a wandering moon bathes you in a misty light. Your head throbs with pain, and your senses are muddled. When your mind eventually sharpens, you find yourself tied to a tree several metres from the track. A short distance away, you see a tall, hooded figure, standing silently in the darkness. He is dressed in long black robes, and beneath the shadows of his hood is a ghastly, withered face. He is soon joined by three more sinister figures. You recognize the creatures as Demonic Soul Stealers. They are foul servants of the Dark Lord Zanack, and their wicked intentions are made clear by the sacrificial daggers that are gripped in their hands! Struck by the desperate nature of your predicament, you struggle violently against your bonds, but you are unable to break free. You can only watch in horror as your captors move closer. They are about to plunge the poisoned blades into your heart, when suddenly… Turn to **329**.

221

Grasping your sword, you swing with all the strength you can muster. The second that your weapon touches the magical barrier, a blue current of energy rushes up the blade and into your body. You are instantly incinerated. Nothing is left of you save for a pile of smoking ashes, but at least death came swift.

222

You turn left, but you have only gone a short distance when you come to a dead end. An impassable wall of crackling, dark magic blocks your way. As you approach the barrier, sparks of black energy leap out of it and burn your skin. (Reduce your **Life Force** by three points. If you are still alive, read on.) There is no way through, so you run back to the last junction and hurry down the other passage, turn to **262**.

223

The passage soon bends to the left, then to the right. You have not gone much further when a young man in drab and tattered clothing sprints out of the gloom ahead. He is unarmed, and his face is fraught with terror. You guess by his emaciated appearance that he is an escaped prisoner, who has been locked up for some time in this dark castle. He is running as if for his life, but you cannot see anything chasing him.

As he sprints by, he looks back yelling "Run! Run! Before it gets you too!" Then he speeds away and disappears from sight.

Suddenly, a blast of wind hits you with such force that you are almost knocked off your feet. Something large has just swept past. Whatever it was, it must have been moving at an incredible pace, for you did not even glimpse it.

The prisoner's footsteps begin to fade, then suddenly his agonised screams echo down the passage.

Will you:

Run back to help him, turn to **350**.

Or hurry on your way, turn to **244**.

224

Carefully, you climb down the fleshy, living wall. You can see blood pumping through the giant veins as you grip onto them. You still cannot see the bottom of the shaft, and you start to imagine what might await you below. It feels as if you are climbing down the throat of a gigantic beast, willingly making your way towards the acidic pit of its monstrous stomach. You try to shake the thought away. A faint red glow lights your way, but it is not clear as to the source of the illumination. Suddenly, the light dims and the walls gurgle and vibrate. Your hand slips on the pulpy surface and you totter backwards, as if you are about to fall!

Do you possess the special ability of **Scale**?

If you do, turn to **191**.

If not, turn to **279**.

225

You spring forward, and with an almighty swipe you bring your sword crashing down onto the beast's head. To your horror, your weapon bounces off of the monster's scales, scarcely scratching it! The guardian grunts and surges to its feet with a vicious snarl. The gigantic hound gleams like a golden statue that has come to life, and its brutal fangs are sharp enough to tear a person in two! You will have to fight hard if you are going to defeat this mighty opponent!

GOLDEN GUARDIAN

LIFE FORCE 13   STRIKING SPEED 10

Focus	Move	Damage
1	Powerful Ram	2
2-3	Ripping Claws	3
4-5	Rending Fangs	3
6	Crushing Bite	4

If you manage to win this epic battle, turn to **211**.

226

As you roll to a halt, you see that your arms and legs are on fire, but you quickly pat out the flames. Battered and bruised, you stagger to your feet.

You are standing in a derelict living room, and through the broken window you can see your enemies landing in the street. Two of the beasts still circle overhead, spewing flames across the roof of the building. The room begins to grow very hot and smoke starts to seep through the rafters as the dwelling crackles into fiery life. If you stay here for much longer you will be cooked to death!

You must decide quickly on a course of action.

Will you:

Leap back into the enemy infested street, turn to **405**.

Or head deeper into the flaming building, in search of a rear exit to the dwelling, turn to **138**.

227

The corridor soon opens into a small, circular chamber. A solitary candle, mounted on the eastern wall, flickers and dances as you enter. A plinth sits nearby, but the inscriptions on its surface have been worn by age and are illegible. Looking north, you see an open door which leads to a gloomy, warm passage. Something seems strange about this room. You have an odd suspicion that there is a secret door nearby, but for all your searching, you cannot find it.

If you have a **Spiderweb Bracelet**, subtract **142** from the number on the artifact, then turn to that page.

If you do not have this artifact, you decide to explore the warm passage, turn to **276**.

Hanging on the side of the cart is a little pouch, inside which you find a small orb of black glass that is humming quietly. You recognize it immediately as a demonic artifact, used for enhancing the potency of dark spells. You do not want this item returning to the hands of its insidious owner, so you throw it to the ground and crush it beneath your boot.

A moment later, you hear the creak of an opening door. You turn to see a young man standing in the entrance of his house, his features bathed in the yellow light of his lantern. His skin looks pale with worry, and you can see by his expression that he is very anxious.

"What are you doing?" he says in a low voice. "Are you insane? Quick, come inside!"

Will you:

Follow him into the house, turn to **14**.

Or continue to search the cart, turn to **71**.

You step through the opening into an enormous, ancient cavern, which sits far beneath the foundations of the castle. The builders of the fortress must have unexpectedly tunneled down into this natural cavern when the ghastly castle was being built. Looking up, you see that the domed roof is unimaginably high, with long stalactites that reach down like the pointing fingers of an Elemental Giant. At the centre of the cave is an enormous lake, the banks of which are carpeted in moss. Huge mushrooms, taller than a man, have grown up all around the water's edge, and they are glowing with different colours. Their enchanting radiance completely illuminates the vast interior. As you look around, you see two stone archways on the far side of the cave, both leading to gloomy stairways that head upwards. A trail leads around the lake towards them, cutting a narrow path through the thick carpet of moss. You set off along the track and soon it is winding through the forest of giant mushrooms. You are bathed in their glow, and the nearby surface of the lake sparkles and shimmers with a magical beauty as it reflects the light. You do not sense any danger here, at least not for the moment.

If you wish to pause by the lake to quench your thirst, turn to **366**.

If you want to taste the giant mushrooms, turn to **312**.

If you would rather continue around the bank towards the doors, turn to **301**.

At the end of the battlements, you discover that the heavy oak door has been decorated with human skulls. It is securely locked, but a brief search of the knight's body reveals a set of rusty keys. You try each one in turn until the door opens with a click, then you step inside.

You are standing at the foot of a short flight of steps, and you can hear menacing voices ahead. You creep upwards and pause on a dark landing at the top. There is only one door that leads on, so you crouch in the shadows and peer inside. You are looking into a large, gloomy chamber with a row of arched windows in the east wall. Standing in the centre of the room, you see your ultimate nemesis: the Demon Sorcerer himself! Zanack! He is a tall, grey skinned Demon, clad in sleeveless black robes. His huge shoulders look impossibly broad and his arms are thick with muscle. Lightning bathes the room, revealing a gruesome crown of twisting thorns upon his terrible, horned head.

He is talking to his legion commander, a stocky Orc with a sheathed sword, who is clad in heavy armour. They are speaking in a guttural, sinister language, and they are completely engrossed by the conversation.

They are not yet aware of your presence.

If you have the special ability of **Greater Wisdom**, you may listen in on their private conversation by turning to **258**.

Otherwise, you may leap into the room and attack the legion commander, turn to **207**.

Or leap into the room and attack Zanack, turn to **275**.

The gloomy passage leads on for several minutes before ending at a tall, wooden door. You turn the handle and find that it is unlocked. Wondering what lies beyond, you step through the opening. Turn to **239**.

232

You are in luck. Although you have no control over the power of the ring, it seems to have an uncanny ability of knowing when you need its help. The little ring starts to sparkle and glow. It only releases a faint light, but it is enough for you to make a reasonable judgment of your surroundings. You can now see that you have stumbled into another circular chamber. This room has three exits, all leading to shadowy passageways. In the centre of the chamber is a stone plinth with an inscription on its surface. Although most of the verse has been worn away by age, you can still make out some of the words. This is what you can read:

In fl--h and bo--, it can al--ys be found,
In d--th and d--ay, it is carefully bound.

After pondering over the inscription, which way will you head?

North, turn to **217**.

East, turn to **227**.

Or west, turn to **267**.

233

Leaving the unconscious Orc slumped on the floor, you chase the woman down a network of twisting, branching tunnels. She has a head start on you, and she is possessed by a desperate fear. You begin to catch up with her, but then you lose sight of her at a T-junction. You head in the direction of her footfalls, but you are met with even more branching tunnels. You continue running around for some time, but eventually lose her in the maze of passages. When her footfalls fade into nothingness, you are forced to give up on the pursuit. You come to a halt and catch your breath. You are standing in a gloomy passage. You could be a long distance from where you started the chase, but it is hard to tell. In the confusing passageways, you could have run in circles and not known it. You will just have to do your best to regain your bearings. Turn to **256**.

234

You find yourself running down another passage. Suddenly, it bends sharply and you stumble and fall as you negotiate the curve at high speed. You are sent crashing to the floor.

(If you possess a **Crossbow**, it has been broken in the fall, so you must deduct it immediately from your equipment list.)

The approaching footfalls grow suddenly louder, so you leap up as quickly as you can. Your enemies are now only seconds behind, so you summon the last reserves of your energy and break into an almighty sprint. You accelerate. Faster. Faster. Until the muscles in your legs burn like fire. The passage floor passes under you in a blur of speed, and it does not take long before the pursuing footfalls fade into the distance. Up ahead, the passage forks. There is no time to think at this speed, so you instinctively veer down the right-hand corridor. Your enemies are too far behind to see which way you went, and by the time they reach the fork you are long gone. They choose the wrong turning and head in the other direction. You race on for a little while longer, to ensure you have shaken them from your trail. Eventually, when your legs can take no more, you stop and sag against a wall, panting with exhaustion. When you have caught your breath, you listen to the deep silence that lingers around you. You have escaped, but the guards are now aware of your presence, and they will be searching for you with murderous intent. You decide that you had best find Zanack as swiftly as possible, so that you can complete your quest and escape the fortress. Turn to **269**.

You are in no mood to be intimidated, so you strike out with your sword. Your blade sweeps through the creature as if it were made of thin air, then the Demon fades like a dream, until there is no trace left of it. The creature was a mere illusion, conjured up by the Witch to scare you off.

The smirk now fades from the crone's face and her lips curl into a frustrated snarl. "You have worn out my patience, you petulant scab!" she snaps in a livid tone. She looks like she is going to say something else, but her temper suddenly explodes, then she jumps over the table and rushes at you with a furious shriek. You sweep at her with your sword, but she ducks the blade and springs on top of you, grasping for your throat!

WITCH

| LIFE FORCE 6 | STRIKING SPEED 8 | |

Focus	Move	Damage
1	Strangling Grasp	1
2-3	Hag's Curse	2
4-5	Spell of Destruction	5
6	Spell of Defiance	See Below*

*(*Special Move: If your enemy casts a Spell of Defiance, she will cast it upon herself, increasing her Life Force by six points.)*

If you win, turn to **32**.

The door suddenly crashes open and ten armour-clad Orcs burst into the room. They surge towards you, roaring savagely whilst swinging their axes. Using the Doom Shield, you block a swipe for your neck, then you retaliate by lopping off the head of your nearest enemy. You dispatch two more guards in the same manner, but more reinforcements are pouring into the chamber, drawn by the sound of battle. Though many fall beneath the bloody swathe of your sword, their numbers start to overwhelm you. Orcs, Demons and other foul creatures swarm to your position. Soon you are surrounded and engulfed by the sea of evil bodies. You fall under a rain of bludgeoning axes, and as your life slips away, you see the Orcs licking their lips. They are the first to wash over you, their eyes gleaming like scavenging birds upon the carcass of a fallen beast. Your fate has been sealed.

They glow with a beautiful red light, whilst releasing a hypnotic scent. They taste pleasantly sweet, but your head starts to ache after just one mouthful and you realise that they are mildly poisonous. Fortunately, they cause you no serious harm and the symptoms quickly pass. You decide to leave these ones alone.

Will you:

Taste a different mushroom, turn to **312**.

Drink from the lake (if you have not already done so), turn to **366**.

Or press onwards, turn to **301**.

238

You head up the wooden staircase. The steps groan in protest, but they hold your weight. After a short while you hear a clanking from above. When the steps curve to the right, you pause and peer around the bend. A group of short, red skinned creatures are toiling away, chiseling and hammering at a blockage of rubble. They are dressed in filthy rags, and have pointed ears and small black horns. This staircase is obviously unfinished, and the little Demons have been tasked with the job of completing it. There are three of them in all, and they are no taller than children. However, they are very stocky and must be incredibly strong, as they are cutting their way swiftly through the rocks. There is no way forward, so you quietly retrace your footsteps, being careful not to gain the attention of the workers. Back in the cave, you turn to the other archway. Here, the steps of black stone stretch upwards, and you sense a tingling of dark magic in the air. You have a feeling that this staircase is guarded, but it seems that your destiny lies in this direction. You rest your hand warily on the hilt of your sword, then step forward to investigate. Turn to **218**.

239

You have found your way into a circular chamber, lit by wall-mounted candles. On the ceiling is a message scrawled in dried blood. It reads: *Welcome to the Labyrinth of Despair*. There are four exits from the room, each leading to narrow passages.

In the centre of the room is a stone plinth with what appears to be a riddle carved into its surface:

In the beginning they were close,
Two twins, morose,
But only one existed
In the end.

Their enemies searched cities,
And they scanned afar,
But the twins were not there, they had fled far.
One was seen hiding in mountains and towns,
The other hid cleverly,
Where it could not be found.

While you are studying the strange inscription, a small creature, no bigger than your forearm, flutters into the room on buzzing wings. It is a flying Imp, with red skin and large eyes. You watch as it replaces a dying candle with a new one, then it lights it with its breath before fluttering off down the north passage. It seemed too busy to show any interest in you.

You are now faced with a choice.

Will you take the passage heading:

North, turn to **206**.

East, turn to **267**.

South, turn to **302**.

West, turn to **314**.

As you hack your way through the vines, more rise up to block your way. You see that the trees are starting to peter out and come to an end, so you dodge past the remaining obstacles and make a dash along the dark trail. A few moments later you burst from the tree line and jump out of reach of the writhing creepers. Behind you, the wood looms darkly, as if disgruntled by your escape. You sheathe your sword and scan the moonlit road ahead. Rolling fields lay before you, and in the distance you can see the rooftops of Grimbree, nestled under a dark sky.

You are eager to move away from the sinister wood, so you follow the road into the village. The hour is late and the streets are deserted and silent. You wander along a twisting lane that leads into the market square. An old looking inn stands nearby, but the windows are dark and a sign on the door reads: *"Closed Early."*

While you are looking around, you see the now familiar cart, abandoned nearby. A cover has been laid over the top to conceal its contents, but the driver and horse are nowhere to be seen. As you are looking at it, the faint yellow glow of a candle appears at the upstairs window of the inn.

If you wish to investigate the cart, turn to **228**.

If you wish to knock at the inn, turn to **316**.

241

As you tiptoe past the monster, the beast draws in a long, slumbering breath. Its nose twitches as it picks up your scent, then it begins to wake from its dream. You grasp your sword, but just as the beast is about to open its eyes, your magical locket begins to sparkle. A faint song briefly emanates from the artifact, causing the guardian to go back to sleep. Relieved, you tiptoe past the hound and open the door. Turn to **265**.

242
Illustration Overleaf

The Dragon suddenly spews a wave of flames from its monstrous jaws. You look certain to be incinerated, but a beam of light erupts from the ring and momentarily blinds your enemy. The Dragon's aim is ruined, the fire misses you, then the beast lets forth a roar of frustration. You hold on for dear life as Snowfire veers wildly into another mass of cloud, hoping to elude the apex predator. But there is no escaping this opponent. The colossal monster continues its pursuit, determined to tear you limb from limb.

(On the following page you will find the stats for Snowfire and for your pursuer. You must roll to determine the conclusion of their battle. Treat this fight as you would any normal combat, but roll for Snowfire instead of yourself. If the Dragon is about to inflict damage with a **Move**, you may use the **Ring** to dazzle your enemy, causing it to miss. You may only do this five times, as the **Ring's** magic will then be depleted.)

Let the battle commence!

SNOWFIRE

LIFE FORCE 9   STRIKING SPEED 10

Focus	Move	Damage
1	Powerful Front Kick	2
2-3	Magical Blast	3
4-5	Hind Leg Kick	3
6	Battering Hooves	4

VS

RED DRAGON

LIFE FORCE 30   STRIKING SPEED 9

Focus	Move	Damage
1	Life Withering Roar	2
2-3	Spiked Tail Whip	6
4-5	Rending Claws	8
6	Flaming Breath	15

If Snowfire wins, turn to **450**.
If Snowfire loses, turn to **271**.

As you follow the trail along the base of a hill, a great fork of lightning streaks down from the violent sky. In the crackling glow, you see a huge dark figure, the size of fifty men, standing on the peak of the slope above you. At first your heart jumps with alarm, but then you realise it is a lifeless statue. The sculpture looks ancient, like a long forgotten god, built by a primeval race which has long since vanished from these lands. You stare at it for a moment, noting the strange, giant head, the branch like horns, and the features eroded by centuries of harsh weather. As the wind whips the hillside, a second fork of lightning suddenly blazes downwards. The crackling bolt strikes the head of the statue with a calamitous bang, causing the colossus to crack under the impact. The huge head, arms and body crash down the hillside and in the next instant you are swept off the trail by the debris. You tumble and plummet down a steep slope, and when you eventually come to a halt you are lying on your back next to the giant, cracked head.

Roll one dice to see if luck is on your side.

If you roll a three or less, you have sustained injuries from the fall: reduce your **Life Force** by three points.

If you roll a four or higher, you have managed to avoid any notable wounds.

As you clamber back up to the path, you can see the lightning striking the hilltops with vengeful force. The storm is growing more savage every minute.

You must find a place of shelter quickly.

Turn to **278**.

244

You proceed along the passage until you come to a steep flight of stairs heading downwards. The steps seem to go on forever, as if they are leading into the bowels of the world. As you descend, you become aware of the smell of death and decay. Something cracks under your foot, causing you to look down. The steps are littered with human skeletons, and the skulls number more than you would wish to count. In the distance, a chilling moan echoes eerily. Before long, you see two sinister forms lurching up the steps in your direction. The stench of decay rises like a mist from their festering bodies, and you realise that you have chanced upon a pair of dreaded Zombies. They are clad in tattered rags. One has a missing eye, and you are sure that you can see maggots wriggling in the cavity. The other abomination has only one arm, but despite their mangled limbs, you know that these wretched things will fight with mindless savagery. Zombies are driven by a single and insatiable desire to feed upon human flesh, and these two horrors are no exception. They head towards you, arms outstretched, with expressions of feverous evil!

You must draw your sword and defend yourself.

ZOMBIES

LIFE FORCE 16   STRIKING SPEED 8

Focus	Move	Damage
1	Diseased Breath	1
2-3	Raking Nails	1
4-5	Choking Grasp	2
6	Frenzied Mauling	4

If you win, you follow the stairs for a long time. At length you come to a door at the bottom. Turn to **229**.

245

Having dispatched the villainous robbers, you have made the highland trail a little bit safer for other travellers. You have done a good deed. You search the bodies and find **ten Crimson Coins** which you may add to your possessions. (This is in addition to any money that the Bandits may have stolen from you, you take that back also.) Eager to move on, you leave the blighted valley and follow the path ever higher into the hills. Thankfully, the remainder of the day passes without incident, but the air is growing colder now. Dusk falls and you see a tide of black clouds sweeping in from the east. Thunder rolls out of the distance.

If you have the word **Venom** written on your Character Sheet, turn to **122**.

If not, you can make camp by the roadside, turn to **70**.

Or keep walking, to look for a better place to sleep, turn to **98**.

Through the archway, you look out into the stormy night. You are staring across the battlements, but you are unable to see the end of it through the cloak of rain. Dark clouds still boil, blotting out the sky. You duck your head against the gale and make your way hurriedly across the wet and slippery stone. To your right, you can hear the lake beating in great plumes of white spray upon the island's rocky shores. To your left, you can see down into a paved courtyard, far, far below.

You soon see a large oak door at the end of the battlements. But it does not stand unguarded. A huge figure looms through the sheet of rain. His heavy armour is as black as the sky, and his face is covered by a fearsome helm. You sense that he is in no mood to talk, so you reach swiftly for your sword. He steps forward and hoists his dark axe above his head, eager to cleave you in two!

ZOMBIE KNIGHT

LIFE FORCE 10   STRIKING SPEED 9

Focus	Move	Damage
1	**Mighty Headbutt**	2
2-3	**Spiked Elbow Slam**	3
4-5	**Downward Axe Chop**	3
6	**Axe Blade Sideswipe**	4

If you defeat this powerful opponent, turn to **230**.

247

You do not have to wait long until a burly, armour-clad Orc comes into view. His back is turned to you, and he is dragging a female prisoner by the arms who is kicking and screaming.

You smash the Orc across the back of the head with the pommel of your sword. The blow goes in hard and the brute falls without a sound, crumpling to the floor in a heap.

The terrified woman is so frightened that she does not look to see who rescued her. She scrambles to her feet and runs away down the corridor, wild with panic.

Will you:

Run after her, turn to **233**.

Or remove the Orc's weapons and wake him up, in the hope of gaining some information from the brutish creature, turn to **287**.

248

As you take the rounded doorknob in your hand, the Troll's mouth suddenly opens. Its sharp, needle-like teeth bite into the soft flesh of your palm, causing you to pull away with a jolt. As you look at the puncture marks in your skin, the world begins to spin confusingly. You stumble sideways and fall to your knees, and your surroundings transform into a blur of colours and indistinct shapes. The venom from the bite has already seeped into your veins, and your arms and legs have become numb and useless! It is not long before a dark mist closes on your mind, and you spiral into a web of terrible dreams. Though you try to wake up, you are unable to do so. Death creeps through your veins, stealing your **Life Force** with merciless ease. The dark castle has claimed its latest victim…

249

You feel as though you are drowning, but somehow you load and fire the Crossbow. The bolt flies through the neck of your enemy, knocking him from the horse. Air rushes back into your lungs, but the steed is now stomping towards you, with red mist streaming from its mouth! You must defend yourself with your sword!

DEMON STEED

LIFE FORCE 7   STRIKING SPEED 9

Focus	Move	Damage
1	**Breath of Deadly Mist**	2
2-3	**Ram**	3
4-5	**Kick**	3
6	**Battering Hooves**	3

If you win, turn to **309**.

About two metres ahead, in the wall to your left, you notice a set of small, circular holes. You halt. Although it could be nothing, something about the scene makes you suspicious. You scan the floor and notice a thin trip wire. It spans the corridor, about six inches from the ground, and it is almost invisible in the gloom. You kneel beneath the holes and twang the wire with the point of your sword. Black tipped darts, possibly laced with poison, shoot instantly out of the little holes and whoosh over your head, clattering harmlessly against the walls. Had you caught the wire with your foot, the darts would have made a pincushion out of your body. You grin and rise, stepping carefully over the wire.

After a short while you come to a smoke stained door at the end of the passage. The entrance is slightly ajar, so you peek through the gap.

You are looking into a chemical laboratory. Benches are pushed up against the walls, and they are covered with complicated apparatus and bubbling vials of liquid. A strange, hunchbacked creature with four arms is mixing potions on the work surface. The beast has its back to you and is unaware of your presence.

If you wish to burst into the room and take the creature by surprise, turn to **266**.

If you wish to quietly head back the way you came, and continue along the previous passage, turn to **223**.

251

The beast starts talking in a terrified voice, but you can make no sense of his primitive language. Your attempts to communicate prove futile, and you conclude that you are wasting precious time. You silence the Orc's whimpering with a hard blow from the butt of your sword, knocking him unconscious once more. Sheathing your weapon, you set off again on your quest, none the wiser for your troubles.

Turn to **231**.

252

You speed down another passage. Up ahead, the corridor splits again. You hear raised voices down the left fork, so you veer to the right.

Suddenly, the passage bends sharply, causing you to stumble and fall. Your pursuers are now only seconds behind. You will not escape them now, so you leap up, spin around, and prepare for battle! Turn to **214**.

"I don't care if you're lost!" She shrieks. "Get out of my sight before I kill you!"

You suddenly notice the Witch's hand reaching for something on the cluttered tabletop.

If you possess a **Sinister Idol**, turn to **177**.

If not, turn to **213**.

254

Zanack's Shadow Demons advance towards you. They look like the misty silhouettes of tall men, brandishing swords of flickering black fire.

You swing your blade to hack a path through their ranks, but the ghostly beings are immune to the cut of your sword!

If you possess the **Doom Shield**, turn to **260**.

If not, turn to **313**.

255

You are exhausted after the battle. (If you possess a **Crossbow**, you discover that it has been broken during the fight. Deduct it from your equipment list.) To your dismay, you suddenly hear stomping feet and clinking armour. Twenty more guards are heading your way, and their guttural voices are growing louder. You do not wait for the rabble to arrive. You quickly turn and make your escape, sprinting left and right along random corridors in the hope of eluding your pursuers. Eventually, after running up a narrow staircase, you find that you have made your way into a quiet part of the castle. There are no guards here as far as you can tell, so you halt in a candlelit corridor to catch your breath. You have escaped for the moment, but now that the guards are aware of your presence they will be searching for you with murderous determination. You decide that you had best find Zanack as swiftly as possible, so that you can complete your quest and escape this wicked fortress.

Turn to **269**.

256

The new passage grows ever narrower. Eventually the deep gloom turns into utter blackness and you have to feel your way along the moss covered wall. Before long you see a glimmer of light at the end of the tunnel. When you finally reach it, the walls have narrowed so much it is a tight squeeze to get through the opening into the bright, candlelit room beyond. Turn to **239**.

Illustration Opposite

As soon as the key has fallen into the gaping jaws, the mouth slowly begins to close. The fangs soon lock together in a tight lipped snarl, then the statue becomes still once more.

For a moment nothing happens, then, behind you, the magical barrier flickers and vanishes. You step forward and triumphantly lift the Doom Shield from its resting place. You are surprised to find that it is as light as a feather, whilst being tougher and more durable than the hardest steel.

(Add the **Doom Shield** to your list of possessions.)

The shield's magical aura flows around you, focusing your mind and spirit. You have been blessed by its awesome enchanted powers! Increase your **Life Force** by twenty points, then turn to **111**.

From your position, you can easily hear the conversation.

"My Lord," grunts the Orc, "the guards 'ave reported sightings of an intruder in the castle. They said the trespasser was last seen moving in this direction."

Zanack laughs. It is a deep, guttural sound, full of derision. "An intruder, in the midst of my fortress? The fool will not survive the night. When the wretch is caught, come back and inform me. I shall enjoy feeding it to my Pool Beast. Now tell me news of Shellhaven."

"The town is overrun," says the brutish monster. "The Night Demons have secured the area but a few of the townsfolk escaped and scattered north, saved by the Captain of the Guard. I have given orders for them to be hunted down."

"Let them flee," grins the Demon, "their stories will spread fear into the hearts of all they meet. Soon my reach will extend across the land, then the rivers will run red with the blood of my enemies. They will wish they had curled up and died in Shellhaven, when the shadow of war marches upon them."

They begin to make plans for an attack on the Wizard's castle, and they are completely engrossed by the conversation. You cannot allow these evil schemes to be put into action! The time has come to strike, but before you can act, the Orc suddenly sniffs the air and gives a disgusted look.

"I smell human flesh!" he grunts.

Turn to **275**.

259

You follow a dark passageway. There are no candles here, and you have to feel your way along the wall. Eventually you come into a pitch-black chamber. You can see nothing at all in the thick darkness.

If you are wearing a **Magic Ring**, turn to **232**.

If not, turn to **209**.

260

The shadows swirl around you, besieging you from all sides. Several dark phantoms lift their swords to strike you, but you are not so easily slain!

You raise the Doom Shield, which suddenly shines with a wonderous radiance. In a matter of seconds, a perfect white light fills the chamber. Zanack's Shadow Demons reel back in horror, shrieking in spectral pain. The foul creatures begin to flicker and fade, their outlines becoming less obvious. A moment later, the intense light burns them away to nothingness.

The light from the Doom Shield now fades to a faint glow, allowing you to stare clearly across the chamber and into the eyes of your hated enemy. Zanack looks worried. For a brief second he stands silent, unsettled by the defeat of his powerful minions.

Taking advantage of his hesitation, you step forward. But Zanack is not done yet! He shakes himself to his senses and fixes you with a terrible stare. Before you can reach him, bolts of flame leap from his eyes and flash across the chamber towards you!

If you try to dodge the flaming bolts, turn to **384**.

If you shelter behind the Doom Shield, turn to **373**.

261

You cup your hands and drink your fill. The water is pure and invigorating, and you are immediately filled with a sense of well-being. The enchanted water is poisonous only to those with an evil heart. Those who are good are duly blessed by its magic.

(Increase your **Life Force** by four points).

Feeling refreshed, you decide that it is time to investigate the docks. With any luck, you might find a boat which you can use to cross the lake. Turn to **145**.

262

You speed down a twisting passage. Wall-mounted candles are sparsely placed along this corridor, and you have to be careful of your footing in the dim light. You reach another junction. The way to the right looks more ominous, so you make a split second decision and turn left. Shortly after, you come to a bend in the passage.

Back at the last junction, your pursuers halt, unable to decide which way you have turned. They sound furious, brimming with rage at the possibility that you might escape. They decide to split up, in order to explore both routes.

Will you:

Turn and wait for the remaining pursuers to catch up, so that you can ambush them as they come round the curve in the passage, turn to **285**.

Or keep running, in the hope that you can lose the rest of them, turn to **212**.

263

Fortunately you are a master of all languages, and you have no trouble in deciphering the beast's native tongue.

"Don't kills me! Don't cuts me throat!" it whimpers. "Rog will tells you anything, anything you wants to know! But you have to promise, yesss? Promise nots to kills me after?"

Your captive seems eager enough to talk, so you reluctantly agree to his terms.

What will you ask?

Where to find the Doom Shield, turn to **210**.

Or where to find Zanack, turn to **296**.

264

You soon come to a narrow rope bridge that spans a deep fissure. The rickety bridge is rattling and swinging in the wind and rain, but this appears to be the only way forward. You begin to edge across, gripping the ropes on either side. The precarious crossing sways and creaks, and you regret the moment you look down and see the black void beneath you.

You have almost reached the far side, and you are moments away from congratulating yourself on your bravery, when disaster strikes! A bolt of lightning sears down from the vengeful sky and strikes the centre of the bridge. Immediately the ropes burst apart and the rickety crossing collapses into the gaping blackness.

You throw yourself forward and just manage to grab the far edge of the fissure. You glance down and see the flailing remnants of the bridge vanishing into the rain swept darkness. It would have been certain death, had you gone down with it! Your hands and arms are cut and bleeding from clinging onto the sharp rocks. (Reduce your **Life Force** by two points.) If you are still alive, you manage to drag yourself up onto the path. The wind is becoming incredibly cold, and you realise that if you do not find shelter soon, there is a real possibility of hyperthermia setting in. Shivering against the bitter gusts, you quickly press onwards. Turn to **278**.

265

Once inside, you close the door behind you. The room in which you are standing is filled with white light, and the glare is so intense that you are forced to shield your eyes. As best as you can, you try to make out your surroundings. You have entered a massive, circular chamber with a domed roof. A closed door is positioned to your far left, and the blinding light seems to be radiating from a mysterious object at the centre of the room. Although it is painful to look at, you squint your eyes to see what it is.

On a stone plinth rests a magnificent white shield, which shimmers as brightly as the sun. As you step towards it, it senses your goodness and the light fades to a gentle glow. The shield is encased in a magical barrier that flickers and crackles with blue energy. The barrier is cylindrical, reaching from the floor to the ceiling. You have found the legendary Doom Shield, but now you must find a way to get it.

Will you:

Attempt to destroy the barrier with your sword, turn to **221**.

Or search the room for a different option, turn to **294**.

266

You throw the door open and leap into the room. The monster suddenly spins towards you in surprise. He has a multitude of evil eyes, and his mouth is lined with vicious fangs. He hisses at you and grabs a dagger from the worktop, but before he can make use of it, you bring your blade crashing down on his head. Your heavy sword strike kills him in one hit, and he crumples to the floor in a heap. You search the body but find nothing of use, so you turn your attention to the bubbling apparatus.

You now have a choice. There are countless potions here. Some are poisonous, others will improve your health, but there are no labels to indicate the good from the bad. If you wish to dice with death and drink one of the potions, you must roll one dice and consult the table on the following page. If you have **Sixth Sense**, you may add one to your dice roll. You can drink as many potions as you want, (there are countless ones to try), but each time you must roll a new dice, risking glory or death.

If you try this dangerous strategy, just remember that your **Life Force** cannot exceed thirty.

Dice Roll	Potion's Effect	Result
1	You have been transformed into a mindless zombie	Your quest is over
2-3	You have been poisoned	Minus 3 Life Force
4	You have been healed	Plus 1 Life Force
5 or higher	You have been healed	Plus 4 Life Force

When you have finished with the potions, you notice a narrow door in the corner of the room.

If you want to investigate, turn to **308**.

If you would rather return the way you came and explore the other corridor, turn to **223**.

267

You follow a narrowing passage which ends at a tiny door. You squeeze into a minuscule square chamber that is lit by glowing mosses on the damp walls. There are four small doors exiting the room, all widening out into more appropriately sized corridors. You can feel magic tingling in the air, and it makes your head swim. You shake yourself to clear the daze, and when you look again, you see that two of the doorways have vanished! Something odd is happening here. You decide to leave this chamber as quickly as possible, in case the other exits disappear as well!

Will you go:

South, turn to **311**.

Or west, turn to **239**.

The castle is shuddering so violently that it is hard to keep your grip. You look down. You are hundreds of feet up, and the whole fortress is tearing itself apart. Off to your left, a dark tower cracks away from the main building and crashes down in a deafening clamour, smashing on the rocks, far, far below. The Doom Shield, which is slung over your shoulder, suddenly disappears, and you know now for certain that Zanack is dead. But you cannot rejoice yet. Suddenly you notice an archer aiming at you from the north watch tower! A black shafted arrow whizzes for your head. It misses by a mere inch, but as it clashes with the wall it throws an array of hot sparks into your eyes. You cry out in pain, your grip slipping! You try to hold on, but the stone crumbles beneath your fingers. With nothing to cling to, you topple backwards and begin falling. You hurtle downwards, picking up speed as you go. Faster and faster you descend, until you are spinning out of control... then cold, foaming water suddenly engulfs you, and you realize that you have crashed into the freezing lake, just missing the rocky shore. The weight of your weapons drags you into the watery darkness, and your lungs are at bursting point. You are drowning, but you do not give in to panic. In a desperate bid for survival, you cast away all of your swords, then you swim upwards and break the surface of the foaming water. (Remove all **Swords, Pommel Upgrades** and **Damage Bonuses** from your Character Sheet.)

Huge segments of rubble are now crashing down into the water around you, and you watch as a massive spire cracks away from the summit of the building. It surges towards you, breaking into two massive sections as it does so. You will never swim fast enough to escape this deluge. After all that you have endured, it looks certain that you will be crushed and buried at the bottom of the lake. However, luck has not abandoned you yet!

You suddenly spot a white shape bursting out of the clouds above you. It hurtles downwards like a bolt of lightning, overtaking the falling spire. A second later, it crashes into the water, sweeps underneath you, and lifts you into the air! You look down, and to your joy and astonishment you find yourself aloft the back of a giant, beautiful winged horse. It is nearly twice the size of a normal steed, and it is glittering with magic. It is Snowfire! Pelanthius's mount from the castle of the Wizards! Turn to **103**.

269

You creep down the passage and soon come to an opening on your left, which leads to another candlelit corridor. You can hear a distant bubbling and popping, coming from that direction.

Will you:

Turn left to investigate the sounds, turn to **286**.

Or ignore the turning and press on, turn to **223**.

270

As you dash up the stairs, the hands claw and grab at you, tearing through your flesh with their stone talons. (Decrease your **Life Force** by two points.) As you run, the sound of howling wind grows wilder and louder. You surge through the sea of arms and make it to the top of the stairs, where you stumble into a short, windswept passage. You are out of reach of the hands here, and they melt back into the walls and vanish from sight. You breathe a sigh of relief and take a moment to wipe the sweat from your brow. At the end of the passage is a doorway which leads out into the night. It must be stormy outside, for the door has been blown open and it is swinging wildly on its hinges. Eager to move away from the haunted stairs, you set off towards it. Turn to **246**.

271

All around you, the clouds are suddenly lit by the flaming breath of your enemy. You hear the mighty roar of the Dragon, then its huge tail crashes into the horse like an enormous, spiked whip.

Snowfire's stricken body plummets like a rock from the sky, limp and unresponsive. You cling to his mane as the victorious Dragon swoops away, leaving you to your fate.

But all is not lost.

To your amazement, you see magic glittering in the steed's feathers, then its wings suddenly spread open. Somehow, your magical companion has revived himself with a tiny trace of life.

With its last shred of energy, the horse angles you towards the edge of the lake, where the water meets the foul marshes. You plunge into the waves and are almost knocked unconscious by the impact, but when you climb onto the sodden bank there is no sign of your saviour. You scramble along the water's edge in search of him, clinging to a shred of hope that he might be alive, but it looks unlikely. With tears in your eyes, you turn to see the last segments of the nightmarish castle disappearing beneath the surface of the Merkwater.

Zanack is dead and the land is safe from the threat of war, but there is sadness as well as joy in your heart. You sink to your knees and rest on the bank for some time. When your strength returns, you rise once more and stand quietly under the brooding sky. Your mission is complete, but your journey is not over quite yet. It will be a long walk back to the Wizard's castle.

You can now turn to the last entry in this book, entitled *Epilogue*.

272

The corridor gradually widens and the flickering candles create a spectacle of dancing shadows. You have not been walking long when you hear the sound of heavy footfalls beyond a twist in the passage.

Will you:

Wait to see what appears, turn to **247**.

Or retreat in the opposite direction, turn to **256**.

You find yourself in a large square room. A big open fireplace is set in the back wall, flooding the area with warmth and lively shadows. In front of the fireplace is an enormous oak desk, and sitting behind it is a little old woman, her face almost lost under the shadow of her pointed hat. She is dressed in jet black robes, with a scraggly mop of dark hair. Her right eye is white and missing a pupil, her nose is long and ugly, and her mouth is full of yellow teeth.

She is stroking a black cat with one hand, whilst holding a book in the other, and she seems so captivated by her read that she has failed to notice your arrival.

You take the moment to view your surroundings, and you see that the ceiling is lost under a cloak of webs, scuttling with hundreds of tiny black spiders.

The old woman looks up at last, her cat's purring alerting her to your presence. The Witch glowers at you malevolently. "What is this? A human in my study?" she hisses with some surprise. "I presume that you have escaped from one of Rog's dungeons. Well, I am too busy to deal with you, I have work to do, so get out of my sight before I turn you into a spider."

Will you:

Do as she says and leave, turn to **426**.

Or ask for directions out of the labyrinth, turn to **253**.

They glow with a purple light, which gets brighter at your approach. You break off a small piece, put it in your mouth and start to chew. There is a strange but not unpleasant taste to it, then you are overcome by a sense of well-being.

(Increase your **Life Force** by four points.)

As you lick your fingers clean, you notice that the red mushrooms have started to emit a poisonous, sharp smelling gas which burns your lungs. You decide that you had better leave this area, before their vapours overcome you.

Before you set off, you still have time to quickly taste one of the black mushrooms.

If you do this, turn to **215**.

If you would rather leave this area and be on your way as quickly as possible, turn to **301**.

You spring from the shadows, swinging your sword in a mighty arc towards Zanack's neck. But your endeavour to behead the unsuspecting Demon with one swipe is suddenly dashed. The loyal Orc leaps forward to shield his master, then his head spins from his shoulders as he absorbs the full impact of the blow.

Zanack leaps away from you with a look of surprise, then his eyes gleam with fury. "A good try, worm," he snarls through barred fangs, "but I am not so easily slain."

He takes several steps backwards, studying you with eyes that swirl with hatred. "So… you must be the Wizard's champion, come to slay me! They should have known better than to have sent a sheep to slay a wolf."

His deep and guttural voice is rich with contempt, and you can hear a fearless and unrestrained savagery in his tone.

As you step towards him, he suddenly calls out in a brutish voice: "HUSHNUCK!" Then he waves his hand swiftly through the air.

Instantly, the gloom in the chamber deepens, then the darkness begins to stir and take on a number of tangible forms. Shadows rise up. Growing. Shivering. Transforming into terrible black creatures.

"If you came seeking death, worm, then you have found it!" He snarls, his eyes wide and psychotic. "Do think of me in the void!"

The Shadow Demons advance towards you. They look like the misty silhouettes of deformed, hunched creatures, brandishing swords of flickering black fire.

You swing your blade to hack a path through their ranks, but the ghostly beings are immune to the cut of your sword!

If you possess the **Doom Shield**, turn to **260**.

If not, turn to **313**.

As you head north along the corridor, the temperature gets progressively warmer. Eventually you come to a closed wooden door with a black iron knocker. The doorknob has been carved into the shape of an ugly Troll's head, and the workmanship has given it an unnervingly realistic look. Pinned to the door is a handwritten note. Although it looks like a curious wish list, you have a suspicion that it is actually some kind of riddle. It reads:

Reminder to self. Don't forget:

> *Killer Nettles*
> *Old Centipede*
> *Konrod's Toad*
> *Withering Imp*
> *Cat's Ears*

The corridor's warmth is due to a shimmering heat that is escaping from a crack under the base of the door.

After reading the note, will you:

Rap on the door with the knocker, turn to **292**.

Or quietly turn the knob, to find out if the door is unlocked, turn to **248**.

277

You follow the twisting stair for some time, up into darkness. The worn steps are uneven and you have to watch your footing. At length you come to a closed wooden hatch in the ceiling, so you push it open and climb through into a brightly lit room. Lying not ten feet away is a huge, sleeping beast. It is dog like in appearance, but it is nearly the size of a full grown lion, and it looks as stocky as a bear. Instead of being covered in hair, it gleams with dragon-like scales, which glow like gold under the flickering candlelight. The brutish creature is positioned in front of a closed door, which it is obviously meant to be guarding. You can only imagine that something of great value must rest in the room beyond. As you watch, the huge beast twitches contentedly in its sleep, merrily distracted by the diabolical events of a ghastly dream.

If you want to try your luck at sneaking past the beast, turn to **395**.

If you would rather attack the sleeping monster, whilst you have the advantage of surprise, turn to **225**.

Illustration Opposite

As you hurry onwards, the rain grows more severe and it is soon dislodging huge boulders from the hillsides. Eager to escape the deluge, you clamber up a tall hill to scan the landscape for signs of shelter. A short distance from the path, upon a lonely craggy summit, you see the unexpected silhouette of a dark castle. Through the sheet of rain, it looks like an ancient building, long ago abandoned. Parts of it have fallen into ruin, but other sections have stood up against the test of time.

With the storm still showing signs of worsening, you head over to investigate. Cautiously, you move in through the open door, taking shelter from the violent, buffeting winds. It is indeed deserted within, and although the abandoned interior has a creepy and ominous look, the thick walls offer the perfect refuge from the savage pummeling of the storm.

In one of the deserted rooms, you find evidence that the Bandits you encountered earlier must have also used this spot as a recent place of shelter. They have left some food here, plus three blankets that they were using for bedding. You can make immediate good use of this find!

Wrapping yourself in the blankets, you lay down to get some rest. All through the night the wind howls as the fearsome tempest rages on. Lightning flickers across the bellies of the blackened clouds, creating an eerie light show over the landscape, but you feel safe and warm in here. You wonder who once owned this dark castle, and why it was abandoned long ago. Maybe you will never know. Listening to the raging wind, you drift off to sleep. You rest deeply that night, and at dawn you wake feeling refreshed and well. You eat the Bandit's food for breakfast, (a meal fit for three), and you feel all the better for it. (Increase your **Life Force** by three points.)

Now that morning has come, you find that the storm has passed, though rain still drizzles gently from the grey sky. You did well by finding this place.

Will you now:

Search the ruined castle before leaving, turn to **433**.

Or set off and press on southward, turn to **42**.

279

You lose your grip and plummet downwards. You pray that you do not have far to fall, and after a few moments you drop out of the bottom of the shaft and crash-land into a gloomy, stone walled passage. You have landed on your back, and the wind is knocked out of you. (Reduce your **Life Force** by one point.)

Looking up at the ceiling, you shiver with revulsion as the shaft closes with a sickening, rasping sound.

You are in a much lower part of the fortress now, where the air is far colder, musty and stale. Wall-mounted candles flicker and dance, stirring the restless shadows. You can head either way along the passage. Whilst considering your options, you hear footfalls to the north.

Will you:

Hold your ground, turn to **247**.

Or hurry away in the opposite direction, turn to **256**.

It is getting late by the time you come out of the valley onto the open meadows again. Throughout the wild grassland, you notice several small bushes packed with berries. The food seems to have little nutritional value, but at least you are not left hungry. The sun eventually falls to the horizon and darkness begins to settle across the land. As you march on, you see that the path is heading towards a deep stream spanned by an old stone bridge.

Suddenly, you duck into the concealing grass by the trackside. Up on the bridge, a dark shadow has unexpectedly materialized. It is a tall, crooked figure, dressed all in black. Its eyes gleam evilly in the gathering dusk, and in its hand is a sword of flickering dark fire. The ominous beast is a Demonic Soul Stealer, a sadistic servant of Zanack himself! The wretched creature has probably been sent to guard the bridge, to intercept heroes travelling along this road. With juddering movements, it turns its back to you and casts its eyes over the land to the south.

There are two ways of dealing with this predicament. You can attempt to sneak up on your enemy while its back is turned, or you can remain hidden in the grass in the hope that the creature eventually leaves. Make your decision now, before turning to **371**. You cannot change your decision once you have left this page.

You have barely taken your first step when the pack changes direction, creating an aggressive spearhead formation. You realise that they have spotted you, and a moment later the beast at the head of the group drops like a stone from the sky. There is a great gust of wind as the massive animal lands in the street ahead of you. It scrambles towards you, its ferocious jaws snapping wildly, but you dodge the attack and leap onto its back, beheading its rider with a wild swipe of your sword. The beast shakes you off, and you topple back onto the earth. As you scramble to your feet, the monster roars with anger. Unlike its rider, this ferocious carnivore will not be so easily slain.

TERRASAUR CHAMPION

LIFE FORCE 16 **STRIKING SPEED** 8

Focus	Move	Damage
1	Whipping Tail	2
2-3	Tearing Claws	3
4-5	Crushing Bite	3
6	Wave of Flames	See Below*

(*Special Move: If you are stuck by the Terrasaur's Wave of Flames, you are instantly killed and melted to a pulp.)

If you win, turn to **409**.

282

The corridor continues in a straight line for some time. Eventually you come to a dead end. The roof of the passage appears to have caved in, leaving no way forward. You check the walls left and right in the hope of finding a secret door, but when your search turns up nothing you are left with no other option but to head back to the previous chamber. You know there must be a way out of this maze, so you try one of the other passages.

Will you head:

North, turn to **206**.

Or south, turn to **239**.

283

You hand over all of your coins, and with a hideous smile the robber takes your money. You step forward, but the Bandit still blocks your way. As he counts your money, a scowl comes over his face. "I don't believe that's all you've got," he says. "Give me the rest."

You tell him that you have given him everything, but the man's eyes darken wickedly. "We'll see," he says.

There is a sudden movement to your left and right, as two more Bandits leap from their cover and rush at you with their knives drawn. The trio engage you simultaneously, and their eyes gleam wickedly as they frantically stab at you with their rusty blades. (You may be outnumbered, but you are far more skilful than your savage and unruly opponents.)

Let the fight commence.

BANDITS

LIFE FORCE 15   STRIKING SPEED 8

Focus	Move	Damage
1	Devious Kick	1
2-3	Wild Punch	1
4-5	Slicing Blade	2
6	Knife To The Back	3

If you win, turn to **245**.

284

As you draw your sword, the bodies of the creatures emerge from the walls. Their roughly hewn forms are humanoid but their stone heads have no faces, no eyes, no mouths, no discernible features at all. Despite the fact that they cannot see, they are drawn to you nonetheless. They are all eight feet tall, with four arms. As the first one reaches towards you, you bring your blade crashing down on its head. The creature's body shatters instantly into hundreds of tiny stone fragments. Although your adversaries look like they are made of solid rock, they are actually surprisingly brittle, and a single blow is enough to fell them. Nonetheless, their great numbers could still cause you a problem. There are nineteen of them left, and they are all groping blindly towards you with savagely clawed hands. You grip your weapon, ready to smash a path through their ranks.

MAGICALLY ANIMATED WALL BEASTS

LIFE FORCE 19   STRIKING SPEED 7

Focus	Move	Damage
1	Raking Claws	1
2-3	Stone Knuckle Slam	2
4-5	Punch To The Skull	2
6	Battering Fists	3

If you win, you step over the shattered remains and head to the top of the stairs. A short passage stretches out before you, with a door at the end which leads into the night. It must be stormy outside, for the door has been blown open and is swinging back and forth on its hinges. Eager to move away from the haunted stairs, you set off towards it. Turn to **246**.

285

Sword in hand, you wait by the bend in the passage, then a tall creature speeds around the corner. It is humanoid, with scaly green armour and a lizard-like face. You catch it by surprise and smash it on the head with the pommel of your sword, knocking it unconscious. As the beast crashes to the floor, three more reptilian creatures hurtle into view. These ones are more cunning than the last, and they are not so easily defeated. They dodge your initial attacks, and from their scabbards they draw savage swords that glitter with an emerald sheen.

Your opponents usually live in the swamps, but they are greedier than Dragons when it comes to the lure of gems, and the promise of wealth quickly enticed them into the service of Zanack. Their callous eyes blaze with cruelty as they lunge towards you.

LIZARD MEN

LIFE FORCE 18   STRIKING SPEED 8

Focus	Move	Damage
1	Spitting Acid	1
2-3	Sweeping Claws	2
4-5	Snapping Jaws	2
6	Striking Scimitar	3

If you win, you suddenly hear more footfalls. It seems that more guards are on their way, drawn by the sounds of battle! You cannot avoid this next fight, as your enemies are approaching from both ends of the corridor. You grasp your sword and prepare to defend yourself. Turn to **214**.

286

You follow the new passage for a couple of minutes, keeping your ears and eyes alert for danger.

Do you possess the special ability of **Sixth Sense**?

If so, turn to **250**.

If not, turn to **298**.

Patiently, you wait for the Orc to regain consciousness. You know this may be a turning point in your luck if you can force some information out of him.

The ugly beast eventually wakes to the sight of your cold blade pressing against his neck, then his eyes light up with terror.

Do you have the special ability of **Greater Wisdom**?

If so, turn to **263**.

If not, turn to **251**.

The entrance is secured by an enormous metal bolt. You slide the bolt out of the lock and open the creaky door. You are peering down a steep flight of stairs which descends into a deep cellar. You can only see the first few steps, then they vanish into a void of utter darkness.

You pause… your senses tingling with unease.

On the steps in front of you, you can see the splattered stains of blood. As you stand at the top of the stairs, wondering whether to descend into the blackness, you hear the sudden rustle of movement. Something is coming up out of the gloom to meet you. And it is moving fast. Before you can act, a sea of shadowy arms suddenly reach out of the darkness and try to drag you into the stairwell!

Do you possess a **Magic Ring**?

If so, turn to **358**.

If not, turn to **392**.

289

You follow a narrow, snaking passage for what seems like a long time. It twists and turns in different directions, making it hard for you to keep your bearings. At length you come to an empty, hexagon shaped chamber. There is a single wall-mounted candle in the room, burning with a dim green flame. By the firelight you can see three exits, each leading to more passages. As you enter the room, you notice a metal grate in the floor in the centre of the chamber. Dark gas suddenly pours out between the slats. In a split second, the room is filled with a dense fog of poisonous fumes! You hold your breath, but not before taking in a little of the burning smog. (Reduce your **Life Force** by two points.) If you are still alive, you quickly stumble towards an exit, eager to escape this cursed chamber.

(As soon as you leave the room, the vapours will be sucked back down the grate. However, at the moment, you cannot see anything through the toxic cloud, therefore you must roll one dice to randomly determine which exit you stagger down.)

If you roll a one or a two, turn to **311**.

If you roll a three or a four, turn to **302**

If you roll a five or a six, turn to **217**.

290

You burst through the door and find yourself sprinting down a gloomy passage that would be completely lightless were it not for the glow of the Doom Shield. Back in the circular chamber, enraged yells rise to an incensed clamour, and you know that the guards have discovered the empty plinth. You glance over your shoulder. On the edge of the light, you see several indistinct shapes burst into the corridor after you. There are too many of them to fight, and you know that your only option is to lose them in the castle's twisting maze of corridors.

Your quick exit from the chamber has given you a head start, but you should not underestimate the determination of the castle guards.

You see a T-junction approaching.

Quickly, which way will you run?

Left, turn to **222**.

Or right, turn to **262**.

291

(If you just used a **Skeleton Key**, remove it from your belongings.)

Do you possess the special ability of **Haste**?

If so, turn to **234**.

If not, turn to **252**.

292

You knock twice.

For a few moments you wait in silence, then, to your surprise, the doorknob moves. You shake your head, wondering if you are imagining things… but you are not. The Troll's eyes flicker open and look up at you. They are fiery red and without pupils.

"You may enter," the Troll hisses. Then it closes its eyes and the door opens by itself. Turn to **273**.

The warrior swaggers confidently to the back of the room, where he proclaims that he will take the first throw. Almost without bothering to look, he hurls his knife across the room, and it slams into the wooden shield, just a fraction of an inch away from the red dot.

You notice the other customer glance over with an impressed look, then he goes back to drinking his ale.

Your opponent gives you his other knife. You are wondering now whether it had been a good idea to challenge the man, but after taking aim, you hurl your blade straight into the center of the shield, piercing the very heart of the red dot.

The man in black looks stunned, and his eyes seem to bulge in their sockets. For a moment he is left staring in silence, then suddenly he laughs in disbelief. It is the first time that you have seen him smile, which is odd considering he just lost the game. True to his word, he gives you **one Crimson Coin** plus his **Golden Locket.** (Add them to your Character Sheet.)

"I see that you are an accomplished warrior," he says, nodding with approval. He collects his knives and downs his drink. "Forgive my earlier rudeness, but personal thoughts have clouded my mind of late, and I had no desire to talk. I would play you again, but I do not think I could afford the losses." The man is stronger than he looks, for when he gives you a friendly pat on the back you can almost feel your ribs shake. "Good night, Blade Thrower," he says, "maybe we will have a rematch in the morning, when my head is clear of ale."

The man turns and heads to bed.

You look around and see that the other customer has also retired for the evening.

You decide to approach the barman and enquire about a room for the night. Turn to **156**.

294

You walk around the room. In a recess in the wall at the back of the chamber sits the solitary marble statue of a kneeling Demon. It is surprisingly lifelike. Its head is tilted towards the ceiling and its fanged mouth is wide open. Oddly, upon its blue marble tongue is the symbol of a key.

If you have a **Blue Marble Key** and wish to drop it into the mouth of the statue, turn to **257**.

If you would rather smash through the magical barrier with your sword, turn to **221**.

Otherwise, you may leave the Doom Shield behind and go in search of Zanack. If you do this, you will have to hope that you can defeat the foul Demon without the help of the legendary shield. If this is your choice, turn to **429**.

The tree is gnarled and twisted and offers plenty of handholds. Even for a child it would be an easy climb and you are soon up in the high branches, surveying the land about you. The fog does not reach up this high; it floats beneath you, crawling for miles across the marsh like a silver sea. A gust of wind blows hauntingly through the night, briefly scattering the mist, and under the gleam of the full moon you catch a glimpse of the path again, just a few minutes walk from where you are. Suddenly, you notice something approaching through the mist. Three dark shapes come into sight, with glowing saliva dripping from their terrible fangs. The Werewolves are speeding east across the sodden landscape, and from your high vantage point you watch as they sweep past you, right under the branches of the tree where you are perched. They do not seem to have noticed you, for they hurry on their way and disappear into the shadowy night. When they have gone you climb out of the tree and set off in the direction of the path.

Turn to **380**.

"Dark place," the Orc hisses, "dark, secret place, I guess."

"Where? What secret place?" you demand.

"Rog does not know," he says. "Nobody tells Rog things like that. Poor Rog," he says. "Rog just nice torturer. But Rog does know lots of other things. Ask me another question, something easier, yessss?"

You can sense no deception in his hideous tone, but before you have time to ask him another question, you hear the sound of footfalls not far away. You listen carefully and deduce that ten guards are patrolling a nearby corridor. They are not yet in sight, but it sounds like they are heading your way. You cannot afford to get into a brawl with that many enemies! You strike the Orc's head with the pommel of your sword, knocking him unconscious, then you make your escape down a gloomy side passage. Turn to **231**.

297

"It is a rare thing indeed to find a helping hand in these parts," says the old man. "These lands have grown less friendly of late."

You ask him where he has come from, and he informs you that he has travelled from a fishing village named Stormwater, several days walk away. "I knew it would be a hard journey for one as old as myself," he says, "but dark powers are growing in the south, so I decided to take my leave from there whilst I could. I am travelling to stay with relatives in Grimbree."

As the man has just come from the direction in which you are headed, you take the opportunity to ask him if there are any dangers lurking on the southerly trail.

"Indeed, there are many dangers!" he answers in no uncertain terms. "If you are heading south, you had best be aware that these hills are riddled with Bandits. And if you are going as far south as the marsh of Harrowmoor, you will find those dark regions haunted by all manner of horrors, Werewolves included. Evil is growing in the southern lands, and rumour has it that Zanack has returned to his dark castle on the lake. Maybe that is true, maybe not, but either way, some dark force is at work there; it is twisting the region and its foul influence grows more ominous with the passing days. If you must head south, let me give you some advice about those Bandits, as you are sure to meet them on the road ahead. They are wicked and malevolent, and even if you give them all the coins in your possession, they will still try to kill you, just for the fun of it. Do not trust them for a moment, draw your sword as quick as you can if you meet them, or else they will be the death of you."

You thank the old man for his stark advice, and you assure him that you will keep on your guard. With a nod of his head, he bids you safe journey and takes his leave. As you watch him shuffle off down the path, a gust of wind makes you blink. When you look again, he has vanished as if into thin air! It seems the old man was a Wizard! You continue down the track, but it is not long before you hear movement nearby. Something is lurking behind a boulder by the side of the trail.

If you investigate, turn to **428**.

If you ignore the sound and press on, turn to **81**.

You hear a sudden click, then you see that your foot has touched a tripwire. To your left, a set of black tipped darts suddenly shoot out of little cracks in the walls. You immediately dive into a forward roll, hoping to dodge their strike.

(There are six darts in all. If you possess the special ability of **Haste**, you manage to avoid all of them. If you do not have this skill you must roll one dice. The total rolled shows how many darts have hit you. Deduct one point from your **Life Force** for every dart that has hit its mark.)

If you are still alive, you pull out any darts that have impaled you. When you have tended to the wounds, you bravely get to your feet and continue on your way. After a short while you come to a smoke stained door at the end of the passage. The entrance is slightly ajar, so you peek through the gap.

You are looking into a chemical laboratory. Benches are pushed up against the walls, and they are covered with bubbling vials of liquid. A strange, hunchbacked creature with four arms is mixing potions on the work surface to your left. The beast has its back to you and is unaware of your presence.

If you wish to burst into the room and take the creature by surprise, turn to **266**.

If you wish to quietly head back the way you came, and continue along the previous passage, turn to **223**.

You row onwards for another ten minutes. As you progress, the fog continues to gather in greater density until you can barely see the end of the dinghy. You are unsure if it is your imagination, but you begin to feel as though you are being watched. Out of the corner of your eye, numerous times you swear that the vapour is forming into the likeness of a thin and grinning Demon, but when you turn to look, there is nothing to be seen. A short time later, when you stop for a brief rest, you notice several long tendrils of mist reaching towards your throat. Suddenly, you feel an icy, phantasmal grip closing around your neck, and you realise that your mind has not been playing tricks on you at all! You tumble back into the boat, and as you do so, you pull yourself free from the clasping hands of your ghostly enemy. The guardian of the lake sweeps around the dinghy, its mouth twisted into a chilling smile. Its voice whispers to you like a faint breeze, haunting and full of shivering lusts. "Mortal souls I can devour, and here one drifts in a darkling hour. A soul I'll steal and then devour, a corpse I'll hang from the highest tower."

Ignoring the taunts, you get to your feet and clasp your weapon. Once more the evil spectre comes forward, its cold hands outstretched!

If you possess a **Rune Broadsword**, **Harn's Sword of Ancient Power** or the **Sword of the Fallen**, turn to **83**.

If you have none of these weapons, turn to **60**.

You sit down at a table by the fireplace and warm your hands over the dancing flames. (If you have just visited the bar and paid for a drink, you may increase your **Life Force** by one point due to the refreshing effects of the brew.) From your seat by the hearth, you overhear snippets of conversation from the other customers.

"…Aye, I heard that as well…" mutters the largest man, an ageing burly fellow, with big hands that have been hardened by years of farming.

"…it killed two men just last night," says another. "I've never known the likes of it!"

The third man also says a few things, but his voice is garbled and slurred by a bellyful of drink.

After a short while, the customers begin to leave, until only one young man is left at the table. He seems downcast, and you notice that he has barely touched his drink. You decide to sit with him, and he introduces himself as Mok, a local farmer. He asks if you are a traveller passing through, and you nod. "You picked a bad time to come to Grimbree, friend," he mutters, before pointing out of the window to a cottage across the street. "That's my home. It used to be a nice place to live, but terrible things have been happening here of late. Every night for two weeks now, a strange figure, swathed in black robes, has ridden into the village and terrorized the folk 'ere. People 'ave been found murdered, and others 'ave simply vanished during the night, stolen from their very beds."

The flames briefly surge in the fireplace, crackling and licking at the air. Warm light and somber shadows dance over the young man's face, and you see that his eyes have been darkened by several sleepless nights. He sips at his ale before continuing. "Two weeks ago a group of us tried to walk to the Wizard's castle to ask for aid, but we are farmers and hard workin' folk of the land, not warriors. The rider attacked us in the woods and killed two of my companions, and the rest of us fled back to Grimbree. You can stay at my house tonight if you wish, for it is too dangerous to leave the village, especially in the darkening hours."

Will you:

Take up Mok's kind offer and spend the night at his place, turn to **66**.

Say your farewells to Mok, and leave Grimbree via the southerly road, turn to **72**.

Or set off to kill the beast in the village, turn to **41**.

301

You make your way along the narrow path until you reach the two archways. Both entrances lead to staircases that head steeply upwards. The steps to the right look rickety and wooden, whereas the steps to the left are carved from solid black rock, chiseled from the very foundations of the fortress.

Will you:

Take the stairs to the right, turn to **238**.

Take the stairs to the left, turn to **218**.

302

You follow the twisting passage until you reach an empty oblong chamber. There are four corridors leading from the room, and a black wall-mounted candle burns dimly beside each exit.

Which passage will you take? The one bearing:

North, turn to **239**.

East, turn to **311**.

South, turn to **289**.

Or west, turn to **206**.

303
Illustration Overleaf

You walk through the moonlit lanes, heading south towards the harbour. It is long after bedtime and most of the residents are asleep. As you round a corner you see a lone man on the far side of the street. He appears to be taking a night-time stroll, but when he sees you he glances nervously at your sheathed sword and ducks into the shadows of a narrow alley. A moment later, to your left, you notice a duo of pale faces peering at you from behind a candlelit window. As soon as you look towards them, the curtains are drawn with a nervous haste and the lights are put out. It seems that the townsfolk have grown wary of strangers. Not wishing to attract attention, you turn onto a lonely back street that is deathly quiet and draped in shadows. The lane continues south towards the docks, but you have not gone far when you see several figures in heavy armour ahead of you.

The men are heading in your direction, and when they see you they pick up their pace. Before you have time to think, you find yourself surrounded by five stern looking soldiers. They are the night watch guards, out on patrol. The captain of the group, a hard eyed, unshaven man in a gold helm, steps towards you, his hand resting on the hilt of his sheathed sword.

"I have not seen your face before, stranger," he says sternly, looking as if he has some reason to be suspicious of you. "Newcomers have not been welcome in Shellhaven since Zanack moved back into these lands and reoccupied his fortress on the lake. We must be suspicious of everyone, in case they are spies from the Dark Castle." His eyes study you untrustingly. "Tell me, how did you get into the town, and how did you get past the guards at the gate?"

Will you:

Tell him that the guards let you in, turn to **332**.

Tell him the truth about how you got into the town, turn to **396**.

Tell him to mind his own business, and advise him to get out of your way, turn to **372**.

Or stay quiet and say nothing at all, turn to **387**.

304

Do you possess the special ability of **Sixth Sense**?

If so, turn to **24**.

If not, turn to **288**.

The sign is pointing south, with the inscription: *Stormwater, ten miles*. Considering this new information, you might reach the settlement by sunrise.

As you stare at the sign, the temperature drops and a chill grows in your bones. Suddenly you freeze. Hovering behind you, near the misty trail, is the ghostly apparition of a young woman. Her abrupt appearance startles you, but the spirit is not evil, and you sense no threat from her. She may have been pretty once, but her eyes are deep wells of sadness now, and her pale lips turn down at the corners with a weight of timeless sorrow. Although her ghostly form is transparent and vague, you can see that she is draped in a tattered pale dress. She floats slowly towards you, her mouth moving silently, She is trying to tell you something, but no sound issues forth.

If you possess the special ability of **Greater Wisdom**, turn to **45**.

If you do not possess this special ability, you cannot understand the spirit's message. Sorrowfully, the ghost recedes and vanishes like a dream. Unnerved by the strange vision, you head on your way, turn to **84**.

306

(If you used a **Skeleton Key**, remove it from your belongings.) Inside the chest is a single, small object, which easily fits into the palm of your hand. You carry it up into the light of the previous chamber, so that you can see it better. You have found a shard of black stone which has been carved into the shape of a strange little beast, with deep pits for eyes, and a very angry expression. You do not like the look of it at all, but you feel compelled to keep it. (Add the **Sinister Idol** to your belongings.) You set off to explore the warm corridor, whilst clutching the sculpture in your hand. Turn to **276**.

307

You reach towards your pocket in the pretence of giving him some money. But as the dim-witted Bandit steps confidently forward to collect his reward, the smirk is abruptly wiped from his face when you land a sudden, massive punch to his jaw. Your attack sends him reeling backwards with a look of horror, his teeth rattling in his skull. Before he can regain his senses, you draw your sword and dispatch him with a death-dealing blow. Your troubles, however, are not over yet. There is movement to your left and right, as two more Bandits leap from their hiding places and rush forward with their knives drawn. As they engage you, they suddenly realise how skilled you are with your sword. A look of horror dawns on their wicked faces, but it is too late for them to back out of the fight now.

It is time for you to teach these evil little goons a lesson.

BANDITS

LIFE FORCE 10   STRIKING SPEED 8

Focus	Move	Damage
1	Kick	1
2-3	Devious Punch	1
4-5	Slicing Blade	2
6	Knife To The Back	3

If you win, turn to **245**.

308

You cautiously open the door and peer into a small, gloomy chamber. There is no one in here, so you step inside to investigate. The space is empty except for a large wooden contraption that dominates the centre of the room. It appears to be some kind of torture device, recently built, which has not yet been put to use.

Using your sword, you smash the main part of the mechanism, rendering the whole hideous creation completely useless.

You decide to search the room thoroughly before leaving, and you find a narrow, secret doorway hidden in the corner of the chamber. As you prize open the dusty exit, you see that it leads to a cramped staircase heading up into the darkness.

You explore the stairs, but after a short while you find

the passage blocked by rubble. Lying on the debris is a damaged **Crystal Ball**. As you lift it, you see a strange vision appearing in its depths. You watch yourself saving an escaped prisoner from a terrible beast, then the man whispers something into your ear. Darkness then fills the orb, so you place it back on the floor.

Above you, a small spider watches with red eyes, as if it finds your appearance strange. Certainly, you must look out of place in this grisly, wicked castle.

You have gone as far as you can in this direction. You head back the way you came, through the lab and down the corridor. When you reach the end you turn left to explore the other passage. Turn to **223**

309

Having slain the rider and his demonic steed, you quickly search the saddlebag and find a potion of healing, which you drink immediately. (Increase your **Life Force** by four points.) You also retrieve the **Bolt** which you fired.

Suddenly you hear footfalls squelching on the marsh. You turn and see several grim shadows moving towards you!

Before you can act, a dart from a blow pipe hits you in the side of the neck. You pull it loose, but a strange sensation immediately overcomes you.

You have been poisoned!

You vision blurs, your legs give way, and you tumble onto the ground. The world is spinning alarmingly, then you suddenly lose conciousness. Turn to **220**.

310

As you place the coin into her hand, it crumbles into a fine dust which she casts into the air. The crimson particles swirl around you and she begins to whisper the words to an ancient spell. Even though you are in a dream, the woman's magic feels strangely real. (Increase your **Life Force** by three points.)

A warm shiver suddenly flows in your veins, causing you to wake up. You are alone by the trail and the sky is still dark, but something feels different; a single coin is missing from your pouch and several of your wounds have healed! (Subtract **one Crimson Coin** from your belongings.) You decide to go back to sleep, in the hope of meeting the strange woman again. But this time your dreams are empty, and you drift in a void until the dawn.

Turn to **93.**

311

You follow a gloomy passage for some time. Eventually you come to a vacant, crescent shaped chamber with a high roof. The area is lit by a single wall-mounted candle that flickers with a faint blue light. There are three shadowy corridors leading from this room.

Will you head:

North, turn to **267**.

South, turn to **289**.

West, turn to **302**.

There are three mushrooms to choose from.

Which will you try?

A black one, turn to **215**.

A purple one, turn to **274**.

A red one, turn to **237**.

In less than a second, the Shadow Warriors swirl around you, besieging you on all sides.

You continue to thrust and slash with your sword, but your efforts are in vain. Your weapon has no effect on your assailants, and they raise their flickering swords above their heads, plunging their blades of dark fire into your body. The last thing that you hear is Zanack's mocking laughter. The world is now his for the taking.

The passage twists and bends in a confusing manner, and after a short time it opens into an empty, triangular shaped chamber. On the walls, three candles are burning with intense red flames, painting everything in a blood-red glow. There are three passages exiting the room.

Will you head:

North, turn to **206**.

East, turn to **282**.

South, turn to **239**.

315

You fight with skill and dogged resolve, but when the reinforcements arrive you are quickly surrounded. There are simply too many for you to overcome, and after a fierce and drawn out brawl you are eventually overpowered. You are dragged to the dungeons where you spend the next fortnight being questioned by the captain of the guard. He seems convinced that you are some evil Demon in disguise, sent to sabotage the town's defences. You tell him that he is wrong, but he is in no mood to believe you. Whilst you sit in the dark prison, Zanack's army expands to an invincible size. Soon the dark legion is on the march, with Zanack commanding from the front. The vast horde is now too powerful to be stopped, and everything in its path is crushed and obliterated. You have failed in your quest.

316

You see a young woman's face in the candlelit window. Her expression is pale and fearful, but you only get a fleeting glance of her. She puts out the light and vanishes into shadow. You knock several times, but there is no response. It would seem that she is too fearful to come to the door. There is a cloak of dread hanging over this village, and you are convinced that it has something to do with the hooded rider.

If you wish to leave the village via the southerly road, and ignore the goings on here, turn to **72**.

If you want to investigate the cart, turn to **228**.

Despite your best hopes, the storm grows worse and rages through the night. Lightning forks from the sky, thunder shakes the ground, and more than once your blanket is nearly blown away by a wild wind. You get little sleep and, with no real shelter, the freezing conditions almost chill you to the point of hyperthermia. (Reduce your **Life Force** by four points!) Only when dawn breaks does the storm finally pass. You catch a snake for breakfast, gather some twigs for a small fire, then cook and eat the reptile. (Regain one **Life Force**). When you are finished, you haul up your rucksack and press on up the road.

You have only been walking a few minutes when you reach the summit of a grey hill. Looking south, you see the remnants of an old castle perched on a nearby rise. It looks abandoned and would have offered good shelter from the storm had you found it the night before! If only you had walked on a little further!

If you wish to explore the ruins before moving on, turn to **433**.

If you would rather not dwell on your misfortune, you may press on without further delay, turn to **42**.

Sword drawn, you step cautiously through the open doors. All is still except for the twitching shadows. There are rows of alcoves in the walls to your left and right, running the length of the room, and in each recess is the iron statue of a Demon. The effigies are huge, warped and misshapen, their expressions captured in snarling, psychotic poses. Many of them have three or more arms, and all sport twisting horns that rise from their temples. Warily, you make your way past them into the heart of the room. At the end of the chamber is the main showpiece: a large, grim looking throne made entirely of skulls. Flickering candles sit on the floor around it, and a fierce black sword leans against the arm of the chair.

If you pick up the sword, turn to **404**.

Otherwise, neither Zanack nor the Doom Shield are to be found in here, so you quietly leave and try the other door, turn to **195**.

As you hurry into the righthand tunnel, the hatchway collapses behind you. Monstrous forms surge into the gloom, but you pick up the pace and stay ahead of them. However, luck is not on your side. You have not gone far when you reach a dead end! You spin around and see a host of Demonic bodies moving towards you, their nightmarish eyes casting a glow over the tunnel walls. You are trapped and there is no way to escape! Dark forms leap towards you, snarling and hissing with rage. Many fall beneath the cut of your blade, but you simply cannot win against such heavy numbers.

Your torn body will be flown back to the lair of the Demon King, and hung on display from the castle walls.

In the weeks that come, Zanack's army will swell to an invincible size. Foul creatures will sweep across the land, scarring the earth with the horns of war. The Wizards will perish beneath the wave of violence, and an age of terror will be ushered in,

Victory will belong to the Demon Sorcerer.

320

With the Demon dead, and the villagers free from its reign of terror, you make your way back through the streets towards Mok's house. When you reach his humble dwelling, Mok looks relieved to see you. You tell him of the beast's demise, and he is overwhelmed with gratitude. He rushes off to pour you a celebratory mug of 'Mok's Mead,' his own home-made brew, but you decline the offer, as you are determined to get some sleep. You spend the night in the quaint little house and you rest well. When you wake at sunrise you find that Mok has prepared a delicious soup for breakfast, which you eat with relish.

(Increase your **Life Force** by two points).

When you have finished the meal, Mok tells you that he is going into the village to spread the word about your heroic events, and he intends to arrange a huge celebration in your honor with the whole of Grimbree invited. You tell him that you will not be able to stay for the party. You are on an important quest, and you cannot afford to be rejoicing just yet. With your mind focused on the mission ahead, you say farewell to your friend and set out from the house. Turn to **21**.

321

You raise your crossbow and take aim. There is a twang from your weapon, then the golden bolt flies through the gloom and finds its mark. It slams into the side of the largest Werewolf and the animal lets loose a howl of pain. (Delete **one Bolt** from your belongings).

The three beasts spin towards you. Their eyes are filled with hatred, and glistening saliva drips from their snarling, nightmarish jaws. As you unsheathe your Rune Broadsword, you see that the symbols on the blade are glowing with a blue light. Old magic still lingers in this ancient weapon, and the sight of it makes even the fierce Werewolves think twice about attacking. Your enemies back off with bitter growls, before fleeing into the night. The runes then cease to glow and you return your weapon to its sheath. Turn to **80**.

322

You hurry into the night, but you have not gone far when you hear the Werewolves howling from multiple directions. You pick up the pace, but disaster strikes! Your foot slips in a boggy hole and you tumble down a bank into a vast pool. When you surface, you see the glowing eyes of your pursuers looming at the water's edge. Suddenly, they pause and sniff the air. A whine of terror escapes them, then they rush off into the night. Treading water, you look around, wondering what could have put such a fear into them.

The stagnant bog emits a terrible smell, and the water suddenly begins to bubble and froth alarmingly. You had better get out of this pool as fast as you can! Turn to **370**.

You are unable to escape the clutches of the nightmare; it is as if a spell has been cast upon you.

"Sleep... sleep," whisper the voices. "We have almost found you. Do not wake now."

You do not stir, even when your bedroom window is opened. Your eyes only widen when you feel the breath of a monstrous creature stooping over you, but by this time it is too late. Before you can act, your throat is torn out by your unseen assailant.

Your adventure is over.

324
Illustration Opposite

The closer you get to the island fortress, the larger and more evil it seems to grow. The building's walls are made from black rock, and pointed spires claw savagely towards the clouds that swirl around its summit. Never have you seen such a vast and menacing structure. Bringing the dinghy to a halt, you climb out onto the rocky shore and lash the boat to the bank. There is no path leading up to the fortress, at least none that you can see, so you are forced to clamber up the steep, jagged rocks in order to reach the ominous building.

If you have the special ability of **Scale**, turn to **440**.

If not, you will have to roll one dice to see if luck is on your side.

If you roll a one, a two or a three, turn to **144**.

If you roll a four, a five or a six, turn to **440**.

The evil monstrosity tumbles to the floor, then a final, gargling breath wheezes from its lungs. You step back, repulsed by the foul stench that is rising from the corpse. Covering your nose, you quickly scan around to make sure no other horrors are hiding in the dark corners. When you are convinced that you are alone, you sheathe your sword. Eager to escape the pit, you pause to decide your course of action.

Will you:

Try to climb the wall, in order to get back to the door, turn to **173**.

Or search the pit for any hidden exits, turn to **5**.

"These Demons came out of nowhere!" says Burlybe as you hurry over to help him. "Who knows what drew them to this place, but one thing is for sure, if they break through the door we will not live to see another dawn!"

You suspect that your attackers are servants of Zanack. If the Dark Lord has heard of your quest, he has probably sent this host of minions to seek you out and kill you.

With no time to waste, you grab the other end of the table and help Burlybe lift it. It is heavy indeed, and you know that if you can wedge it against the entrance, the extra support may stop the enemy from breaking down the door. Burlybe is grateful for your aid, but before you have even moved the table an inch, your blood is chilled by an agonised cry. Before the man in black could finish boarding the last gaps in the windows, a demonic arm has smashed through the pane and grabbed him by the throat. Despite his best efforts, he cannot free himself from the strangling grasp.

Will you:

Drop the table and rush over to help him, turn to **351**.

Or finish helping Burlybe to brace the main door, and hope there is still time to save the man afterwards, turn to **376.**

327

The robed figure whips the horse and charges straight at you! He obviously has no intention of stopping. At the last moment you are left with no option but to leap out of the way.

Just in time you dive clear, then the steed thunders recklessly past. You leap angrily to your feet, but the cart has already vanished into the wood. You stand for a minute, letting your anger subside, but your mood is not helped by the dull pain in your arm. You must have landed heavily on it when you dived to avoid the cart. (Reduce your **Life Force** by one point). Bruised but alive, you set off again on your quest.

Roll one dice to find out what random events the day has in store for you.

If you roll a one, a two or a three, turn to **51**.

If you roll a four, a five or a six, turn to **198**.

You look at the broken form of Lord Elendrik, whose shattered remains are strewn at your feet. The fire has vanished from his eyes, but the candles in the room are still burning intensely. (If your **Striking Speed** was reduced by Elendrik's **Glacial Curse**, the effects will not wear off until the end of this adventure.) There is nothing in here of any use, so you decide to leave the haunted crypt and get back to your quest. Turn to **76**.

"HALT!" cries a woman's voice.

Your adversaries pause, then they turn to see a young woman standing in the gloom. She is nearly six feet tall, with long hair and a beautiful face. She is clad in black knee-high boots, tight-fitting dark trousers, a short-sleeved green top and a black cloak with the hood thrown back.

A furious hiss escapes from one of the Demons. "You!" its snarls, "you will pay for your meddling."

Powerless to help, you watch as three of the creatures advance on the lone woman. Suddenly, a ball of crackling blue light leaps from her hand. There is a blinding flash as it hits the chest of her nearest enemy, then the Demon vaporizes with a hideous shriek. The second creature leaps towards her, swinging its blade at her head, but she ducks under the attack and drives her own blade upwards into the groin of her enemy. The beast falls with a cry, clutching at the fatal wound between its legs. The third beast now leaps onto her back. For a second she looks defeated, but she is a skilled fighter. Reaching behind her, she grabs her ambusher's shoulders and throws him to the ground. The cloaked fiend jumps to its feet, ready to spring at her for a second time, but blue light flashes once more and the creature vaporizes with a howl of pain.

Knowing that it is defeated, the final assassin runs away and vanishes into the night.

Barely out of breath, the woman recovers her dagger and cuts you loose from the tree. Without a word she sheathes her weapon, scans the area, then turns to face you.

"There is no time to explain now," she says. "Follow me. It is not safe to linger here. I will explain everything soon." Turn to **30**.

330

You hurry onwards, following the trail through the marshes. Before long the creeping fog becomes so thick that you cannot see your feet marching along beneath you. You soon lose your bearings, as well as the path. You wander around in the marshes for a long while, tripping and stomping through wet bogs. Somewhere in the distance a terrible howl pierces the darkness, and you rest your hand cautiously on the hilt of your sword. After a few hours you come to the foot of an ancient, gnarled tree. It stands alone, growing up out of a foul bog, and its long, bare branches hang sullenly towards the earth.

If you wish to climb the old tree, turn to **295**.

If you would rather continue walking, turn to **380**.

"A traveller heading south, you say? Well, I would not head that way were I you," says Bayek grimly. "Last night I saw strange shadows, sweeping and soaring in the distant skies to the south. I also saw dim lights shimmering, like burning fires. I had thought that a battle was going on, though I could not be sure."

You thank Bayek for his information, and for his concern, but you have no intention of turning back on your quest.

Bayek looks around and a shiver runs through him. "I have had enough of these foul lands," he tells you. "I for one am heading back home to the west. Whichever way you decide to go, I hope that good luck shines on you, my friend."

Before you part, Bayek informs you that he knows a little magic. He casts a spell on you which makes you immune to lycanthropy, therefore, if you are ever bitten by a Werewolf, you no longer have to worry about contracting the beast's terrible curse. He also gives you a **Jagged Pommel Upgrade**. You can detach and reattach it to any sword that you own. (Add it to your inventory, then increase the **Damage** of your **Sword Hilt Smash** by one point.) You thank Bayek and wish him a safe journey, then he disappears into the night. Knowing that you have done a good deed, you trudge back to the path and set off once more. You can only hope that Bayek escapes these lands as fast as he can.

Turn to **375**.

The dark eyed captain steps closer, and you can see by his stern expression that he has spotted your lie.

"The guards at the gate would not have granted you access," he says. "They have been given strict orders to let no strangers in." His eyes narrow suspiciously. "I can only assume that you snuck in here somehow, and you should know that we do not take kindly to trespassers in Shellhaven." He nods to two of his men and strong arms suddenly grab you on either side, holding you still. "You have lied to me once already," he says in a fierce tone, "but I shall give you one last chance to speak the truth. Why have you come to Shellhaven?" he demands. "If I am not convinced by your story this time, I shall have no misgivings in having you hauled to the dungeons for further questioning."

You can ill afford to be dragged to prison! You must act quickly.

Will you:

Try to break free and make a run for it, turn to **355**.

Draw your sword and fight them, turn to **365**.

Or be truthful about your quest, turn to **445**.

333

You leave the path and push through the ferns, halting at the edge of the gently bubbling pool. On the far bank is a large rock, almost as tall as a man, with strange symbols carved into its mossy surface.

If you possess the special ability of **Greater Wisdom**, turn to **33.**

Otherwise, you may pause by the bank and drink from the glittering pond, turn to **8.**

Or return to the trail and press on through the valley, turn to **137**.

334

Your hurl your sword with all your might. Your aim is true and the blade slams into the chest of the startled Games Master, knocking him off his feet. The hooded menace slumps to the floor and exhales a last, rasping breath, before lying motionless. The blade must have pierced his heart, killing him instantly. As you watch, his robes crumple inwards until they are lying flat and empty on the ground, where his body has turned to dust.

With your foe vanquished, you regain your sword and return it to its sheath. Looking around, you find that all of the exits are still sealed by the Games Master's lingering magic. You hunt around for an escape route, but to no avail. It is beginning to look as though you will end up locked in here forever... but then you come across a small lever in the wall. You give it a firm tug and hope for the best. Immediately, a circular hole opens like a toothless mouth in the centre of the floor. You peer down into the deep, vertical shaft. It has a five foot diameter, and its walls are pulsating and fleshy, covered in a network of throbbing veins. With each pulsation, the walls make a hideous rasping sound.

You have no desire to climb down there. You cannot see where it leads to, but there is no other way out of the chamber. Your options are severly limited. Using the thick veins as hand holds, you reluctantly begin your descent. Turn to **224**.

335

Suddenly, the hatchway collapses into ruins. Dark shapes force their way into the gloom, but the Demons are hindered by the narrowness of the passage, and you manage to stay ahead of them. You follow the warrior, keeping close on his heels, and you soon burst through a door and find yourself back under the night sky. You have come out onto the side of a small hill, half a mile from the wrecked inn. As the Demons surge after you, your comrade pulls a black orb from his rucksack and hurls it back into the tunnel. There is a sudden flash of light - a ripping explosion – which destabilizes the whole tunnel. The walls cave inwards, the ceiling crashes downwards, and in less than a second your demonic pursuers are buried and compressed beneath the weight of tons of black earth. The whole horde was down in that tunnel, and the gnashing fangs and the wild roars have been crushed into silence.

You both fall to the ground to catch your breaths, too exhausted to talk.

You have outmaneuvered your enemy, despite the overwhelming odds that were stacked against you, and a sense of well-earned relief washes over you.

Overhead, you see that the storm is passing, and the first rays of morning light push back the morose darkness.

"What *was* that orb?" you ask, when your breath finally returns.

"Elirium: the rarest substance in the land," answers the swordsman. "We had best get moving. Those beasts were looking for something... or some*one*. Hopefully no more of their friends will turn up, but I am not waiting around to find out!"

He pulls himself to his feet and stomps back towards the path, heading northward. You call after him, but his only desire is to leave this area as swiftly as possible. You do not blame him. You set off in the opposite direction, southbound towards Shellhaven.

Turn to **146**

336

You suddenly drop to your knees as an insatiable hunger grips you. Wild thoughts fill your head, and you have a desire to forget the burdens of your quest. You try to ignore the thoughts, but the curse of the Werewolf is strong indeed! Pain tears through you. Sweat drips from your forehead and your temperature rises to dangerous levels. Your hair is growing wilder too, and your muscles are stretching and thickening as your body takes on a new form.

Soon you will be speeding across the dark landscape, howling at the moon. Late in the night, you attack a human settlement on the outskirts of Harrowmoor. The terrified guards fire at you with their bows as you smash your way in through the main gate, then people flee in all directions as you scramble towards them. Before you can kill any of the petrified townsfolk, you are cut down by a sudden hail of arrows.

Under the reign of the curse, you had no control over your actions, but nonetheless, your ending was most unbefitting for a hero.

337

True to his word, Harn makes sure that the rest of your stay is very comfortable. He makes some swift arrangements and sees to it that you are given lodgings at the local inn, free of charge. Your room is spacious, the bed comfortable, and an open fireplace crackles warmly in your room. Knowing that time is of the essence, you decide to stay in the town for just a couple of hours. You get some sleep, (the best you have had for some time), and when you wake you are treated by the innkeeper to a huge and nourishing meal. (Increase your **Life Force** by three points). The innkeeper will accept no payment for his hospitality. When you are full, you thank him and head outside.

It is early dawn, but it feels more like night-time. Dark clouds linger in the sky, casting evil shadows across the town. The sun is hidden, and a foul mist drifts from the lake and crawls about the huddled dwellings.

The Captain of the Guard is waiting outside to greet you, and you are surprised to find that he is holding a brilliant white sword, which he has brought as a gift for you. "I want you to take this," he says. "This weapon has been in my family for ten generations. An old ancestor of mine forged it, long ago. He was one of the greatest weapon makers in the land, and it is said that he even had the blade blessed by a Wizard. I believe it will be of great use to you." He insists that you accept his offering, and as soon as you take it, you are struck by how light, yet how sturdy it is. This weapon has indeed been enchanted, of that much you are certain, and you can feel its magic flowing through you.

(Make a note that you now possess **Harn's Sword of Ancient Power**, then look at the list of **Moves** on your Character Sheet. Increase the **Damage** of your **Stabbing Thrust** and **Sweeping Blade** by one point each.)

You have been blessed with a mighty gift, and you thank Harn for his generosity.

Most of the townsfolk are still in bed, but across the street, you notice that a shop has opened early.

If you wish to investigate the store, turn to **448**.

If you feel that you have spent enough time in Stormwater, and wish to set off for the dark castle, turn to **399**.

You do your best to strike up a conversation, but the solemn eyed man completely ignores you. He rudely stares into his drink, as if you are not even there.

After draining his mug, he gets up and moves to another table in the corner of the room.

You notice that he has sat down near a round, wooden shield, with a red dot at its centre. It is hanging on the wall, with the word *daggers* written next to it. A notice explains that the shield has been put there as a game for the patrons. The rules sound simple enough: two people throw a knife at the shield and whoever gets closest to the red dot wins the game. Looking again at the man in black, you notice two throwing knives hanging from his belt. You decide to challenge him to a game and to your surprise he stands up and agrees. "Very well," he says. "But if you lose, you must give me three crimson coins. And if I lose, I will give you one crimson coin, plus my locket." He shows you the golden locket that is hanging around his neck. It is glimmering with an aura of magic.

If you accept his terms, turn to **293**.

Otherwise, you may decline his offer and talk to the other customer, turn to **131**.

Or approach the barman and enquire about a room for the night, turn to **156**.

339

You tell the guards that you are not in alliance with Zanack, and you try to convince them that you are not here to cause trouble. When you are done talking, you await their response. A silence follows which seems to last forever. Then you hear it: a rushing sound accompanied by a high-pitched whine. You duck instinctively as an arrow whizzes past your head and thuds into the earth behind you. The guards are no longer firing warning shots; that arrow was meant to kill you! It appears that, despite your best efforts, they did not believe your story.

You quickly retreat into the late night shadows, disappearing from the sight of the archers. You are not going to get into the town via the main gate, that much is clear, so you decide to look for a safer way in.

Turn to **193**.

340

As the hound falls dead, you look up to see the young man driving his own blade into another of the Werewolves. There is now only one beast left, and when it sees that it is outnumbered it backs off with a vicious snarl. You raise your blade, but the creature does not attack. It bars its teeth with fury, then escapes into the mist. If it has any sense, you do not expect to see the foul creature again this night.

Sheathing your sword, you head over to the young swordsman.

At first, all you can get from him is endless gratitude, but after more thanks than your ego can handle, the stranger finally introduces himself as Bayek.

"There are not enough words to express my gratefulness," he says. "If you had not appeared so unexpectedly to help me… well, I would have surely been slain!" You learn that Bayek is not local to these parts. He had set out from his homeland to the west, in search of adventure, after hearing about some lost ruins that had apparently sunk into these marshes long ago. "The tale says that he who finds the fabled ruins will also find its ancient treasure," he tells you. "Maybe it is a fool's tale, but I am a poor man, and my family deserve better than the life I can afford for them. I had hoped to find my fortune here, but alas, since I arrived in this region two days ago I have found nothing but evil upon the marsh. These lands are not safe for good-hearted folk. I fear a dark power is rising in the south. I cannot explain quite why, but for a cold feeling in my bones. Tell me stranger, what brings you out along this grim road after dark?"

Will you:

Tell him about your quest, turn to **361**.

Or will you keep the nature of your mission a secret, and simply inform him that you are a traveller heading south, turn to **331**.

The ring must have belonged to the vanquished Demon, yet there are Elf runes on its surface. You suspect that the ring was stolen from its rightful owner. Suddenly, to your surprise, it slips onto your finger as if with a will of its own. Before you can act, it changes size so that it fits you perfectly.

You are in luck, for this is indeed an Elf Ring, and a magical one at that. It would have been useless in the hands of the Demon, for the Elves crafted such items so that only those with a good heart would be blessed with its power. Now that it has found itself in the hands of a worthy owner, the ring begins to sparkle with magic. You get the feeling that you have found a very important item, but you are not yet sure how to use it... Maybe its hidden powers will be revealed at a later date. Make a note that you possess a **Magic Ring**, then turn to **320**.

342

Suddenly, a flash of light erupts from the ring. You are unharmed by the radiance, but your enemy reels back with a look of pain, its skin and eyes burning and hissing in the white glow. Before it can gather its wits and defend itself, you bring your sword slicing downwards. Your blade buries deep, severing an artery in its thick neck, and the creature stumbles backwards with a deathly howl. Return to **394** and fight the Demon, but reduce its **Life Force** by five points.

343

You raise your sword and unleash a fierce strike. Your blade slices into the liquid, causing its surface to ripple briefly, then it becomes still. You strike it again, and a third time, but the strange obstruction shows no sign of being damaged.

Seeing that your attempts are in vain, will you:

Try to step through the liquid wall, turn to **130**.

Or head back the way you came, turn to **116**.

344

As soon as you put it onto your wrist, you feel a strange tingling sensation in your arm. You have picked up a magical item, of that much you are sure, but it is not immediately evident what it does. Cryptically, you notice the number 194 incorporated into its design. You examine it for a short while, hoping to unlock its secrets, but to no avail. Despite your lack of success, you have a feeling that it may come in useful at a later time, so you leave it on.

(Make a note that you are wearing a **Spiderweb Bracelet** with the number **194** on it.)

You can now hear a strange scraping noise, coming from outside.

If you wish to investigate by heading towards the window, turn to **383**.

If you would rather return to the stairwell and head downwards, turn to **118**.

You hurry through the darkness, watching for signs of another ambush. The mist has thinned a little now, and you are relieved when you find your way back to the path. However, you are now starting to sweat and your temperature is soaring. The glow of the full moon beats down on you and a strange sensation starts to make its way through your body. You slowly realise with a dawning horror that you have fallen foul of lycanthropy (the Werewolf's curse!) You look down at the wounds from your last fight, and to your dismay you see that they are glowing. A moment later you are gripped by a desire to cast off your belongings and run into the night! You call out in dismay, but your voice no longer sounds human. Already the curse is taking effect and your cry echoes across the land like the howl of a wild beast!

You are becoming a Werewolf, and if you do not act fast, you may soon be doomed to roam the moonlit marshes as a savage monstrosity!

Gathering your willpower, you desperately try to resist the might of the curse.

If you possess a **Magic Ring**, turn to **368**.

If you do not possess this item, turn to **336**.

There is a long pause after you have spoken. Most of the guards do not believe you. They look to their leader, awaiting his order to attack.

The dark eyed captain stares at you closely, then at length he turns to his men and tells them to stand down. Loyal to his command, they do as he says.

The captain takes off his helm. "I know an honest tale when I hear one," he says. "I apologise for thinking you a servant of evil, but we must be suspicious of everyone these days." He introduces himself as Harn, Head of the Town's Guard. You soon learn why he is so distrustful of outsiders. "A stranger, claiming to be a traveller, came to the town a few days ago," he tells you. "The man turned out to be a Grakhul, an evil beast which could change its shape at will. It disguised itself as a lone adventurer to get through the gates, then it transformed into its true, hideous form. The beast ran amok, slaying the Town Elder and setting fire to the storehouses. Several people died trying to put out the blaze. It was a servant of Zanack no doubt. Thankfully we managed to slay it before it set the whole place ablaze, but we have been wary of newcomers ever since." His face grows grim. "Zanack is a menace," he says. "As soon as he returned to the castle on the lake, a cloak of evil began spreading across this land. Dark creatures now haunt the marshes at night, putting the fear of death into the townsfolk. If something is not done soon, I fear that most of the residents will up and leave. If you are on a quest to destroy the root of this evil, then I salute you.

You may take a boat from the dock as soon as you wish and use it to row out to Zanack's castle. Though I should warn you, a great beast of fire guards the only entrance to the building and getting past it will be no easy trick! You will need your wits about you, so I advise that you get some rest before setting off. I will see to it personally that you are treated well during your stay."

If you take up Harn's offer and rest in the town before moving on, turn to **337**.

If you would rather head to the docks without delay, then row to the Demon's fortress, turn to **399**.

347

There is no way to avoid the spell. It slams into you and your body is charred to a cinder by the crackling lightning. The last thing you hear is the sound of your enemy's triumphant laughter. Your quest is over.

348

Your dream changes. Your surroundings are swept away, and you find yourself floating in deep space. In the darkness around you, you can see distant stars and wondering planets. You drift aimlessly through the cosmos, or are you being drawn towards an unknown goal, pulled by a mysterious force? You descend towards a lonely planet, sinking through purple clouds until you are sitting on a mountaintop bathed in the light of a dying sun. You are not alone. A tall woman, beautiful beyond reckoning, stands before you. She is swathed in flowing garments and surrounded by the aura of a goddess.

"Darkness haunts your trail," she whispers, in a voice more beautiful than the melody of a thousand songs.

"Are you a dream?" you ask, but she gives no answer.

Her eyes shimmer with an ancient, all-knowing look. "Danger awaits you," she says. "A great beast, cast from gold, protects that which you seek. You will not easily defeat it in battle. Be wary of your confidence, for not all things tremble at the sight of sharpened steel. Seek the path of least resistance, and if you have been clever in your choices, you may well be rewarded." She moves closer and holds out her hand, urging you to give her a crimson coin.

If you do as she asks, turn to **310**.

If you refuse, her image fades away, and you glide into a dreamless sleep, turn to **93**.

349

Rubbing at your weary eyes, you carry on down the trail. However, you have not gone far when you hear a strange and bestial cry in the distance. It is a dreadful, blood-curdling sound, which stops you in your tracks and sets your heart hammering. A moment later, you hear the cry again, rising hauntingly over the marshes. You stare into the thickening night, but it is too dark to see what lurks ahead on the winding trail.

If you wish to proceed along the path, turn to **367**.

If you would rather head back to the inn, turn to **172**.

Illustration Opposite

As you run back down the corridor, the screams halt. The cries are replaced by an ominous silence, and a moment later you come upon the body of the young man. Despite your efforts, it appears that you have arrived too late to save him.

Leaning over the corpse is a strange creature.

Now you know why you did not see it earlier. The beast is invisible! But you can now see its gator-like jaws, as they are painted with the blood of its victim. The creature looks up from its kill, then it pounces towards you with a gutteral roar!

INVISIBLE BEAST

LIFE FORCE 9   STRIKING SPEED 8

Focus	Move	Damage
1	Speeding Ram	1
2-3	Sudden Impact	1
4-5	Invisible Claws	2
6	Tearing Fangs	3

If you win, turn to **203**.

351

Sword in hand, you rush across the room. Your blade sweeps downwards in a mighty arc, then green blood splashes across the floor as you hack through the Demon's arm. The beast lets out a roar of pain that shakes the night, then it withdraws its bloody stump back through the gap.

Saved from the clutches of the Demon, the man recovers his breath and offers his thanks. He hastily boards the last of the windows. Turn to **385**.

352

You step to the side of the road so that the cart can pass safely by, but the driver veers sharply towards you. He seems intent on running you down, but you are too swift-footed. You spring into the nearby field and narrowly avoid being trampled under the stampeding hooves. You draw your sword in annoyance, but the speeding cart is gone within a split second, having vanished along the trail into the wood. You take a moment to calm your anger and sheathe your blade. With the crazed driver gone, you continue your journey.

Roll one dice to find out what random events the day has in store for you.

If you roll a one, a two or a three, turn to **51**.

If you roll a four, a five or a six, turn to **198**.

You are almost at the door when the beast draws in a long, slumbering breath. You have been travelling in the same clothes for several days, and you are ingrained with the rich aromas of wild and strange places. The monster's nostrils twitch inquisitively as it picks up your scent, then its eyes flash open. Before you have time to think, the beast is up on its feet, a terrible snarl etched across its face. With alarming speed, the monstrous hound springs towards you! You are forced to duck and dodge, then you stumble backwards as its mighty fangs try to tear you apart!

GOLDEN GUARDIAN

LIFE FORCE 15   STRIKING SPEED 10

Focus	Move	Damage
1	Powerful Ram	3
2-3	Ripping Claws	3
4-5	Rending Fangs	3
6	Crushing Bite	4

If you defeat this powerful opponent, turn to **211**.

You manage to break the gaze of your enemy. The spell shatters and you immediately regain control of your body. Your thoughts sharpen in an instant and you lunge forward with a heavy sword strike. You intend to behead him before he can transfix you again, but he vanishes, leaving your blade slicing through thin air. Now a cold laugh echoes around the chamber. You spin around and see your nemesis standing twenty feet to your left, draped in shadows. The Games Master whispers another spell and every exit slams shut, sealing you both in the hall.

"You will never leave this castle alive," he hisses evilly. "Zanack will rise to power. The age of the Demons will come. And we will build the foundations of our empire upon the graves of our enemies." The robed figure starts chanting and, as he does so, he slowly raises his hand, pointing his finger in your direction. He is absorbing energy from the darkness around him, in order to unleash a devastating spell to rip the life from your body.

You must stop him before he completes his chant!

Will you:

Run across the chamber to hack him down, turn to **363**.

Throw your sword at him, in the hope of impaling him before he can cast his spell, turn to **334**.

Or, if you have a **Crossbow** and any **Bolts**, you may fire on him from where you stand, turn to **422**.

The guards leap at you, trying to drag you down as you attempt to escape. Despite their efforts, you are too strong to be restrained. You break free and dash along the lane, heading south.

They immediately give chase, but their heavy armour slows them down and you lose them amongst the dark and winding back streets. In a lightless, abandoned alley, you pause to catch your breath. Suddenly, you hear the muttering of quiet voices. You grip your sword, wondering if the guards have caught up with you, but it is only a couple of locals, talking in a house nearby. Their voices float out of an upstairs window and echo into the dark alley. They are unaware of your presence and you cannot help but overhear the conversation.

You soon learn that a stranger, claiming to be a traveller, visited the town a few days ago. The man was welcomed by the locals, but he was no human. He was a Grakhul, a hideous creature that could change its shape at will. He transformed into a giant beast that ran amok in the town, and the guards only slew it after a fierce battle. You imagine that the beast was a servant of Zanack, and it is now no wonder why the townsfolk are so wary of strangers.

You decide that you have overstayed your welcome in Shellhaven, short as your visit may have been. It would be wise to head to the docks and take a boat out of town, before the night watchmen catch up with you.

Turn to **410**.

You hurry down the twisting street, your shadow dancing through the yellow glow of candlelit windows. You soon come to the eastern edge of the village, where strange footprints mark the earth, leading into the dark, surrounding fields. You quickly follow them, and after a short while you come to an abandoned watchtower, a few miles from the edge of Grimbree. As you approach the building, you sense dark magic in the air. You suspect that this is your enemy's hideout. Unbeknownst to you, as you step up to the entrance, a shadowy figure appears at the summit of the tower and drops a huge slab of masonry from the rooftop.

If you have the special ability of **Sixth Sense**, you are alerted to the danger and leap to safety just in time.

If you do *not* have **Sixth Sense**, you must roll one dice. If you roll a five or a six, you have been lucky: your enemy's aim is poor, and the slab misses you by a few inches. If you roll any other number, the block crashes into you and sends you sprawling to the ground: reduce your **Life Force** by three points.

If you survive the attack, you look up and see your cackling enemy disappearing back into the tower. With a vengeful expression, you rush in through the entrance, sword drawn and ready for battle. Turn to **420**.

357

You pause, inanimate as stone. Even though it is one of the most hideous Spiders that you have ever laid eyes upon, you bravely resist the urge to shudder. There are many Spiders that can kill a person with their fatal toxins, so you do not wish to provoke it. Slowly, almost lethargically, it climbs down your arm and drops onto the step at your feet. You watch as it casually dissappears through a crack in the wall. You breathe a sigh of relief, knowing that you did the right thing. You thoroughly scan the dense cobwebs, but you can see no other scuttling Spiders, at least not for the moment.

Suddenly, the candles flicker wildly and almost go out. A cold breeze is now blowing down the stairwell with a haunting whistle. Its icy touch makes you shiver.

If you continue upwards, turn to **374**.

If you would rather turn back and head for the bottom of the stairs, turn to **118**.

358

The ring suddenly emits a dazzling flash of light, blinding your assailants. In that brief second, the shadows are blown away and you glimpse a sea of evil creatures on the staircase before you; countless Zombie-like beasts, with wide, pupil-less eyes and mouths that are lined with bloodied, needle-like teeth. The mindless horrors reel back from the light and release their grip. You slam the door shut, throwing the lock into place. As soon as it is bolted, the gruesome monstrosities begin hammering on the door, trying to break it down.

Their hunger for human flesh is insatiable and there are far too many of them for you to fight, so you cannot go that way. Fortunately the door holds. With no other option, you turn around and head for the stairs.

Turn to **277**.

359

With a sputtering breath, the huge beast sags to the floor. Behind you, the warrior recovers consciousness and rejoins the battle.

You both fight valiantly, and for several minutes your enemies are held back by the thrusts of your swords. Then, to your dismay, the Demons intensify their assault.

Despite your courage and mighty valor, you cannot stop the surge. You are forced back and the Demons pour into the room. You grip the hilt of your blade, standing back-to-back with your comrade.

Besieged, you watch in horror as the demonic mass rises up like a wave of darkness. Death seems suddenly assured, but luck has not abandoned you yet. "We need to get out of here!" says the warrior. "I thought we could hold the inn, but we will have to take our chances on open ground!" Before you have time to process his words, your comrade grabs you by the scuff of the neck and drags you backward. He pulls open a hatchway in the floor behind the bar and hauls you down into the shadows, slamming it shut behind you. He locks it with a bolt, and a moment later you hear a wild scrambling on the far side as your enemies try to claw their way through. You have entered a low ceilinged, narrow escape tunnel, dug by the owner in case the inn was ever ambushed. "Quickly, follow me!" says the warrior. "That hatchway will not last for long!"

You are not entirely sure how he knew of this place, but for the moment you do not care. You race forward and pause at a split in the tunnel. The warrior hesitates, trying to remember which way to go. "Have to guess," he curses, "no time to think."

If you have **Sixth Sense**, turn to **64**.

If not, the warrior takes a guess and turns left.

If you follow him, turn to **335**.

If you turn right, turn to **319**.

360

You decide it is time to teach these foul things a lesson, so you stand firm and wait for your enemies to appear. It is not long before you see the eyes of your hunters, gleaming in the dark. Two terrible beasts come slowly prowling out of the night. Their fur is jet black and their snarling mouths hang open, revealing rows of savage fangs. You grip your heavy sword, steadying your nerves as you take in their monstrous appearance.

Suddenly you hear a snarl from behind, and you look over your shoulder to see a third Werewolf creeping up on you. You spin towards it, but the surprise attack has caught you off guard. The big animal pounces, biting and clawing at your flesh. (Reduce your **Life Force** by two points.) If you survive, you manage to throw the beast off of you. Your attacker is the largest of the three, and its snarling fangs are now red with your blood.

It leaps forward to attack you again.
You must fight!

WEREWOLF

LIFE FORCE 6   STRIKING SPEED 9

Focus	Move	Damage
1	**Speeding Ram**	3
2-3	**Slashing Claws**	3
4-5	**Life Draining Howl**	3
6	**Bite Of The Lycan**	4

If you win, the remaining beasts advance, determined to finish you off.

If you possess a **Rune Broadsword**, turn to **423**.

If not, turn to **390**.

361

You tell him that the Demon Sorcerer has returned to his castle in the south, and that you intend to travel into the heart of his dark fortress, to put an end to the evil that is spreading across the land.

Bayek looks as surprised as he is impressed. "One person, against the dark wrath of a Demon Lord? You are brave indeed, adventurer!" he exclaims. "If my heart were braver then I would come with you, but I am not blessed with your courage." He tells you that if you are heading south you had best be on your guard. "Last night I saw strange shadows, sweeping and soaring in the distant skies. Then dim lights like far away fires. I think a battle was raging near the village of Stormwater. Do not go there. Head south for a mile or so, then take the branching trail that leads west. It will be safer."

You thank Bayek for his information, and for his concern. You advise him to head home immediately, and escape the marsh while he still can.

He nods and takes your advice. Before you part, Bayek informs you that he knows a little magic. He casts a spell on you which makes you immune to lycanthropy: if you are ever bitten by a Werewolf, you no longer have to worry about contracting the beast's terrible curse. In addition to this, Bayek gives you a potion of healing. "If you are heading into the Demon's lair, you will need to be in good health," he says.

You drink the potion immediately, and its magical properties quickly take effect. (Increase your **Life Force** by three points.) "I hope that helps," he says.

You thank him for his aid and wish him a safe journey, then you watch as he heads to the west and vanishes into the dark. Knowing that you have done a good deed by saving the man's life, you trudge back to the path and set off again on your quest. You hope that Bayek finds a safe road home. Turn to **375**.

362

The harbour disappears and you soon become lost on the great lake. The green fog is all around you, and a deathly silence descends.

With powerful strokes, you draw your oars through the dark water. The lake is much larger than you had imagined, and after a few hours your arms begin to ache from the effort of rowing. You eventually halt and stretch your weary muscles. As you look around, you notice a small white shape, no bigger than a clenched fist, hovering in the miasma a short distance ahead of you. It glows with a faint light, but you cannot make out what it is through the fog. The little shape darts through the air, first to the left, then to the right, as if it is seeking something. Whatever it is, it has not seen you, as you are shrouded in a particularly dense pocket of mist.

If you want to row forward to investigate the mysterious shape, turn to **94**.

If you would rather remain hidden, turn to **424**.

363

Do you possess the special ability of **Haste**?

If so, turn to **397**.

If not, turn to **377**.

364

The door has been sealed by a powerful spell. There is no lock to pick, and no amount of effort can get it open. It is too heavy to break down.

If you are wearing a **Spiderweb Bracelet**, you will know the number that is incorporated into its design. Multiply that number by two, then turn to the page that is the same as the answer.

If you do not have a **Spiderweb Bracelet**, you will have to try the door marked with the sword, turn to **3**.

365

You are in for a tough fight. The guards work as a tight knit unit, and they respond to your aggression with equal ferocity. They are skilled swordsmen and their shields and armour make them hardy adversaries.

(If you are still alive after the first three rounds of combat, turn to **381**.)

GUARDS

LIFE FORCE 20	STRIKING SPEED 10

Focus	Move	Damage
1	Pommel Slam	1
2-3	Shield-Wall Battering	2
4-5	Swishing Blade	3
6	Unified Sword Strike	4

366

You kneel by the bank and look into the deep water. It is crystal clear and you can see right to the bottom. No foul denizens lurk here, so you take a moment to quench your thirst. As you drink, you hear a faint whispering coming from the lake itself. These are the spirit-voices of all the humans who have been murdered in the lake over the years. You can hear a desire for vengeance in their dreamlike tone. They are urging you to lower your most fearsome sword into the deep water, and you feel compelled to obey. When you take it out, the blade is shimmering with blue lights, as if it has been coated in a sheen of magic. Your weapon has been imbued with a vengeful power, and it has become even more deadly. (Turn to your Character Sheet and look at the list of moves which you use in battle. Increase the **Damage** of each **Move** by one point.) The faint whispers have moved to the sword itself, and the lake has become deathly silent and as still as glass. You decide what to do next.

Will you now:

Set off around the bank towards the doors, turn to **301**.

Or investigate the giant mushrooms, turn to **312**.

367

You edge along the dark trail. The strange wail grows louder and more eerie, and the glow of the moon adds to the spine-chilling atmosphere. You have not gone far when you hear several more of the strange calls. You listen to the baying, and you count at least ten demented voices, somewhere on the dark trail ahead. The creatures sound large, hungry and dangerous. They are unaware of your presence for the moment, but if you are discovered, you will be heavily outnumbered. You cannot leave the path to navigate around them, as you cannot risk becoming stuck in the mud traps.

Will you:

Head back to the inn and resume your trek in the morning, turn to **172**.

Or continue forward, and take your chances with whatever awaits you, turn to **398**.

An insatiable hunger grips you. Burning pain makes your muscles cramp and your temperature rises to near fatal levels.

You are on the verge of blacking out when the ring on your finger starts to glow with a faint light. You feel its magical power washing through you, and a moment later your temperature begins to fall. The ring continues to grow brighter until you are forced to close your eyes. Then a strange sensation overcomes you, and you lose consciousness.

When you wake, the light has ceased. All is dark, save for the glow of the moon. The power of the ring has saved you, having dispelled the curse from your body.

You sit up slowly. You have been left disorientated and shaken, and it is a while before you can get to your feet again. After everything that has happened, you have no desire to come face-to-face with another Werewolf.

Turn to **375**.

369

The stern faced man has broken up one of the tables and is nailing slats of wood to seal the windows. He has almost finished boarding one window when a demonic arm reaches through a gap and grabs him by the throat. The Demon's grip is vice-like, and you can see the man's face suddenly changing colour, as the life is choked out of him.

Sword in hand, you leap bravely forward. There is a flash of steel as you swing your blade, then green blood sprays across the room as you hack through the monstrous arm. The beast lets out a roar of pain and withdraws its bloody stump back through the gap.

Saved from the clutches of the Demon, the man bombards you with thanks. You help him board the gap and seal the remaining windows. Turn to **385**.

370

As you are scrambling up the bank, a giant hand suddenly grabs your ankle and pulls you back, dragging you deep under the water. You draw your sword and your sharp blade slashes down, biting into thick leathery flesh. Your assailant instantly lets go, then you burst to the surface, coughing and spluttering. You crawl onto the bank, but as you look back, you see a huge black creature rising up from the foaming water. It is at least ten feet tall, humanoid, but with grotesque features. Its nose is upturned like a pig, its lidless eyes are bulbous and black, and its mouth is filled with jagged fangs. It would seem that there are worse things than

Werewolves in the dark places of the mire! With a gurgling, hideous roar, it storms towards you through the water, its hand leaking green blood where you have just hacked off its thumb!

(If you possess a **Crossbow**, you have time to fire one **Bolt** before the beast is upon you. If you wish to do this, reduce your enemy's **Life Force** by two points, erase the **Bolt** from your belongings, then finish the battle with your sword!)

GIANT MARSH BEAST

LIFE FORCE 13   STRIKING SPEED 8

Focus	Move	Damage
1	Swiping Claws	2
2-3	Powerful Back Hand	3
4-5	Fists Of Fury	3
6	Punching Frenzy	4

If you manage to slay this savage opponent, the monstrous beast crashes back into the water and vanishes beneath the inky surface. You are soaked, shivering and exhausted after the clash. You set off again and before long you find your way back to the path.

Eager to escape the foul marsh, you swiftly head down the track. Turn to **375**.

If you chose to sneak up on your enemy, you chose wisely: just as you reach the bridge, the creature turns and spots you. You leap forward and strike before the beast can raise its sword. Roll one dice to see what **Move** you perform and reduce your opponent's **Life Force** accordingly, then continue the combat as per the normal rules.

If you chose to remain hidden, your rival does not leave the bridge and it eventually senses your presence. You have lost the chance to catch the fiend by surprise, and you will now have to fight it anyway. It sweeps into the field to attack you.

SERVANT OF THE DARK LORD

LIFE FORCE 9   STRIKING SPEED 8

Focus	Move	Damage
1	Demonic Curse	2
2-3	Spell Of Agony	2
4-5	Soul Draining Stare	3
6	Blade Of ShadowFire	4

If you win, the shadowy Demon throws up its arms in despair, then it crumbles into dust. Its flaming sword spins away and splashes into the river, sending up a cloud of steam as it vanishes beneath the water. Wasting no time, you hurry across to the far side of the bridge.

Turn to **155**.

The captain is momentarily stunned by your curt response. Then his expression becomes fierce. "The watchmen at the gate have been given strict orders to let no strangers into the town," he says, "which means that *you* must have snuck in here, and we do not take kindly to trespassers in Shellhaven."

He nods to his men, and their strong arms suddenly grab you from either side, holding you still. "Tell me your business here, and be swift about it. Why have you come to Shellhaven?" he demands. "If I am not convinced by your story, then I shall have no misgivings in sending you to the dungeons."

You might have been able to talk your way out of trouble earlier, but not now. You have insulted the captain and it is pointless trying to converse with him. He is in no mood to believe anything that you have to say. You will have to resort to drastic actions to get out of this mess. But what will you do?

Draw your sword and attack the guards, turn to **365**.

Or try to break free and make a run for it, turn to **355**.

Illustration Opposite

The Doom Shield completely absorbs the damage of the fire spell, saving you from incineration.

Zanack looks stunned, and you can see the disbelief etched into his face. For a moment he stands motionless... then his frustration turns to anger. A fiery light appears around him, as though he is literally smoldering with rage. Retractable claws slash from his fingers, and with a furious roar he rushes across the chamber, intent on using his savage power to beat you into submission. You must fight for your life!

ZANACK

LIFE FORCE 20   STRIKING SPEED 9

Focus	Move	Damage
1	Slashing Claws	3
2	Jaw Breaking Uppercut	4
3	Rib Shattering Punch	4
4	Bone Crushing Grapple	4
5	Agonising Curse	4
6	Wild Fury	See below*

(*Special Move: If Zanack unleashes his Wild Fury, you are assaulted by a sudden flurry of brutal punches. In desperation, you attempt to dodge and block the attacks. Roll one dice and add one to the total: this is the amount of damage that he manages to inflict on you.) If you win, turn to 400.

You finally approach the summit and see an arched door, half open and creaking in the breeze. After hearing the scream earlier, you decide to draw your sword before peering through the entrance. You are looking into a medium sized chamber with no exits. The wind is coming through a large open window, and thick clouds are swirling around outside.

The room is empty save for the bodies of two, ugly Orcs, who are sprawled on the floor. They have died very recently from puncture wounds to their necks, but there is no sign of their killer. You cautiously search the bodies and find **three Crimson Coins,** which you may add to your belongings if you wish. You also discover a Spiderweb Bracelet.

If you wish to put the bracelet on, turn to **344**.

If you leave it where it is, turn to **383**.

You make your way southward through the marshes. The fog continues to linger, and every now and then you hear the distant, shattering howl of more Werewolves.

You keep your eyes sharp and your sword drawn as you walk along. Late in the night, you come to a split in the path.

Will you:

Continue south, turn to **430.**

Or take the boggy, narrow trail that branches into the west, turn to **197**.

376

The door is shaking so violently, it could break from its hinges at any moment. Just in time you wedge the table against it, jamming the door shut. With the entrance now barricaded, you spin your attention back towards the man in black. But you are too late to save him. The poor fellow has had the life throttled out of him, and a second later his body is dragged through the gap, vanishing forever into the black night.

To your further dismay, you watch as a horde of Demons smash their way through one of the un-boarded windows and start to pour into the room.

"We cannot let them get a footing inside the building," cries Burlybe, "they will surround us and we will be doomed!"

Heeding Burlybe's warning, you spring into action. Turn to **27**.

377

You rush towards the Games Master, but he completes his chant before you can reach him. Blinding lightning leaps from his fingertips and sears towards you!

Are you wearing **Gorath's Savage Helm**?

If you are, turn to **382**.

If you are not, turn to **347**.

378

You wander around the streets for quite some time, but there is no sign of the sinister menace. You are beginning to think that you have been led on a wild goose chase, but then you catch sight of a tall, dark shadow sweeping through the gloomy street ahead of you. You only get a brief glimpse of it, as it quickly disappears down a side turning. Sensing an aura of evil from that sinister figure, you head after it. Hurrying into the side turning, you come to a T-junction. The figure is nowhere in sight. Not knowing which way it has gone, you listen in the hope of hearing footfalls. But the night is oppressively quiet.

Having to rely on a hunch, will you:

Take the turning on your right, turn to **356**.

Or the turning on your left, turn to **13**.

379

As you draw closer, you see a defensive wall around the outskirts of the settlement, which has been erected quite recently. Living so close to Zanack's fortress has obviously made the locals fearful for their lives.

The trail winds up to a large wooden gate which is the only entrance to the town. It is barred shut and stands twenty feet in height, lit on both sides by flaming beacons. In the thickening gloom you can make out the silhouettes of two bowmen positioned on the rampart above the gate. They are talking quietly and have not yet seen you.

Will you approach the gate and tell them that you wish to be let in, turn to **104**.

Or will you avoid the main gate and look for another way into the settlement, turn to **193**.

380

You hurry away from the tree, but you have only gone twenty paces when you see something that makes you pause in your tracks. You have stumbled upon the gruesome remains of a young man, most likely the same poor fellow who was surrounded on the lonely hill. He must have fled deeper into the mire in a bid to escape his pursuers, but to no avail.

If you wish to search the body for anything useful, turn to **403**.

If you do not want to linger here, you may head on your way, turn to **322**.

381

As the battle continues, you hear the sound of footfalls echoing in a nearby street. Your noisy brawl has attracted more guards, and they will soon be arriving to help their colleagues. In a few moments you will be outnumbered fifteen to one!

Will you:

Break away from the fight and flee towards the docks, turn to **355**.

Or keep fighting, turn to **315**.

The helmet suddenly glows with a protective energy and the lightning veers away from your body. Your enemy casts his spell once more, but again it veers harmlessly away. It seems that the armour has a magical power of its own, that can protect its wearer against certain mystical attacks. The robed menace pauses, and you sense his confusion and horror. He cannot comprehend how you have thwarted his spells. Taking advantage of his hesitation, you leap at him before he can gather his wits. With a death-dealing swipe, you cleave through the torso of your demonic adversary. A cry of agony escapes him, then his robes crumple to the floor in a heap, where his body has turned to dust.

You sheathe your sword. Looking around, you find that the exits are still sealed by the Games Master's lingering magic. You hunt around in search of an escape route, but to no avail. It is beginning to look as though you will end up locked in here forever, but then you find a small lever in the wall. You give it a firm tug, and a circular hole opens up like a toothless mouth in the chamber floor. You walk to the opening and peer down into the deep, vertical shaft. It has a five foot diameter and its walls are pulsating and fleshy, covered in a network of throbbing veins. With each pulsation, the walls make a hideous rasping sound. You have no desire to climb down it, but there is no other way out of the chamber. Using the thick veins as hand holds, you reluctantly begin your descent. Turn to **224**.

Suddenly, you are greeted by the sight of several, long, hairy legs coming up through the open window. A moment later, the body of a large Spider squeezes nimbly through the opening. Unlike its small relative, who dropped onto your shoulder in the stairwell, this foul beast is the size of a full grown man! You are briefly frozen with alarm. Its enormous fangs move in the dim light, and venomous green slime drips from its jaws!

If you have **Haste**, you may dash down the stairwell by turning to **118**. (The creature will not follow.)

If you do not have **Haste**, the scuttling horror spits a toxic web over the exit, trapping you in the room before you can escape. You are then forced to fight!

GIANT SPIDER

LIFE FORCE 5   STRIKING SPEED 9

Focus	Move	Damage
1	**Scuttling Body Slam**	1
2-3	**Toxic Web**	2
4-5	**Burning Saliva**	2
6	**Puncturing Fangs**	See Below*

(*Special Move: If you are stricken by the Spider's Puncturing Fangs, the arachnid will inject its lethal venom directly into your veins, killing you instantly.)

If you win, you hack through the web and head back down the stairwell. Turn to **118**.

You throw yourself out of the path of the fireballs, but the flaming missiles curve after you! Realising that there is no way to avoid them, you raise the Doom Shield… but you are now too late. You are engulfed in flames, your body blazing like a human torch.

Zanack's hideous laughter rebounds around the chamber as you are incinerated in the blaze.

You came so close to success, but evil prevailed.

Behind you, there is the sound of splitting wood. Burlybe, who is still dragging the table towards the door, lets loose a howl of terror. The door groans with the force of a concentrated attack, and it explodes off of its hinges. Before you can act, a host of demonic arms reach in through the shattered entrance and drag Burlybe out into the night, where his cries for mercy are swiftly silenced.

Incensed by the slaughter of this innocent man, you raise your sword and charge at the door with a battle cry. As the Demons try to flood in through the shattered entrance, you vent your fury and send several heads rolling across the floor of the inn. The warrior in black hesitates. He is briefly frozen in awe, stunned by your awesome swordsmanship, but then he leaps to your side and puts his own sword to use.

The Demon horde thrash around, trying to force their way into the tavern, but your swords keep them at bay.

"We must stay strong!" cries the man at your side,

as he hacks into a monstrous form. "We cannot let our enemies push us back!"

Roll three dice to see if luck is on your side.

If the total is seven or less, turn to **53**.

If the total is eight or higher, turn to **394**.

386

Without warning, you swing your sword at the advancing monster. Fragments of stone shatter from its stomach, but the beast seems unperturbed. Its huge hand leaps out, catching you by the throat in a vice-like grip. It lifts you effortlessly from your feet. For a moment you are left dangling helplessly in the air. Then it swings you into the side of the passage, crushing your head into the wall. Your adventure has met a swift end.

387

The guards are unimpressed by your lack of cooperation

"If you will not answer, you leave me no choice," says the captain. "Surrender yourself, and we will take you to the dungeons. We have good reason to be suspicious of strangers in Shellhaven. Our enemy Zanack has many cunning servants, and I will not have you walking around until I have determined whether you are a friend or a foe. I am sure that you will feel ready to talk after a few nights in the cell."

They begin to close in on you, their many swords gleaming in the moonlight!

You can ill afford to be dragged off to prison! You must act quickly.

Will you:

Make a run for it, turn to **355**.

Or draw your sword and stand your ground, turn to **365**.

388

You are suddenly aware of a strange power emanating from the bracelet. A moment later, the door shudders and creaks slightly ajar. The bracelet must be some kind of magical key, allowing entry into sealed off parts of the castle! However, the way forward does not look appealing. Looking through the opening, you can see a gloomy corridor that is positively dense with cobwebs.

You pause for a moment, deciding what to do.

Will you:

Head through this door, turn to **12**.

Or open the door marked with the sword, turn to **3**.

389

As you sit on the cold stone, you take in the deep quiet of your surroundings. An oppressive silence hangs like a weight in this foul maze, but at least the castle's wretched inhabitants are not creeping around in the nearby corridors. Your body is grateful for the short rest, and you are soon glad that you stopped. After a while you are ready to move on again. You stand up, eager to get underway, but you suddenly notice something forming on the surface of the plinth. An inscription is appearing as if by magic. The scrawling letters are glowing with a faint blue light, and when the writing has fully revealed itself, you can see that it is another enigmatic verse. You study it inquisitively, wondering whether you will be able to unravel its cryptic message.

It reads:

In shadows and darkness it eternally lays,
Coming to rest at the end of days,
Tis the beginning of sadness yet the end of woes,
In the heart of existence its image it shows.

Tis the end of chaos yet the beginning of storms,
Where it twists and flows in serpentine forms.
It is never in view and always in disguise,
But in essence seen easily with the keenest of eyes.

After pondering over the words, you must decide which way to head.

Will you take:

The north passage, turn to **206**.

The east passage, turn to **289**.

The south passage, turn to **259**.

The west passage, turn to **267**.

You grip your weapon as the beasts leap towards you!

WEREWOLVES

LIFE FORCE 10   STRIKING SPEED 9

Focus	Move	Damage
1	Tumbling Grapple	1
2-3	Slashing Claws	2
4-5	Tearing Fangs	2
6	Enraged Mauling	2

If you manage to win this epic skirmish, you pause to regain your breath. Even though you were outnumbered, your fierce resolve and skilled swordsmanship have won through. But you are not out of danger yet. Somewhere in the distance you hear a faint howl. Your eyes narrow. It appears there are still more Werewolves about. You cannot spend the whole night fighting off these foul beasts! Eager to escape the dangerous marsh, you quickly set off in search of the path. Turn to **345**.

As you brush it off, its sharp fangs stab into your hand, drawing blood. (Reduce your **Life Force** by one point.)

Having been swiped from your shoulder, the nimble beast lands on the steps and scuttles quickly towards a crack in the wall, through which it vanishes.

You briefly wonder if the Spider was venomous, but

you suffer nothing more than a stinging hand.

You look at the cobwebs on the ceiling, but you can see no other scuttling Spiders, at least not for the moment...

Suddenly, the candles flicker wildly and almost go out. A cold breeze has started to blow down the stairwell. Its whistle is haunting and its icy touch makes you shiver.

If you continue upwards, turn to **374**.

If you would rather turn around and head downwards, turn to **118**.

392

As strong as you are, you cannot stop yourself from being dragged into the darkness. You have opened the door to Zanack's Cellar of Doom, where he keeps his most powerful mutant creations. These Zombie-like creatures are always hungry, and now that you have unleashed them, they are eager to feed.

Having been bundled into the lightless basement, you are immediately set upon by countless, unseen beasts. The savage monsters tear and bite at your flesh, slashing and ripping with claw and fang. A skilled fighter you may be, but there are simply too many to defeat, and they make short work of you! You should never have opened the door marked with the red hand.

393

You begin your sweep of the perimeter. The settlement is surrounded by grassy plains and farmland, with a group of huddled trees scattered here and there. The land seems quiet and tranquil, and there is no sign of the foul beast that Mok described. Just as you are about to complete your circuit, you hear a whispering voice drifting on a faint breeze. Curious, you head towards the sound. You trudge through a wild field, then the ground begins to rise, and you realise that you have come to the base of a small hill, half a mile from the border of Grimbree. Up on the rise is the hallowed ground where the villagers bury their beloved dead. You can see the dark shapes of boulders, which mark the graves of the fallen. By the sound of it, the whispering voice is coming from up on the hill.

Will you:

Investigate the burial ground, turn to **443**.

Return to the village and search the streets, turn to **378**.

Or give up on the hunt, and retreat to Mok's house for the night, turn to **66**.

394

The silhouette of an enormous Demon appears before you, filling the frame of the shattered entrance. It is one of the largest beasts that you have seen this night. Lightning sears the sky, and in that momentary glare you watch as it rakes the air with its terrible red claws, its blood-red horns gleaming in the rain lashed night.

Your comrade dives forward, determined to run it through with his sword. But this Demon is a powerful adversary, and with a mighty swing of its muscled arm it sends the warrior sprawling backwards across the floor, knocking him half unconscious.

You cannot let this evil break across the threshold.

If you possess a **Magic Ring**, turn to **342**.

If you do not possess this item, you must fight!

RUNE-SCARRED NIGHT DEMON

LIFE FORCE 10   STRIKING SPEED 9

Focus	Move	Damage
1	Monstrous Punch	2
2-3	Stabbing Horns	3
4-5	Crushing Grapple	3
6	Mauling Frenzy	3

If you win, turn to **359**.

395

Do you possess the special ability of **Stealth**?

If so, turn to **418** .

If not, turn to **353**.

396

The dark eyed guard steps towards you. His eyes look fierce but he does not draw his sword.

"So, you admit to sneaking into the town," he says. "I knew that you must have snuck in here somehow, for the watchmen at the gate have been given strict orders to let no strangers in." He nods to the other guards, who draw their swords but do not advance. "We do not look kindly upon trespassers," he says, "but as you have been truthful with me, I will give you one chance to explain yourself."

Will you:

Tell them the truth about your quest, turn to **346**.

Or tell them that your business is private, turn to **387**.

397

You race across the chamber so fast that you reach the Games Master before he can cast his spell. Your foe is completely caught off guard by the speed of your approach. You hack through your adversary, felling him with a death-dealing blow. A cry of disbelief echoes upwards, then his robes crumple to the floor in an empty heap, where his body has turned to dust.

With your foe vanquished, you sheathe your sword and breathe a sigh of relief. Looking around, you find that the exits are still sealed by the Games Master's lingering magic. You hunt around for an alternative escape route, and you eventually find a small lever in the wall. You give it a tug, then you turn to see a circular hole opening up like a toothless mouth in the floor. You peer into the deep vertical shaft, which has a five foot diameter. Its walls are pulsating and fleshy, covered in a network of thick, throbbing veins. With each pulsation, the walls make a hideous rasping sound. You have no desire to climb down there, but there is no other way out of the chamber. Using the thick veins as hand holds, you reluctantly begin your descent. Turn to **224**.

Turn to **224**.

398

You carry on up the trail. The strange cries continue for a short time longer… then an abrupt silence settles over the marshland. Unbeknownst to you, the approaching storm has blown your scent towards the enemy, and the smell has driven your foe into a frenzy. Moments later, you see glowing eyes emerging from the darkness. You comprehend with horror that the baying was not that of several creatures, but rather of one creature with many mouths.

You are faced with a true horror of the marshes: a bloated creature ten feet in height and width, straight from the realms of a nightmare. Despite its gluttonous bulk, it scurries across the ground with frightening speed, dragged along by its writhing tentacle-like arms. Its many eyes glitter with murderous intentions, and its numerous jaws hang wide, drooling with madness and insatiable hunger.

As it closes in on you, your sword thrusts outward, hacking one of its arms clean off. To your horror, two more limbs instantly grow back to replace the last! Panic grips you, for you know that your attacks are only going to increase the strength of your enemy! Before you can think of another course of action, you are suddenly hoisted into the air, then you find yourself gazing down into the life draining stare of your opponent. Your very soul is sucked out of you by the gaze of the Marshland Horror, and your body collapses into a shriveled husk.

Your adventure has met a grisly end.

399

Harn respects your decision and accompanies you to the town's harbour. Once there he shows you to a small dinghy. As you climb on board, he bows to you and wishes you the best of luck. Alone in the dinghy, you row out onto the misty lake.

Turn to **362**.

400

Zanack falls backwards, his wounds oozing thick green blood. But even as he hits the floor, he manages in his last, dying breaths, to utter one final spell of destruction.

Suddenly the walls of the fortress begin to rumble and shake, then the whole castle starts to tear itself apart! You have to get out of here, and fast! You glance towards the door, but part of the ceiling collapses and blocks the exit. You hear dismayed voices on the far side, as the guards try to get in to reach their master. You could almost pity them. If only they knew, it was the hand of their own beloved ruler, the Demon Sorcerer, which sealed their doom.

The walls of the room are splitting apart and crashing down all around you. If you do not escape this place quickly, you will be buried alive with the rest of the castle's inhabitants. Dust is billowing and swirling, adding to a sense of confusion and chaos. Leaping the broken rubble, you dash for the nearby window and scramble through it just before the rest of the ceiling crashes in. As quickly as you can, you begin climbing down the trembling face of the outer wall.

Turn to **268**.

401

After rowing for another ten minutes, you come across a tiny island which sits alone on the vast lake. It is no more than thirty feet across, with mossy banks and a grassy summit. The little island looks empty, apart from a strange black object which stands at its centre. The four sided rock is about four feet wide and ten feet tall, and it has been chiseled into the shape of an obelisk: a tall thin shard with a sharp point at the top. It is not clear as to the purpose of this strange monument, but there is a faint hum emanating from it.

If you wish to investigate, turn to **427**.

If you would rather ignore the island and row onwards, turn to **115**.

402

"Good," hisses the figure. There is no hint of surprise in its tone. "Then my suspicions were correct."

You suddenly suspect that someone, or something, is sneaking up on you from behind. Before you can spin around to look, you are struck by a heavy blow across the back of the head. You stumble forward, then the world mists before your eyes. Darkness fills your mind, and your unconscious body hits the earth with a dull thud. Turn to **220**.

403

You find a glass vial which may have contained a potion of healing, but it has been broken and the liquid has leaked out. You look around for his sword, but it has sunk into a bog. Hoping for better luck, you search his pockets and find **three Crimson Coins**, which you may take if you wish.

Now you spin on your heel. A savage howling, belonging to a pack of Werewolves, fills the sky. Your delay here has cost you dear, for the beasts of the marsh have caught your scent and are now approaching,

What will you do?

Draw your sword and hold your ground, turn to **360**.

Or sprint away from the sounds, in the hope of eluding the pack, turn to **322**.

404

Upon closer inspection, the brutal sword looks even more fearsome. Its blade has jagged edges on both sides, designed to inflict massive damage. Thinking that it might be of use to you, you grasp the hilt. But this sword belongs to Zanack, and the Demon has put a curse on it so that only he may wield it!

If you have **Sixth Sense**, you quickly drop the weapon before it can cause any harm.

If you do not have **Sixth Sense**, you feel the sword's dark power flowing into you - reduce your **Life Force** by four points - then you throw it to the ground.

If you are still alive, you hear a sudden rumbling. By touching the sword, you have awoken the guardian of the throne room. With deep, clanking movements, one of the demonic statues comes to life and steps out of the alcove behind you. The deformed sculpture towers almost to the ceiling. Its great weight hinders its movements, but it looks immensely powerful. The beast is fuelled by dark magic. It has three arms and a pitiless hatred for all life. Its snarling, demonic features make the hairs rise on the nape of your neck. There is only one way out of this cursed chamber, (back the way you came), and the horror is blocking your way. You have no choice but to fight it!

IRON GUARDIAN

LIFE FORCE 14   STRIKING SPEED 7

Focus	Move	Damage
1	**Brutal Punch**	3
2-3	**Striking Claws**	4
4-5	**Hurl The Enemy**	4
6	**Iron Fist Smash**	5

If you win, you take a moment to recover your breath. Fortunately, the noise of the battle has not attracted any more guards. There is nothing of use to you in here, so you leave the throne room and try the other door.

Turn to **195**.

405

You escape the burning building just before it collapses in a mess of blazing timbers. But now you are in the open road again, and the fleet briskly surrounds you. With no avenue of escape, you draw your blade and start fighting. You slay many enemies, and they quickly rue the moment they set eyes on you. However, in the end, you are simply too heavily outnumbered to win this fight.

It was foul chance that you were spotted by the patrolling fleet.

406

With a hideous rasping sound, the tentacle loosens its grip and retreats into the water. As the other tentacles writhe towards you, you quickly turn and scramble to safety through the open doorway. From here, you are out of the Pool Beast's reach, but your troubles are not over yet. To your dismay, the castle guards suddenly break through the door at the far end of the chamber. You grasp your sword, ready for battle, but luck is on your side. As the horde rush through the opening, they are ambushed and dragged into the water by the thrashing tentacles. The chamber is suddenly filled with screams. The Pool Beast is one of Zanack's favourite pets, and although it has recently been fed, it seems all too happy at the prospect of another meal. You quickly run down the corridor, whilst the guards are preoccupied with the monstrous abomination. Turn to **446**.

407

"Wrong!" leers the Fire Demon. Without warning it breathes out, and you are blasted by the intense heat of its breath. Your whole body bursts into flames. Your flesh smokes and melts. Then your remains sag to the floor as a bubbling pulp.

408

You cast away the vial and are about to press onwards when you notice that something is missing. All of your money has vanished! The Witch must have stolen it, though you are not sure how. Maybe she robbed you with the use of some devious spell? (Remove all **Crimson Coins** from your belongings.) You curse the Witch for her treacherous greed, but you are glad that you did not drink her potion; no doubt it would have led to an even greater misfortune! You scan the marsh, but there is no sign of her, so you continue down the trail.

Either side of you, hideous pools bubble and spit, belching foul fumes into the atmosphere. Weird and bestial cries continue to haunt your trail, but no more strange creatures bother you tonight, and you safely navigate the last of the darkling hours.

When dawn tentatively breaks over the ghostly grey world, you finally see the rooftops of a settlement nestled in the distance. You guess that it must be the village of Stormwater, so you set off towards it.

Turn to **57**.

409

The fleet has been circling overhead, awaiting the outcome of the fight. At your victory, the sky is filled with furious roars, then a large Terrasaur spews a raging ball of fire straight in your direction! You dodge to the left as the molten blast slams into some nearby barrels. You see fragments of wreckage being flung into the air by the force of the explosion, and the smoking debris clatters down all around you. You sprint across the street, closely followed by a wave of flame. Veering to the left, you dive to safety through the window of a rickety building.

You are sheltered here for the moment, but you will not be safe for long. You are standing in a derelict living room, and through the open window you can see your enemies landing in the street. Two of the beasts still circle overhead, spewing flames across the roof of the building. The room grows very hot and smoke starts to seep through the rafters as the dwelling crackles into fiery life. If you stay here for much longer you will be cooked to death.

Will you:

Leap out through the shattered window, back into the enemy infested street, turn to **405**.

Or head deeper into the flaming building, in search of a rear exit to the dwelling, turn to **138**.

410

It is not long before you reach the small harbour on the southern edge of the settlement. You stare across the misty water and there you see, on an island in the middle of the lake, Zanack's fortress, rising ominously against the night sky. You scan the dock and see a small dinghy which could be used to row out to the island. You are about to step towards it when you notice a large guard who has fallen asleep on duty. He is snoring quietly by the quay.

Will you:

Kill him in his sleep, then take the dinghy, turn to **436**.

Or try to sneak to the dinghy without waking him, turn to **114**.

411
Illustration Opposite

You move with the reflexes of a wild tiger, and your quick reaction saves your life. The bolt misses you by the narrowest of margins, and there is a clang as it shatters against the wall behind you.

Ragroda curses and steps back. Suddenly, before your very eyes, she begins to change. Her slender body starts to swell and grow. Her face begins to stretch and her soft skin turns rough and leathery. In a few seconds she has transformed into a massive, terrifying beast. She is at least seven feet tall, with hulking arms that have burst through the stitching of her clothes. Her wolf-like head turns towards you, crowned with curving horns, then she storms forward. Her booming footfalls echo like the drums of war, and you barely have time to raise your sword before the beast is upon you!

RAGRODA

LIFE FORCE 10   STRIKING SPEED 9

Focus	Move	Damage
1	Rending Talons	2
2-3	Ramming Horns	3
4-5	Crushing Grapple	3
6	Mauling Fangs	3

If you win, turn to **151**.

412

After gulping down the concoction, you suddenly collapse to the earth.

For some time you lay in a comatose state. When your eyes eventually open, you find yourself lying by the sodden trail. But you are not alone. The mossy haired woman has returned, and she is stooped over you, muttering to herself in an excited voice. "Ah! A nice meal this one will make, yes yes," she croaks merrily. "It always works. I read their minds, tell them what they want to hear, and then they drink. They always trust old Haggadus," she laughs.

You realise that Haggadus is talking to herself. She still believes that you are asleep, and she is unaware that her drug has worn off early. "Now," she asks herself, "how shall I get you to my hut? You're too big to lift, and too heavy to drag. But I'll find a way." She stoops over you and begins to push you with her hands, as if to test your weight. You decide to take her by surprise and with a sudden movement you draw your sword to strike. Haggadus leaps backwards with a shriek of alarm, and with a wave of her hand she vanishes before you can catch her. You stagger up and take a deep breath. You came very close to a grim end. Had the old crone's potion not worn off early, you would surely have been turned into a ghastly stew. (The potion has left your arms and shoulder joints feeling stiff and sore, and it may take several days for the effects to fully ware off: reduce your **Striking Speed** by one point.) You scan the darkness, but there is no sign of the deceitful hag, It is a shame that you do not have time to go in search of her. You tell yourself to be more cautious in the future, then you set off along the trail. As you are walking, you realise that your bad luck has not yet ended, for the Witch has stolen all of your **Crimson Coins**. If you were carrying a **Magic Ring**, that has vanished as well! (Remove these items from your adventure sheet.) Feeling dismayed, you trudge onwards. A few hours later, the glow of dawn breaks over the ghostly grey world and you catch sight of a settlement nestled in the distance. Faraway rooftops lay silhouetted against the faint rays of morning light, and you guess that you have stumbled upon the village of Stormwater. You set off towards it. Turn to **57**.

413

When you wake, your vision is blurred and you feel profoundly disorientated. You are lying at the bottom of a square, dark pit. Thirty feet above, you see light coming through the broken doorway. The slippery walls are almost sheer, and they are covered with damp moss. It would be a treacherous climb to get back to the opening. As you get to your feet, something cracks under your boot. You look down and see that the floor is littered with human skeletons. From a lightless corner of the chamber, you hear a deep and unsettling growl.

You are not alone! Something is in the pit with you! You hear the sound of rushing footfalls and you spin on your heel, just in time to see a monstrous form. You use your arm to block a fierce punch that is aimed at your head, then you leap backwards.

A twisted monstrosity stands before you. Its skin is dark green, which makes it almost invisible in the gloom. As it comes forward, you see that its flesh is sagging from its body like melted wax. Its head leans to one side, and its face is a nightmare of twisted features. Hideous fangs jut from its deformed jaw, and a multitude of eyes fix you with a ravenous look. The claws on its webbed hands grope for your throat as it lurches out of the darkness. You must fight this abomination!

RABID PIT FIEND

LIFE FORCE 11   STRIKING SPEED 8

Focus	Move	Damage
1	Disease Soaked Grapple	1
2-3	Throttling Grasp	2
4-5	Blood Sucking Maw	2
6	Psychotic Frenzy	3

If you win, turn to **325**.

You sprint towards the rear of the building and come to a narrow door with a heavy lock. As soon as you open it, a sea of arms reach in and drag you out into the storm. (Countless fangs tear into you: reduce your **Life Force** by four points, then, if you are still alive, read on.) Your sword sings through the air, beheading two Demons with a single strike. You are momentarily freed from the grip of your enemies, then you stumble backwards into the safety of the corridor. Demonic forms leap after you, but you slam the door just in time, then force the lock into place. A throng of bodies try to bash their way through, but the back door is extremely sturdy. It is clear that you will not escape this way! Your only hope of survival is to barricade the rooms and stop the horde from flooding into the building

You return to the main bar area.

"Where did you go?" says Burlybe. Fortunately, he does not give you time to answer. "Quickly!" he says, "help us to secure this room!"

If you help Burlybe to reinforce the front door, turn to **326**.

If you help the man in black to board the remaining windows, turn to **369**.

The pack suddenly backs away, clearly startled by your fierce swordsmanship. With a series of yelps, the surviving Wolves retreat into the darkness, vanishing as quickly as they came.

With the danger passed, you take a moment to gather your wits. Dawn is not far away, and after your bloody encounter you are eager to move on. You cut a slab of meat from a slain Wolf, as it will make a nourishing meal for later, then you haul up your rucksack and set off along the winding trail. The clouds of yesterday have faded and the sun's welcome heat is soon warming your skin. At midday you find a safe spot to build a fire and cook the Wolf meat. You eat the lot, and the meal proves most nutritious. (Increase your **Life Force** by two points.) One hour later you come to a split in the trail. To the southwest, the path winds through fields and meadows. To the east, it leads into the foothills.

Will you:

Take the southwest road, turn to **87**.

Or the eastern road, turn to **48**.

A dark vision enters your mind, warning you that something shadowy and terrible lurks in the deep water beneath the bridge. A monster lays in wait there, ready to ambush unwary travellers. You decide to unsheathe your blade, and your decision comes not a moment too soon. Behind you, a huge glistening Snake, with two heads, suddenly rises from the bubbling water. Before the beast can strike, you spin on your heel and hack into the monstrous form, causing it to recoil. Your quick reaction saves your life, but your enemy shows no sign of retreating. It lunges towards you, possessed by a ravenous fury. (Because you struck first, reduce your enemy's **Life Force** by three points, then finish the fight as normal.)

WOUNDED SERPENT

LIFE FORCE 10   STRIKING SPEED 8

Focus	Move	Damage
1	**Glancing Fangs**	1
2-3	**Left Headed bite**	2
4-5	**Right Headed Bite**	3
6	**Two Headed Strike**	5

If you win, the Snake crashes into the deep water, its green blood oozing into the stream as it sinks beneath the surface. You hurry across to the far side of the bridge.

Turn to **155**.

It is some time before you find yourself back on the trail. When you do, the hour is very late. You march on for several hours, then, deep in the night, you see the rooftops of Shellhaven emerging from the blackness. The town is nestled on the banks of a vast lake. Far out on that murky water is the island fortress where Zanack resides, plotting and scheming in his castle of terror.

Shellhaven could be a safe place to rest and recover, In addition, you might be able to rent a boat in the morning, then row out to the castle on the lake. With these thoughts in mind, you follow the trail towards the town. Turn to **379**.

418

You inch forward. Your movements are not disturbing the slumbering beast, but you cannot relax just yet. The guardian possesses a keen sense of smell and, if it detects your scent, it may yet awaken from its slumber.

If you are wearing an **Amulet of the Crescent Moon**, turn to **439**.

If you possess a **Golden Locket**, turn to **241**.

If you have neither of these items, turn to **353**.

The lid seems to weigh a ton. You are not sure if an army of men could lift it. Undeterred, you search around the base of the plinth and after a few minutes you find a discreet catch which releases a lock on the top of the coffin. You give the lid another tug and this time you heave it off. You cover your nose as you peer inside. The remnants of a large, ancient Demon rest within. The centuries have all but turned its bones to dust, but the ominous skull is still intact. It is wearing a brutal looking black helmet, which is adorned with horn-like spikes and strange engravings. As you remove it from its deceased owner, the skull crumbles into prehistoric dust. The helmet is far too big for you, but you feel compelled to put it on. As you slip it over your brow, you feel it changing shape and moulding to the contours of your head, so that it fits you perfectly. Luck has befallen you! You are wearing an ancient, enchanted piece of armour, and its magic flows into you. (Increase your **Life Force** by five points and make a note that you are wearing **Gorath's Savage Helm**.)

There is nothing else of interest to be found here, so you decide to leave. As you retrace your steps out of the chamber, you feel battle ready and unnaturally vibrant.

Turn to **181**.

420
Illustration Opposite

It is dark inside, and it takes a few moments for your eyes to adjust. A flight of steps spiral upwards, so you ascend cautiously, alert and ready for danger. You have not gone far when you hear a noise from above. Suddenly, a dark shape drops out of the gloom and lands on the steps in front of you. The creature throws back its hood, revealing its hideous features. Its skin is taught over its face, and its large, jet black eyes stare with psychotic intensity. Two small horns rise from its bald head, and burned into its brow is the letter Z, the scolding mark worn by those whom serve the Dark Lord Zanack. Worse still, the menacing figure has acquired a large, rusty scythe from within the building. The creature is probably a scout, sent by Zanack to spy on the roads between Grimbree and Merkwater. You imagine that its orders were to keep a lookout for heroes to slay, but it has not been doing a very good job at all, having been merrily sidetracked into terrorizing the poor folk of this village.

You must slay this terror!

(If you have made an alliance with the **Vengeful Dead**, you should reduce your opponent's **Life Force** immediately by two points, as a ghostly wind is swirling around the stairwell and sapping the Demon's energy.)

DEMON SCOUT

LIFE FORCE 9   STRIKING SPEED 8

Focus	Move	Damage
1	Swift Kick	1
2-3	Elbow To The Throat	2
4-5	Savage Bite	2
6	Sweeping Scythe	3

If you win, turn to **59**.

421

As you stagger to your feet, the rider hauls on the reigns and points his hand towards you. You suddenly feel a constricting force around your throat, as if an invisible hand has grabbed you with vice-like strength. Unable to breathe, you stagger forwards and drop to your knees. Your vision begins to mist. You try to raise your sword, but you are choking to death and are unable to get to your feet!

If you possess a **Crossbow** and a **Bolt**, turn to **249**.

If not, darkness suddenly drowns your thoughts, then you topple sideways to the earth, turn to **220**.

422

You load the bolt and swiftly take aim. Before you can fire, the robed figure suddenly completes his chant. A streak of lightning leaps from his fingers and strikes your crossbow, turning it to dust in your hands!

(Remove the **Crossbow** and one **Bolt** from your inventory.)

Cold laughter echoes around the hall. "Fool! You cannot kill me!" jeers your foe. Your opponent begins another dark chant, its voice slowly ascending in volume. Dismayed, you decide on a different course of action.

Will you:

Run towards him with your sword raised, turn to **363**.

Or throw your sword, in the hope of impaling him before he casts his next spell, turn to **334**.

423

As you raise your Rune Broadsword, the etchings on the blade suddenly glow with a faint blue light. Traces of old magic must still linger in this ancient weapon! The Werewolves pause, their lips curling into fearful snarls. The glowing blade has diminished their confidence, so you step forward, slashing it through the air. Your enemies back up and retreat into the night, then the blade stops glowing. You look at the weapon with an impressed expression, but you have little time to revel in your victory. You set off once more in search of the path, eager to find a way out of the dangerous marsh.

Turn to **345**.

424

You sit motionless, not wanting to attract its attention. The glowing shape flitters around for a moment longer, then it darts away. When you are certain it has gone, you start rowing once more.

There is still no sign of the elusive fortress, and it soon becomes clear that you have rowed off course. You decide to turn the dinghy and explore in a different direction.

If you veer to the right, and explore that area of the lake where the mist hangs deepest, turn to **299**.

If you row to the left, where the mist is slightly less dense, turn to **401**.

425

You shout your answer and the monster immediately halts. For a moment it just stands there, staring silently. Then, with a deep rumbling, it melts back into the floor and vanishes.

Breathing deeply, you continue down the corridor. The strange guardian does not reappear, so you deduce that you passed its test. After a while the cobwebs grow less dense, and you realise that the passage has started to slope downwards. Before long you come to a T-junction. The tunnel to your left appears dark and narrow whilst the tunnel to your right is better lit.

Will you:

Go left, turn to **256**.

Or right, turn to **272**.

As you make for the exit, the Witch suddenly springs from her chair with a cackle. A streak of black energy leaps from her hand and strikes you in the back, causing you to stumble through the door and crash-land into the passage. As you leap to your feet, you realise that something strange is happening. The world around you seems to be getting bigger. The corridor appears to be widening and the ceiling is getting higher.

Only after a few seconds do you realise the horror of what is occurring. The world around you is not getting bigger. *You* are getting smaller. Your eyesight is changing too; it is becoming sharper and strangely sophisticated. You look around, and realise that you have shrunk down to the size of a man's thumb. Worse still, you are no longer sure that you are human. To your shock, you realise that the Witch has transformed you into a furry little Spider. The chuckling old crone hops around the corner and starts leaping all over the corridor, trying to squash you under her booted feet. She is enjoying the challenge of stomping on you. You scuttle around on your numerous, spindly legs, panicking and wondering how in the world you are ever going to escape this frightful situation. You sight a crack in a wall and speed towards it. But will you get there in time?

Roll one dice.

If you roll a three or less, you see a large foot looming over you, then you know no more.

If you roll a four or more, you live out the rest of your days in the castle walls, eating flies for dinner.

You haul the dinghy onto the bank and walk to the centre of the island. Now up close, you see that the shard is actually made from a black, glass-like material. Demonic symbols have been etched into its surface, but before you can examine them properly, you begin to feel extremely ill. The humming increases from the obelisk, and you realise that a dark power is emanating from it. This is clearly a thing of evil, put here to ward off humans. (If you are wearing **Gorath's Savage Helm**, you are immune to the effects of this cursed structure, and it is unable to cause you any harm. If you are not wearing **Gorath's Helm**, you must immediately reduce your **Life Force** by three points. If you are still alive, read on.) You swiftly draw your sword and strike the black shard. It instantly shatters, scattering to the ground into a million pieces. There is nothing else on this blighted mound, so you return to your dinghy and push off. As you row on, you see more little islands, each one housing an identical obelisk. The monuments hum with insidious power, so you keep at a safe distance. Before long, the fog begins to creep towards you, causing you to lose sight of the islands. You continue blindly through the murk, but your luck eventually changes. By pure chance, you finally come upon the centre of the lake, then a huge rocky island emerges through the mist. At its summit sits Zanack's forbidding castle.

Gathering your courage, you row towards it.

Turn to **324**.

428

As you peek around the rock, you hear an ominous hiss. You pause and scan the ground. A few feet ahead, a small Snake is basking on the earth. It is impressively camouflaged, and you might well have stepped on it had you not heard its warning. You decide to give it a wide berth, but it suddenly rears up and slides forward, pausing within striking distance.

If you draw your sword to strike it, turn to **437**.

If you stand absolutely still, turn to **128**.

429

As you turn to leave, you hear footfalls just outside the room. You must have tripped a silent alarm when you entered the chamber, attracting the attention of the castle guards! You make a swift exit through the door at the far side of the room.

Down a gloomy passage you sprint, speeding along as fast as you can. There are no candles here, and your eyes struggle against the thick veil of shadows. Looking back, you see several indistinct shapes burst into the corridor after you. There are too many opponents to fight, so your only option is to lose them in the castle's maze of twisting corridors.

You suddenly bump into a wall, and for a fleeting second you think that you have reached a dead end. Fortunately this is not the case.

You are at a T-junction.

If you turn left, turn to **222**.

If you turn right, turn to **262**.

430

You push on southbound. After a few hours you approach an old signpost by the side of the road. Something is written on it, but due to the mist and the gloom, you cannot read it without closer inspection.

If you investigate the sign, turn to **305**.

If you keep on the move, turn to **84**.

431

"Do not move, human. Do not even flinch if you value your life." Her grin widens when she sees the look of surprise on your face. "Confused? You don't have to tell me. A single expression can tell a thousand words... or a thousand lies." She releases a wicked cackle that echoes around the chamber. "My name is not Avion, it is Ragroda! I am a Shape-Shifter! Three days ago I chanced upon the real Avion. I took the form of a young peasant girl, and Avion told me of her quest to help you. A plan began to form in my mind, and I realised that if I were to gain the password for myself and slay Zanack, I could take his form and set myself up as ruler of the world! But I could not get into this crypt and obtain the password alone, so I slew Avion and took her form. I came to find you, in the hope that I could trick you into helping me. Thank you for your aid, but now your job is done. I need you no longer, and useless items are best discarded."

There is a sudden twang as she releases the string of her crossbow. You have been betrayed!

You see the flash of the bolt as it spins towards your

head. You have a split second to avoid being shot.

You must dodge the speeding bolt, but which way will you duck?

To the left, turn to **29**.

Or to the right, turn to **411**.

432

You hunker in the gloom and watch the road from a safe distance. The thumping hooves grow louder and an enormous black stallion soon bursts out of the darkness. The steed's eyes are burning red, and a crimson mist rises from its nostrils and out of its foaming mouth. Aloft the nightmarish steed sits a tall, twisted figure, swathed in black robes and a hood. The horseman halts and scans the area.

Suddenly, you hear the sound of footsteps squelching in the sodden marsh behind you. The rider is not alone! You glance backwards and see a hooded figure leaping out of the gloom. You swerve instinctively, narrowly avoiding the thrust of his dagger, then you spring to your feet and slam the pommel of your sword into his chest. As he staggers backwards, your blade sweeps through him, killing him with one hit!

His body crumbles into ash, but your troubles are not over yet!

Turn to **28**.

433

If you explore the upper levels first, turn to **129**.

If you explore the ground floor first, turn to **15**.

You leave the path and begin to climb the hill, but the slope is very steep. (If you have the word **venom** written on your Character Sheet, you begin to feel hot and fatigued, and you must reduce your **Life Force** by another point.) You eventually come to the summit and you look down on the path below. You can see that the trail snakes around the base of the hill before dipping into a valley. Suddenly you hear a whine, then a black tipped arrow whizzes past your head. A group of Bandits are down in the gorge, firing up at you with their longbows. You duck behind a large boulder as more shafts whiz through the air and shatter into the nearby rocks.

The falling arrows suddenly halt. "Come out from your hiding!" echoes a voice from below.

"Yes, come out," says a second voice, "and we will promise to kill you swiftly."

You are not overly keen on the man's offer, so you decide to stay where you are. You sit there for what seems like a long time. There is nowhere for you to go, for the Bandits will shoot you as soon as you leave your cover. Suddenly, an idea comes to you. You realize that the boulder is teetering right on the crest of the hill, and with enough force you might be able to push it off the top, down onto the murderous gang below. You thrust with all your might, pushing until you are red-faced with the effort, then the boulder begins to move. Seconds later it is rolling down the hillside, setting off a landslide of rocks along the way, and the thundering chaos crashes into the valley, onto the shocked looking thieves. When the rubble has settled you look down and see that the Bandits have all perished, their bows smashes into splinters by the rocks.

You decide to search the bodies. Turn to **245**.

435

Within the compartment is a diary. A name was written on the cover, but moss and damp has partially rotted the leather, making the inscription unreadable. When you open the book, you find the writing inside more legible. As you turn the decaying pages, you feel a cold sensation growing in your veins. On page after page, line after line, the same words have been written, over and over, hundreds of times, in a disturbing scrawl:

Blood. Pain. Lust.

The cavity is deep, so you reach back in to see what else you can find.

Roll one dice to see if luck is on your side.

If you roll a five or a six, you find an **Amulet of the Crescent Moon**, which you may wear around your neck. (Add it to your belongings.)

If you roll a four or less, the amulet is just out of reach and you are bitten by an angry Spider. You quickly withdraw your hand. (Reduce your **Life Force** by one point.)

There is nothing else to be found in the room, so you head back to the stairwell. You may now:

Explore the ground floor, turn to **15**.

Or leave the ruins and continue your quest, turn to **42**.

436

As you are sneaking up on the guard, he is woken by the echo of raised voices. The shouts belong to the night watchmen who were chasing you earlier, and your dithering has allowed them to catch up with you. They rush out of a side street and suddenly surround you. You are overwhelmed and dragged to the dungeons, where you spend the next fortnight being questioned by the captain of the guard. He is convinced that you are a Demon in disguise, and he is in no mood to believe anything that you have to say. You are under constant watch, so there is no escape. In the days that come, Zanack's army expands to an invincible size. A tide of evil soon sweeps across the land, burning and crushing everything in its path. Your quest has failed.

437

The Serpent's head suddenly darts forward in a blur of speed, then its needle sharp fangs puncture your hand. Before you can exact revenge, the Snake vanishes under a boulder by the trackside.

With no sign of your enemy, you press on up the trail. However, you have not walked far when your fingers start to swell and your arm becomes stiff and sore. The Snake was venomous! (Reduce your **Life Force** by two points, then write the word **Venom** in the notes box on your Character Sheet.)

As you continue, your veins start to burn from the effects of the bite. You can only hope that the symptoms wear off soon. Turn to **81**.

Burlybe's voice suddenly rings out above the chaos. "Quickly!" he cries! "Follow me!" He fights his way towards one of the smashed windows and you both leap out of the building. Your pursuers attempt to follow, but, as they spring towards the opening, the ceiling suddenly crashes down and crushes them under a mess of blazing timber. A second later, part of the roof collapses, destroying half of the building.

You hear several Demons howling and roaring, trapped within the fiery chaos. A few of them break into the open by smashing through the wreckage, but their bodies have been lit up like blazing torches! They collapse on the earth, writhing and burning, and you hasten their ends with the merciful swipe of your blade.

Soon the inferno has destroyed the entire structure, and there is nothing left of your enemies save from smoldering husks on the ground. You stand with a dark, stoic expression as you gaze upon the remnants of the inn. You have narrowly survived the night. But not without cost.

Burlybe is bleeding badly from his many battle wounds. Kneeling beside him, you see that his injuries are too deep to heal, and he sags into your arms.

"We fought well, my friend," he tells you weakly. "But it seems that my luck has run out at last."

His eyes gently close… never to open again.

Angered by his senseless death, you rise to your feet with a fierce expression.

The storm is now moving away. The rain has gone and the red glow of dawn is painting the eastern sky.

You feel more determined than ever to put an end to the heartless evil that is spreading across the land. You say a few words for your departed friend, then with an icy look you set off south through the marshes.

Turn to **146**.

439

The crescent moon pulses with a dim glow, then the hound's breathing becomes slower and more laboured. The magical artifact has somehow lulled the guardian into a deeper sleep.

Did the amulet's past owner use it to sneak around at night, without being detected? You may never know, but you are certainly glad that you found it.

The amulet continues to pulse until you reach the door, then the glow ceases. Turn to **265**.

440

The rocks are razor-sharp and many thrust upwards like stabbing fangs. You take your time, moving with great care to avoid injury. After nearly an hour of climbing, you finally come to a flat ridge high above the mist covered lake. You have reached the foot of the fortress, and you are confronted by a huge doorway of black stone. Strange as it seems, the entrance has been left open and it appears unguarded.

As you move forward, you notice a wide circle of stones, scattered on the ground. A strange quiet hangs in the air, then suddenly... turn to **106**.

441

"You speak the OLD password," snarls the Demon. The enormous brute is not about to give you a second guess, so it reaches down to grab you.

You are left with no option but to defend yourself! Turn to **89**.

442

There are six green toadstools to choose from, so you pick one at random and pop it into your mouth.

You have barely taken a bite when your body starts to shake. A moment later you collapse by the trail and are violently sick. (For eating the poisonous toadstool, you must reduce your **Life Force** by four points! If you are still alive, read on.)

It takes a full hour for the symptoms to pass, but you eventually stagger to your feet and continue on your way. Turn to **75**.

As you make your way up the hill, the whispering ceases. Mist is at your feet as you walk among the many boulders, and you cannot shake the feeling that you are being watched. Some of the stones are weather-beaten, but you notice that many have been put here recently. You kneel by the newest grave, to read the inscription:

Here Lies Torin RavenSword,
Once The Innkeeper Of Grimbree,
Now Lost To The Land Of Shadow.
May He Forever Rest In Peace.

Suddenly, a cold feeling enters your bones. You turn, and there, at the centre of the stones, is the faded and ghostly form of a burly man.

"Do not fear me," he says, his voice distant like a breathless whisper. "My mortal body may be broken in the earth at your feet, but my spirit still wanders this plane. The beast that you seek is the one who took me from the land of the living. If you wish to destroy the evil that plagues this village, then I will aid you. If I have my vengeance, my spirit might at last be freed from the chains of this world."

He turns slowly and drifts away from you, pausing on the edge of the slope to look back. With an ethereal whisper he beckons for you to follow.

If you wish to follow the spectral figure, turn to **133**.

If you would rather flee from the hill, and return to the safety of Mok's house, turn to **66**.

Before long the innkeeper stops shouting and you hear him hurry away down the corridor. Glad to be rid of him, you settle back to sleep. You soon feel yourself sinking into a dark dream. The vision of a long passage stretches out before you, with a pinprick of light in the distance. You walk towards the glimmer, but evil shadows form in the gloom and pull you backwards.

"Dream," whispers their cold voices. "Sleep forever. And let the arms of death cradle your soul."

You twist and turn in your sleep, while the storm rages beyond your window.

Roll one dice to see if luck is on your side.

If you roll a two or higher, you are lucky: the innkeeper returns and this time he is more desperate. He kicks the door with such force that the lock is snapped in two! Turn to **201**.

If you roll a one, no one comes back to wake you: the inn becomes strangely quiet and you fall deeper into the morose dream, turn to **323**.

445

You tell them about your mission, but they are deeply suspicious of your story. Because you lied to them, you will now have to work hard to regain their trust.

To see if luck is on your side, roll one dice four times.

If you roll a six on at least one occasion, turn to **346**.

If you do not roll a six on any occasion, you fail to convince the guards. They presume that you are a spy of the enemy and they try to drag you off to prison. You cannot afford to be thrown into jail, so you have no choice but to resist arrest:

If you wish to fight the guards, turn to **365**

If you try to flee, turn to **355**.

446

As you run away from the chaotic scene, you pass a door to your right. Glancing through the opening, you see a host of wretched Demons in black clothes. They burst out of the room to attack you, but you speed away along a random network of corridors. Twice you stumble and fall as you dash round the sharp bends. (If you possess a **Crossbow**, it is broken during one of your tumbles, so you must deduct it from your equipment list.) Eventually, you escape up a stairwell into a quiet part of the castle. All is silent, so you pause to catch your breath.

You are safe for the moment. Turn to **269**.

447

You soon drift into an uneasy sleep. Your mind is troubled by violent nightmares, with creeping shadows that haunt the corridors of your subconscious. Your dreams may be unpleasant, but you sleep for a while and your body is grateful for the rest. (Increase your **Life Force** by one point.) When you wake, the watchers in the mist have gone. Turn to **179**.

448

"That's old Martha's shop," says Harn, as you turn towards it. "She collects and sells all sorts of things, though I doubt she'll have anything to interest you."

Despite his lack of optimism, you decide to have a look. The store is run by an eccentric, thin lady who is dressed in a patchwork of colourful clothes. All sorts of clutter fill the interior, leaving barely enough room to manoeuvre through the shop. Most of the items are of no interest, but one curious trinket catches your eye. It is a small green pebble, no bigger than your thumb, which has been hand crafted into the shape of a skull. The artifact is attached to a chain which is designed to hang from a belt. The shopkeeper tells you that she found it washed up on the shore of the lake.

If you want it (and can afford the price) add the **Skull Charm** to your list of possessions, then reduce your money by **two Crimson Coins**. When you are done, you leave the shop.

Time is pressing, so you inform Harn that you are now ready to leave. Turn to **399**.

The spectral vision of the dead innkeeper forms in the darkness in front of you. His transparent features are hard to define, but you can see a look of relief in his eyes. As you watch, tendrils of light begin to drift from his hands. As the light moves around you, you become filled with a sense of wellbeing. (Increase your **Life Force** by two points.) The ghost smiles at you, then his image grows fainter.

By slaying the horror that stalked these streets, you have brought peace to the vengeful spirit of Torin RavenSword, and he is no longer bound to the land of the living.

There is a final look of gratitude in his eyes, then he vanishes forever.

If you now wish to pick up the ring, turn to **341**.

Otherwise, turn to **320**.

Overcome by the skill of the winged steed, the Dragon spirals downwards and hits the lake with a colossal boom. The beast vanishes beneath the surface, then the impact creates huge waves that beat towards the shore. You wipe the sweat from your brow, scarcely believing that you survived the conflict.

Snowfire soars higher, swooping above the great expanse of Harrowmoor, and you sigh with relief as he carries you homeward. Thanks to you, Zanack is dead and many of his minions lay slain beneath the debris of the ruined castle. The few survivors will have no choice but to flee back to the wastes from whence they came, lost without their leader. Your nerves start to relax and you begin to think about all of the great perils that you have overcome.

The sun is now glowing on the horizon, painting the sky in hues of purple and gold, and you savour the fresh air on your face.

You look forward to seeing the Wizards once more, for they are sure to give you a hero's welcome.

Turn to the *Epilogue*, which is the last entry in this book.

Epilogue

Over the marshes, the fields and the hills, you make your way. On a late evening, as the moon rises into a purple sky, you find yourself back by the gates of the Wizard's castle.

Pelanthius is already waiting by the entrance, as if anticipating your return, and he is enormously relieved to see your face.

That night, wondrous bursts of light illuminate the glittering towers in celebration of your return. A large feast is laid out in the hall and you eat your fill, whilst telling tales of your journey. Your bearded friends listen with great intensity and occasional gasps of dismay, then a century old bottle of Hoggle-Berry Brew is brought up from the vault, which you all partake in.

There seems no end to the Wizard's supply of sumptuous food and interesting drink!

At length, a great tiredness comes upon you, and Pelanthius escorts you to your chambers.

"You may stay as long as you wish," he says. "Forever if you like! For we are eternally in your debt."

You thank him before collapsing into your bed, where you remain for the next few days.

In the weeks that follow, you get plenty of rest in the high tower. You sleep lots and never rise early. Occasionally you sit on the balcony of your private room, gazing northward towards the Enchanted Forest. The air is fresh and glittering with magic, and you can feel your wounds healing at speed.

As the news of your heroics spread, people start to turn up at the gates to ask if what they have heard is true. You learn that the Elves in the Golden Forests have started to write songs of your bravery and even the Faires in the deep woods are dancing and rejoicing.

Your quest has been a complete success, and your name will be enshrined in legend forever more.

The two special abilities which you used to complete this book are now yours forever. The boxes next to them should be marked with a '**P**' (for permanent) on your Character Sheet. You will never lose them, and you may take them with you into your next adventure.

This page is effectively a 'save point.' When you start the next book, you will choose another two abilities to add to the ones that you already have. And this is good news, for while the eyes of the world were focused on the threat from Zanack, an even darker power was stirring deep beneath the earth. A force of unthinkable evil will soon be unleashed. And when it comes, all hope will once again rest on you!

Your story continues in book two, entitled:
Army of Bones.

Printed in Great Britain
by Amazon

74889321R10220